CW00537481

DEEP BLACK LIES

CJ CARVER

BLOODHOUND
— BOOKS —

Print ISBN 978-1-913419-23-3

PRAISE FOR CJ CARVER

'A terrific page-turner'
   Harlan Coben

'Solid gold'
   Lee Child

'A gripping thriller, perfect for fans of Lee Child and Mason Cross'
   The Guardian

'A top-notch thriller writer. Carver is one of the best'
   Simon Kernick

'A page-turning thrill'
   Mick Herron

'Don't expect to sleep, because this is unputdownable'
   Frost **Magazine**

1

The last thing Harry Hope expected as he walked up Gloucester Street at 6.15pm on a chill spring evening was to be knifed. He'd heard the footsteps behind him, padding swiftly, and assumed they belonged to a worker hurrying home at the end of the day. When he felt the man's hand on his shoulder he honestly believed it was someone he knew catching him up, perhaps a friend wanting to say hello and ask him out for a pint.

He didn't feel any danger, his instincts lulled by his routine evening walk to his car, a walk he must have done a thousand times. He didn't take in the drizzle dampening the Georgian buildings of Bath, or see the porticoed entrance just ahead because, as usual, his mind was taken up with the clients he'd seen through the day. The depressed teenager, the sad divorcé, the obese woman desperate to lose weight.

The one that had hit him hardest was the loving husband and father who'd just discovered that his three children, all now university students, were not his own but his wife's lover's. It had made Harry think about his own three kids. Like most fathers he assumed they were his, but how would he know for sure without a paternity test? And would he actually want to know if one or, God forbid, all of them had been sired by another man?

He may be divorced but even so. He loved his children fiercely and would do pretty much anything for them. Talk about opening a can of worms. Harry couldn't get his patient out of his mind. The poor man hadn't just been cuckolded, but betrayed on a monumental scale. Little wonder he was feeling homicidal. Harry sighed, thinking he would probably feel like killing someone too.

'You...' The man's voice was low and hard, breaking through Harry's thoughts, and at the same time his hand yanked Harry backwards.

Shocked, Harry lost his balance, stumbled to one side. At the same time, he saw the flash of metal slice past his waist. A blade gleamed in the streetlights. A knife. The man had tried to knife him.

Harry didn't hesitate.

With all his strength he thrust himself to the side, driving his elbow into his attacker's midriff, using his shoulder to punch his attacker off balance. They fell together, Harry on top and delivering a vicious blow with his fist straight into the man's face. He felt the crunch of snapping cartilage followed by the rush of warm liquid that he knew was blood. The man cried out but Harry had no intention of pausing, not with a knife around, and he punched the man again, and again.

Footsteps hammered. Voices shouted.

'Hey, stop! Stop!'

Harry felt himself being heaved up but his adrenaline was still surging and he lashed out at the person hanging on to his arm.

'Harry, stop! It's me!'

Harry hauled himself under control. 'Doug?' he gasped.

'What's going on?' Doug demanded. Doug was a fellow

ALSO BY CJ CARVER

THE HARRY HOPE SERIES

Deep Black Lies

Cold Echo

THE DAN FORRESTER SERIES

Spare Me The Truth

Tell Me A Lie

Know Me Now

THE JAY MCCAULAY SERIES

Gone Without Trace

Back With Vengeance

The Honest Assassin

THE INDIA KANE SERIES

Blood Junction

Black Tide

OTHER NOVELS

psychologist at the Wellbeing Centre. He was helping Harry's attacker to his feet. The young man was clutching his nose, which was pouring blood. Early twenties, jeans, sneakers, grey hoody. He was watching Harry with such loathing, Harry found it hard not to recoil.

'He had a knife.' Harry's breathing was choppy and shallow as the adrenaline began to ebb. 'He tried to knife me.'

'A knife?' Doug stepped back.

'No knife,' the attacker mumbled. 'He just went for me. No reason. He's crazy. He should be locked up.'

'Liar.' Anger made Harry bunch his fists again. 'Turn out your pockets.'

'No way.' The young man tried to back away but Harry grabbed his hoody in his left hand and raised his right fist threateningly. 'Do it.'

Trembling, sweat sheening his face, the young man emptied his pockets onto the ground. Harry dragged him aside. Looked down to see a wallet, a set of keys and a balled-up tissue. 'And the knife,' Harry told him.

'I already said!' The loathing Harry had seen had vanished beneath a blanket of fright that made the young man's voice wobble. 'I haven't got a bloody knife, okay?'

'Just do it,' Harry snarled.

'Pat me down, then! See if I'm wrong!'

Harry pushed him in the chest and when the young man lurched backwards, offering no resistance, moved behind him and began searching for the knife. Nothing in his pockets. Nothing tucked in his waistband. Harry ducked down and ran his hands up and down the man's legs, his arms, his spine.

Shit, he thought. *I can't believe this.*

No knife.

2

Harry was looking around, trying to see where the young man had thrown the knife, when Doug spoke up.

'Shall I call the police?'

Harry scowled. *Where was the sodding knife?*

'Harry?' Doug had his phone out.

Heart thudding, Harry made to pick up the young man's wallet, wanting to see some identification, but his attacker was faster and ducked down and snatched it up. For a second, their eyes met. The man's face was already swelling, blood pouring from his nose and down his chin. And then he spun on his heel and ran.

He was fast. Much faster than Harry. And he was young. Harry used to play rugby but too long ago for it to be any use today. He didn't stop though. Anger spurred him on. He charged along Rivers Street, following knife-man as he swung right, heading into town, pounding down the hill past the Queensberry Hotel. He nearly lost him on the next crossroads but a woman's yelp directed him down the cut-through past the Assembly Rooms where, in the distance, knife-man was pelting hell for leather.

Harry kept running until he lost sight of his quarry at the bottom of Bartlett Street. Heart pounding, breath hot in his throat, he paused, scanning the handfuls of tourists, the street filled with rush hour traffic, searching for any movement that seemed out of place.

'Harry,' a man gasped behind him.

Harry spun round to see Doug bent double, panting, his face puce. 'You lost him?'

'Yes.'

'Bugger,' Doug wheezed. 'God, I really must do more exercise. I'm so bloody unfit, I can't tell you.'

'Thanks for helping out.' Then Harry frowned. 'I thought you were in Zurich this week.'

'Symposium was cancelled. I was taking Mum and Dad to Patrick's for their wedding anniversary. You know, that restaurant–'

'Yes, I know Patrick's.'

Harry hadn't dined there, and although Doug was a fellow psychologist Harry decided not to tell him that he only knew the place because he was giving their pastry chef some relationship therapy.

'I parked up Lansdown,' Doug continued, 'and was walking down when I saw two men fighting. Didn't realise it was you. I didn't know you were quite so, er... physical.' He gave Harry an appraising look.

'The result of a misspent youth,' Harry admitted. 'I got into a bit of a rough gang who taught me a few tricks.'

Doug's eyebrows rose. 'Rather more than tricks from what I saw.'

Harry wasn't going to go into that period of his life with Doug. He'd carried a huge burden of guilt for something that happened when he was a child, and had turned into an insufferable teenager, running wild with the wrong crowd and ignoring his long-suffering parents' pleas. It was only thanks to one of their friends, a psychologist at the Royal United Hospital, that he was pulled back from the brink. Yet that became the bedrock for his future in psychotherapy, underpinned by a driving urge to atone by helping others.

Harry ran a hand over his head. His sweat was starting to cool, his pulse returning to normal. Doug, however, was still wheezing. Harry had to admit he was surprised at Doug's intervention. He might be a big, gruff man but appearances were deceptive. Over the years Harry had come to see Doug as placid, a man of trust, but also a bit of a wimp, if he was being honest. Like Dave, Harry's ex-best friend who, even though he was a qualified judo instructor, still hid upstairs whenever Harry appeared. Not that he made a habit of going to his ex-wife's home, but occasionally he had to go there to pick up the kids.

'Did he really attack you?' Doug was frowning. 'I have to admit that it looked as though...' He trailed off, hesitating.

'As though what?' Harry hadn't expected the words to come out quite so aggressively but he wasn't surprised, considering what he'd just gone through.

'Well, you were punching him, weren't you?'

'Yes. Because he attacked me.'

Doug flicked his eyes up and down Harry's burly frame. Harry got the message. The young man might have been tall but he hadn't had Harry's muscular bulk. He'd been like a greyhound to Harry's bull mastiff.

'Are you going to report it?' Doug asked anxiously. 'Because if you are, I'm not sure what I should say... I mean, I didn't see a knife. I just saw you on the ground, hitting him.'

Great. Knowing Doug, who was a stickler for protocol, he'd probably have him done for assault.

'No, I won't report it,' Harry said wearily, but back at home –

after searching Gloucester Street for the knife to no avail – he changed his mind.

3

'You're saying I'm one of how many knife attacks?'

'It's not me saying it, Harry. It's the news.'

Jessie brought out her phone and tapped. Turned the screen to him.

Man attacked with knife while sitting on a bench in Bath.

Youth pulls knife on cyclist in Weston.

She tapped some more.

Victim describes 'terrifying knife attack' outside his judo school.

Harry looked at the photograph of the third victim, a fit-looking man wearing a judo kimono. Definitely not Dave. Besides, if Dave had been attacked, Harry would have heard about it.

'They don't look related,' he said, trying not to be distracted by Jessie's perfume. Or the way her jumper clung so agreeably to her. She was wearing a vibrantly coloured scarf, skinny jeans and ankle boots, and looked as delicious as a rosy apple just plucked from the tree. Sometimes, like now, he couldn't believe his luck. Not just that they'd met, but that she seemed to like him. And he liked her back. Lots.

'But three knifings in a fortnight?' She gave him a droll look. His ex, Nicole, didn't do droll. She didn't tease him, tell jokes or have sex anywhere but the bedroom. Jessie had been a revelation. They'd made love in front of the fire in the sitting room, on the sofa, in the kitchen, on the stairs and in the shower. When summer eventually arrived, he had no doubt she'd incorporate the garden. Was her adventurousness to do with her being Australian? Or was it because she was simply a vibrant young woman in love with life?

He'd never had such a generous lover before and now he wondered about the power of culture and how it affected sexual development and relationships. Social factors were of vital importance too. What were her parents like?

He'd met Jessie last year, when one of his clients, a seventeen-year-old boy, had gone missing. She worked for Eddie's Farm, a charity that turned difficult kids around and gave them a taste of a different life through farming and physical achievement. Back then Jessie had been a fund-raiser cum general dogsbody, and the instant they'd met, he'd been bowled over by her.

'Hello? Earth to Harry. Are you receiving me?'

Jessie was standing with her hands on her hips, brows drawn.

'Sorry.' He raised a hand, let it fall. 'Miles away.'

'Really?' Another droll look. 'I hadn't noticed.'

He snaked an arm around her waist. Drew her close. His hands and knuckles were sore but he barely noticed. 'Do you know what I was thinking about?'

Her mouth opened and closed. 'No way!'

'Yes way.'

He bent his head and kissed the tender skin behind her ear the way she liked. Scooped her closer. 'Hmm,' he murmured. 'You smell good enough to eat.'

She leaned back and linked her arms around his neck. She was smiling.

'Well, you know what they say about those who've just had a near-death experience...'

Her creamy breasts pushed against him and as he looked at her mouth, lush and glistening, he felt a rush of heat. Lust, love, desire, a screaming need for release took hold of him, shocking him with its strength. When Jessie took his tongue into her mouth, winding her body around his, he practically tore their clothes off and was groaning, gasping in haste. His lovemaking was fierce and urgent, and nothing like he'd experienced before.

Afterwards, Harry carried Jessie up to bed where he held her, tucking her head against his chest and stroking her hair. 'Sorry. It was a bit quick.'

She twisted to meet his eye. 'Never apologise, Harry. Getting carried away is extremely sexy. Makes me feel ultra-feminine.'

'You're kind.' He gently kissed her lips.

'Not kind.' She smiled. 'Just honest.'

Which was one of the things he loved the most about her. To him it was an invaluable asset, especially after all of Nicole's lies. They lay quietly for a while. Then Jessie stirred.

'I'll come with you, if you like,' she said.

'Where?' He was baffled.

'To the cop shop. Make a report on your attack.'

He thought it over. Then he fetched his phone. Checked out the other attacks. He couldn't see that they were related because the attackers appeared to be different people, plus the attack outside the judo school had been committed by a gang of youths, not a single, young, white male.

That said, he knew he should report it in case (a) it happened again or (b) happened to someone else.

'Wait here.'

Harry went and fetched his laptop and a bottle of wine, two glasses. While they sipped, feet entangled beneath the duvet, he filled in the *Report a Crime* form. Part of his mind wondered whether his young attacker was doing the same. He had, after all, come off a lot worse than Harry. It didn't take long, and he clicked on the big blue *submit* button with a flourish.

'So,' Jessie mused. 'They weren't a pissed-off client, then.'

'No.'

'The son of a pissed-off client?'

He thought of the undiluted vitriol in the young man's face. 'Possibly.'

They polished off the wine, chatting inconsequentially about their days. A flurry of hail rattled the windows and they snuggled down, content to stay in bed. Darkness had fallen and even though it wasn't particularly late they fell asleep, Harry on his side and Jessie spooning him.

When the doorbell rang Harry was deeply asleep, no dreams. Blearily, he checked his phone to see it was just after 7am and the sky was a pale blue above the beech tree at the end of the garden. They hadn't closed the curtains before they went to sleep.

The bell rang again.

Harry struggled up. Various parts of his body ached from where it had hit the pavement the night before, and the knuckles on his right hand were purple and blue. What in God's name his clients were going to make of that, he couldn't imagine.

'What the...?' Jessie popped upright like an auburn meerkat, curly hair awry.

'I'll go.'

Pulling on a dressing gown, Harry went to the window on the landing, peered outside. Thanks to the porch covering the front door he couldn't see who was there, but he got a clue from the car they were driving which had fluorescent yellow and blue checks down each side and a band of blue lights on its roof.

A police car.

4

Harry yanked on clothes without thought. Trousers, shirt, sweater. He wasn't going to answer the door half-dressed in case he got carted off. He skittered down the stairs, his mind whirling. Had knife-man accused him of assault?

He opened the door to the sound of birds and a slab of bright sunshine that hit him straight in the eyes, making him squint.

'Nice look, Harry.'

Detective Sergeant Elizabeth Harding. Five foot six in her Dr Martens police boots, she had dark wavy hair and sharp blackbird eyes that were, at this moment, sweeping from his bare feet to the top of his head, where he knew his hair would be sticking up in tufts.

'Libby.' He felt his shoulders slump in relief. 'You got me going there for a moment.'

'Been up to no good?' She briefly looked amused and then she took in his hand. 'Bloody hell. And there was I thinking it was you who got assaulted. I even brought sympathy buns.' She raised a paper bag. 'Cinnamon. Your favourite.'

His appetite suddenly kicked in, making him realise he hadn't had supper last night. He was ravenous.

Stepping back, he let her in. 'Coffee?'

'Only if Jessie's making it.'

He blinked.

'Her car's outside.' Libby cleared her throat. 'And there's, um, evidence of a female…'

Belatedly, Harry remembered last night's urgent lovemaking and realised their clothing still lay crumpled at the bottom of the stairs, including Jessie's bra and knickers.

'I'll go to the kitchen and leave you to tidy up.' Libby was brisk.

Gratefully, Harry scooped up the clothes and tore upstairs, dumped them in the bedroom. Jessie was already in the shower. He could hear her singing.

Downstairs, Harry switched on the coffee machine. 'Sorry, you'll have to have it made by me. Lungo? Vivalto?'

Libby gave an exaggerated long-suffering sigh. 'Ah well. As long as it's got caffeine.'

He was grateful she left him his privacy with Jessie. He'd known Libby for three years now, having helped her and her boss, DI Theo McCannon, on a murder case last year, and a mass shooting the year before. Libby cheerfully called Harry the department's psychic, and despite the fact he'd insisted that all he'd called on was a basic knowledge of human psychology, she remained convinced he was able to see inside a criminal's mind.

Coffee to hand and settled at the kitchen table, Harry devoured his first bun while Libby brought out her notebook and pen. 'I saw your crime report.'

'How come?'

'We're investigating a murder that happened last night. We think it might be linked to the recent knife attacks.'

Harry was startled. 'They're connected?'

14

'We're not sure, but something's off. The attacks started on April the first.'

April Fool's day.

'How many on the day?' Harry asked.

'Three.'

Harry whistled. That was definitely 'off'.

'There was another attack in Bath last night. The victim died.'

Harry felt something akin to a spider scurry down his spine.

'How?'

'They were pushed into the Kennet and Avon Canal. They couldn't swim. They drowned.'

Harry raised his eyebrows.

'We saw it on CCTV. We've over two hundred secret cameras around Bath, in case you didn't know. The attack was caught on one of them. Unfortunately, we didn't get there in time to nab the bastards or save the vic. They wore a tweed coat and went down like a stone.'

He felt another shiver. 'I thought canals were only a few feet deep.'

'Not this bit. The depth was increased to two metres to allow heavier cargoes.'

She fell silent when footsteps pummelled down the stairs followed by the rattle of a drawer and keys jingling. The next instant Jessie scooted into the kitchen doorway, curly hair wet, booties on, handbag over her shoulder.

'Hi, Libby.' She gave her a finger wave.

'Hi, Jessie.'

'Don't get up,' Jessie told Harry. 'I'll text you later, okay?' She blew him a kiss, and vanished. Three seconds later, the front door slammed.

Libby looked at the space where Jessie had been. 'Can you keep her?'

'Er...'

'Not only does she make the best coffee around, but she's not jealous, she's not stuck-up, and best of all, she's not–'

'Nicole, I know.' Libby had never got on with Nicole but liked her even less after the way Nicole had treated him through the divorce.

'Jessie's visa's up to date, isn't it?'

'What?' Harry was startled.

'Don't want her being chucked back to Australia, do we?' Her gaze turned sly. 'Not now we're addicted to her excellent coffee.'

Harry rolled his eyes. 'If you have to know, she's got a British passport. Her mum's British.'

'That's all right, then. Just don't want you, er, you know...'

She didn't want to see him hurt again. He was immeasurably touched. 'Jessie's not going anywhere,' he told her. 'Not as far as I know, anyway.'

'Good.' Libby flipped a page over on her notebook. 'So, moving right along. What can you tell me about your attacker?'

Harry gave a description. Young white male. Floppy brown hair. Six one or two. Harry was six foot and his attacker had been taller. Hazel eyes. Soft hands. Cut-glass English accent.

'He reminded me of those boys in *Brideshead Revisited*,' Harry told her.

'Posh, then.'

'Yes.'

'Clothes?'

Harry thought back to the little logo stitched on the breast pocket of the young man's hoody.

'Designer. Understated. Expensive.'

'Trainers?'

'Running shoes, yes. He went off at one hell of a lick.'

'Didn't want another hammering.' She snickered as she looked at his knuckles. 'You break his nose?'

Harry recalled the gristle crunch. 'Probably.'

She nodded. Made another note. Looked up, expression serious. 'The boss wants you to come in.'

Harry blinked. 'Why? I've already made a report.'

'No, it's not that. He wants you to look at the cases. See if you can give us a bit of a hand looking into what's going on. Use your psychological insight, was how he put it.'

'Absolutely not,' he snapped.

'Don't be like that.' She affected hurt. 'You were brilliant last time, remember?'

'I nearly died, remember?'

She looked away.

'No. Final answer.' He put his hands on the table. 'Now, I must get to work.'

She flipped her book closed with a sigh before putting her pen in her bag. 'He'll roast me for it. He told me not to take no for an answer or he'd have to take another look at my performance assessments.'

'Don't you dare try to make me feel guilty.'

'It was worth a shot.' She grinned, unrepentant.

'Go on.' He shooed her out of the kitchen and down the corridor. 'Go and annoy someone else.'

She kissed his cheek at the front door.

'Do me a favour? Try to keep out of trouble.'

5

Harry's first client was the pastry chef from Patrick's. Alvin was in his thirties and had been unable to hold down a long-term relationship. He wanted to get married and have kids, but every time he got engaged, it never lasted more than a month or two before he broke it off. He'd been engaged five times.

When Harry asked how things had been, beginning the session, Alvin's eyes closed – and then opened again.

'Things are difficult at the moment,' he confessed. 'I've got massive credit card debts.'

'What have you been spending your money on?'

Alvin's face brightened. 'I've met someone wonderful. Sakiya. She's a fashion designer. She's really pretty... She likes nice things, you know? We've been dating for a while. I've been taking her out to nice restaurants. Actually, top restaurants. Michelin-starred... and I've been buying her gifts. We've been making plans for the future. Talking about what our lives are going to be like, together.'

'Did you do this with Paula?' Harry referred to Alvin's most recent fiancée.

'Well, yes. But this is different.'

'Different, how?'

Alvin tilted his head back and gazed at the ceiling. 'It
She's a unique person. I've never known anyone like her.'

'Didn't you think the same about Paula? That sh
unique?'

'I may have done.' He shifted uncomfortably.

'How about with Helen? The fiancée before?'

'Of course I wined and dined Helen. Took her or
abroad. She was terrific. But she wasn't the *one*.'

To Harry's satisfaction, a clear picture was beginn
emerge. He just had to unpeel another few layers and ho
Alvin would come to the same realisation: that he
commitment-phobic, he was simply addicted to falling i
the romance of sending roses; the gifts of jewellery;
deeply into his lover's eyes over a candle-lit table. Bu
they'd said *yes* to his marriage proposal, once he'd wo
love, he lost interest. To achieve the same emotional im
had to repeat the whole process with another woman.

Before he left, Alvin handed Harry a bakery box.
peeked inside to see a large, beautifully made pie.

'Venison and red wine.'

'I can't.'

'You have to, because I can't pay you until next time.'

Knowing how important it was psychologically that
paid for their sessions in some way, he accepted the pie
it on his desk. 'You will come?'

Alvin took the question seriously. 'Yes. But if I can't
next time, can I pay you in kind again?'

When Harry hesitated, he said, 'I could teach you
make a pie like this. It's easy, you know. But you must us
makes such a difference, I can't tell you.'

Harry was sorry when he had to refuse. He'd like

more than to learn how to make a cracking pie, but he needed to keep things simple.

'Look me up on YouTube.' It was as though Alvin had heard Harry's thoughts. 'I'll show you how.'

Harry was typing up his notes on Alvin's session when Jagoda buzzed him. 'Your policeman friend. He is here. He wants to see you.'

He was used to Jagoda's bullet-point announcements. She'd come from the Ukraine eighteen months ago, looking for temporary work, and had taken up the job to be the Centre's cleaner cum receptionist with alacrity. Although they hadn't been able to afford to give her much of a pay rise since she'd started, she'd stayed.

'I like how it smells,' she'd announced brightly. 'And where else can I get a massage at lunchtime?'

The Wellbeing Centre offered acupuncture, aromatherapy and shiatsu as well as clinical psychology (which is where Doug and Harry came in) and Jagoda took regular advantage of the staff discount. Trisha's oils and lotions permeated the atmosphere most days and although Harry couldn't tell the difference between bergamot and boronia, he agreed with Jagoda; it smelled nice.

'Tell DI McCannon I'm busy,' he told her.

'But Harry...' She dropped her voice to an urgent whisper. 'I already tell him you have a cancellation.'

'Oh, Jagoda.' He raised his eyes to the ceiling. 'You really must ask me first.'

'I'm so sorry.' She was still whispering. 'What shall I tell him?'

Harry groaned. 'I guess you'd better send him in.'

'Oh, thank you. So sorry. Thank you.'

When DI Theo McCannon tapped on his door, Harry closed the lid of his laptop and called, 'Come in.'

He swivelled his chair around as Theo stepped inside. His friend, three years younger than Harry at thirty-six, was wearing a suit and tie and a pair of smart-looking lace-up shoes.

'No,' Harry said.

He was surprised when Theo didn't respond. He'd expected Theo to try to persuade him to join the murder team but instead the DI stepped to the window and looked left down Margaret Buildings, a pedestrian street lined with pretty boutique shops, then right to study the square, the cherry trees draped in blossom, the clumps of vivid yellow daffodils. Like Harry, he was broad-shouldered, but where Harry had a fair complexion – light brown wavy hair, brown eyes – Theo had dark, brooding looks with thick black hair and stubble that looked as hard as the bristles on a scrubbing brush. His profile was tense, Harry noticed, his mouth narrowed. Finally, he turned to Harry.

'I'm afraid I'm here about something else.'

It was Theo's sombre expression that made Harry alarmed. 'What is it?'

'I'm sorry... but one of the people attacked was Lorraine Brown.'

'Not the Lorraine who was Nicole's bridesmaid?' Harry was horrified.

Theo's expression softened. 'I'm sorry.'

Harry could picture Lorraine now, her narrow face mischievous, unapologetic when he'd caught her snogging the head waiter in the kitchen after their wedding. Gavin Brown. Harry always maintained it must have been a fantastic snog since Lorraine and Gavin ended up getting married eighteen months later. He and Nicole had gone to their wedding and, six years after that, Nicole became godmother to Lorraine's daughter, Esme.

'Is she all right?'

When Theo cleared his throat and looked at the ground,

Harry's heart squeezed. 'No,' he breathed. 'Please. Not Lorraine...'

'I'm sorry. She died last night. Drowned in the canal. She was pushed.'

After a long silence, Harry said, 'Libby told me someone drowned but she never mentioned a name.'

'She didn't know you knew her.'

'She mentioned a tweed coat...'

'It was full-length. Weighed a ton. Even if she could swim, she would have really struggled.'

Gavin, Harry recalled, had bought it for her one Christmas. Poor Lorraine. Poor Gavin.

Theo held Harry's gaze. 'Don't you want to catch the people who killed her?'

Harry thought of Nicole mourning her best friend. And what about poor Esme, Lorraine's daughter? She was a good kid, two years younger than his own daughter Lottie, but they were still friends of a sort, in spite of the age difference. Could he really stand by and not get involved?

'What do you want me to do?' Harry relented.

'Meet me at the station first thing tomorrow for an eight o'clock briefing. I'm the SIO.'

'But you're in Bristol,' Harry protested. Theo had been transferred from Keynsham last month. Keynsham had been dead handy being barely seven miles west of Bath, but Bristol? It may look like no distance on a map being another seven miles on from Keynsham, but the traffic on the A4 was, invariably, awful. A lot of people forwent the A4 to drive three times further on the motorway because it was less hassle.

'It's not on the moon.'

Harry sighed. Checked his online calendar. 'I can reschedule most of my morning but I have a client at midday.'

'We'll be done well before then.' Theo walked across and briefly gripped Harry's shoulder. 'Thanks, pal.'

6

The major incident room smelled of coffee and hard work. Sounds were muted, expressions intense. At first glance it appeared incredibly disorganised with files, notepads and piles of paper everywhere, but Harry knew from past experience that despite the mess, everyone knew exactly where everything was because each person in the room had to be able to account for every piece of paper they created.

Harry walked across the room, heading for Theo, who was talking to a uniformed constable. Harry's eyes felt gritty after a restless night, haunted by dreams of his attacker and Lorraine's murder. Jessie had been a godsend yesterday, quietly supportive and loving, and instead of haring off to Eddie's Farm this morning she'd stayed and shared tea and toast with him, leaving the house at the same time. Her company had been remarkably soothing and now he felt steadier, more able to cope.

Theo looked up and when he saw Harry, terminated his conversation and turned to the room.

'Listen up,' he called.

Anyone who wasn't on the phone paused in what they were doing and looked up.

'You need to know we have Dr Harry Hope on our team.' He pointed at Harry. A roomful of heads swivelled to look at him. Harry raised a hand, feeling more self-conscious than he ever had standing in front of hundreds of people at a convention.

'Harry helped us with the NATS case last year so he comes with top credentials.'

A few nods and murmurs greeted this statement, encouraging Harry to think he might not be rejected outright. Unlike Libby, not every police officer saw the value in having a psychologist working alongside them. Some found it downright uncomfortable, thinking that Harry could read their minds. Which wasn't strictly true. Yes, he could read the subtext in a lot of personal conversations and interpret people's facial expressions and body language to a minute degree, but clairvoyance? Don't make him laugh.

'Harry has volunteered to help us with the Lorraine Brown case as well as look into the rash of knife attacks in the area. Help him where you can, please, and include him where you think appropriate. You will find him invaluable, but only if you involve him.'

With a nod to convey he'd finished, Theo stepped over to Harry. 'Briefing's downstairs. Are you okay to see the CCTV? It's pretty harrowing, but unless you do, you won't know what we're up against.'

Harry didn't want to watch Lorraine's attack, but he also didn't want the perpetrators to get away with murdering her, so he said, 'I'll be fine.'

The briefing was for uniformed officers who were responsible for door-knocking, checking witness statements and following up leads given to them from the officers in the MIR. A uniformed sergeant was standing at the front of the room. Harry tried not to look at the photographs of Lorraine on the board, smiling somewhere sunny, looking as mischievous as ever. How had it come to this? An attractive young mother pushed into the canal and left to drown?

Once again Theo introduced Harry – more nods and murmurs – after which the sergeant continued.

'So, what sort of person are we looking for? Let's have a look at the CCTV...'

A large screen flickered into life. Even though he'd braced himself, Harry still felt horror flood through every vein.

There she was, petite, vivacious Lorraine, walking briskly along the towpath seemingly unaware of three figures behind her in the shadows, stalking her. There was enough light from streetlamps for him to see they all wore hoodies, sneakers and jeans. Young men, like his own attacker. Each wore a mask. Halloween masks of skulls, blood and sharp teeth.

The time on the screen read 22.10.

As the men narrowed the space between them and their prey, he wanted to shout at Lorraine to turn around, to see them, to run, *anything*, but the next second, they were upon her like a pack of feral dogs.

She tried to fight back but she was barely five four and slim as a wand. She didn't stand a chance. Two of the figures simply picked her up and lobbed her into the canal. Harry's gaze went to the third. Another hit of horror. The third man was holding up his phone. He was recording it all.

Lorraine floundered. Harry couldn't bear to watch. Clamping down his emotions, he studied the youths. They all stood with their phones trained on her until, to Harry's shock, the third man stepped forward and started taking selfies – or was he filming himself? – with the drowning Lorraine behind him.

Abruptly, she vanished.

For a second, maybe two, the youths stared at the water slopping lazily. They became agitated, waving their hands and shouting between themselves. And then they ran.

Harry put a hand on the wall to steady himself. He felt like reaching into the film and grabbing each of those young men and holding their heads beneath the filthy canal water until their lungs filled.

The sergeant tapped the board. 'We need to find if elements of this crime might indicate the type of suspect. If they've pushed someone into the canal before. Whether they've threatened to do it before. Was Lorraine targeted, or was it a case of wrong place, wrong time?'

Harry listened to the sergeant allocating jobs to the team, who would interview who and where, who would map the area and get the geography of the crime sorted, and who would check the internet for any posting of the mobile phone footage.

At last, the room began to empty.

'Thoughts?' Theo asked Harry.

'I want to watch the footage again.'

Harry watched it, then watched it again. And again. He watched it until his eyes ached. Finally, he turned to Theo, who'd been watching with him.

'Although everything moves incredibly fast, it's obvious they're acting like it's a prank.' Harry pointed at the screen. 'You see the third man? He was egging them on. If the two who threw her in had been on their own, they'd never have done it.'

'Group think.'

'Yes. When she goes under, they were shocked. They didn't expect her to drown.'

Theo blinked.

'But when she did, none of them went to help her.'

He looked into Theo's eyes.

'I hope you hang them for that.'

7

In the car, Harry rang Nicole. He hadn't called her sooner because he'd wanted to have a clear run at the police side of things. Once she knew he was working with them she'd bombard him with questions and he wanted to be able to give her something to bite onto. Nicole wouldn't just be devastated at Lorraine's murder, she would be filled with rage.

She answered on the second ring.

'Harry.'

'I am so sorry, Nicole. Theo told me.' When she started to speak he rode over her, wanting to get his information across first not just to save time, but to save her further angst. 'He's also signed me up to help. I visited the station and they've got a massive team dedicated to finding Lorraine's attackers.'

'Do they have any idea who they were?' Her voice was stiff and he knew she was struggling to retain her control. Hurt, grief and anger mingling.

'Not yet. But they will, Nicole. You can rest assured of that.'

'And you're helping them?'

'Yes. Can I come and see you?'

'Of course.'

'I'm on my way.'

'Park in Dave's spot. He'll move his car for you.'

Harry felt a childish smugness that Nicole hadn't asked Dave but commanded him, putting Harry first. *Careful*, he told himself. *You don't want to stir up the mud in that particular pond. It'll only stick to you.*

If he counselled someone in the same position, he'd be telling them that their watchword should be indifference. Could he practise what he preached? Be indifferent to the man who had, effectively, stolen his wife? Although Harry had found the glorious Jessie and finally come to terms with the divorce, he still hadn't got over Dave's betrayal. The fact that his friend had been conducting an affair with Nicole for fourteen months – over a bloody year! – before they'd publicly declared their undying love for one another, continued to make his blood boil.

How could Dave have gone to the rugby with him, had a pint with him, while shagging Harry's wife? It beggared belief and right now he could feel his face flush and his pulse rise. He tried some deep breathing but he was still holding the steering wheel far too tightly when he pulled up outside their detached villa in Holburne Park.

He climbed out of the car into a brisk wind peppered with sleet. He turned up his collar. It might be April but the temperature was barely above freezing. Harry walked past the neatly clipped box hedge and up the path to the brand new home crafted from golden Bath stone. Four floors of sleek modern living for £1.4 million and they didn't even get a garden shed.

You can do indifference, he told himself. *You're a grown-up, remember?*

He scowled at Dave's new purchase; a brand spanking new BMW coupé M Sport, which cost over twice as much as what Harry earned in a year. Some days, Harry wondered if he'd chosen the right profession.

Nicole opened the door. For a moment, she stood there, tall and chic, her ice-blonde beauty as breath-taking as ever, but the instant their eyes met she crumpled.

'Oh, Harry.'

Gone was the composed and elegant woman and in her place was the young student in her twenties who had instantly captured his heart.

He strode to her, opening his arms. She stepped into his embrace as naturally as though they'd never been apart. He held her close, cupping the back of her head as she clutched his jumper and wept. He rocked her, murmuring nonsense, waiting for the storm to pass. Through the open door he could see a man watching them. Tall, strong shoulders. Dave might have played rugby but he had a tennis player's build. Harry didn't give any indication he'd seen him and after another few seconds, Dave disappeared. To hide in the attic, no doubt.

Finally, Nicole stepped back, wiping her eyes.

'God, I must look a mess,' she said.

'Never. You always look beautiful.'

She gave a wobbly smile. 'Ever gallant, Harry.'

'Ever truthful.'

'Yes.' Tears filled her eyes again.

'Oh, sweetheart.' He gave her another hug. 'I'm so sorry.'

'I'm sorry too, for crying all over you. I didn't realise how upset I was. Dave doesn't really do tears.'

I am indifferent to Dave, he told himself. He kept up the chant as Nicole led him inside and past a massive painting propped with its face against the wall. A pile of DIY tools lay beside it. He wondered briefly what the picture portrayed – he didn't think Dave was interested in art but perhaps he'd underestimated him.

In the kitchen Nicole put on some coffee. Harry stood by the fridge looking at a child's painting of a rainbow, with sheep and pigs at the bottom. He smiled inside, pleased that Lottie didn't seem to be expressing anything psychologically worrying through her art. They'd told all three children at the same time about the divorce fifteen months ago, trying to cushion the shock and provide a sense of family continuity. The fact Harry had kept the family home in Batheaston, a village two miles east of Bath, helped a lot, and when Lottie regressed to whining, her older brothers told her to look on the bright side. 'You'll have two homes,' Tim had said. 'That means two TVs,' Ben added, 'two bedrooms, two unicorns...'

Lottie had been obsessed with unicorns back then and the thought of having another one had diverted her nicely.

'Tell me what happened.' Nicole's voice cut through Harry's memories.

He didn't mince his words. He knew she wouldn't want that. Nicole would hate to be ambushed by something leaked to the press. She'd want to know it all, no matter how appalling. So he told her about the attack, the masks, the mobile phones.

She went as white as chalk. 'I hope you get them, Harry.'

'I'll do my best. Do you know what she was doing on the towpath?'

'Walking Bailey.'

Harry had forgotten about the family cockapoo. 'I didn't see Bailey on the CCTV.'

'He probably ran away, useless creature. When he came home alone Gavin knew something was wrong and went looking for her. You'll see Gav, won't you?'

'Absolutely.'

Harry stayed for another hour, talking things through and giving Nicole some impromptu grief counselling. 'There's no right or wrong way to feel,' he concluded. 'It's okay to be angry. It's okay to feel exhausted... And it's okay to ring me any time.'

Nicole kissed his cheek.

She was walking Harry outside when he spotted the cordless drill his father had given him one birthday. He didn't hesitate but bent down and picked it up.

'Harry!' Nicole looked shocked.

'I'm only reclaiming it,' he said reasonably.

In the car, cordless drill on the passenger seat, Harry started the engine but paused when a young man appeared at the bottom of the street. He wore a padded jacket and walked with an easy, loose-limbed pace. He had bruises around both eyes, and twin strips of tape over the bridge of his nose.

For a moment, Harry couldn't believe it.

It was his attacker.

Knife-man.

8

H arry grabbed his phone and dialled Libby. Prayed she was in Bath, investigating the stabbings and not tied up elsewhere arresting some scumbag or chasing another down the street. He could have screamed when her messaging service kicked in but as he started to speak, there was a click and she said, 'Hey, Harry. Brushed your hair yet?'

'My attacker,' he hissed. 'He's here. Outside Nicole's house.'

'Yay!' she exclaimed. 'I'm still in town!'

He rattled off the address.

'On my way,' she told him. 'Five minutes max. Don't lose him...'

Harry shoved the phone into his back pocket. Squirrelled as low as he could in the car, trying to hide, trying to keep his eyes averted and not draw attention to himself. Knife-man loped closer. He was thumbing his phone's screen, seemingly absorbed. As he neared Harry's car, Harry heard Libby's voice.

Don't lose him.

Harry already knew he couldn't run as fast as the youth, so following him on foot when he might be spotted was out of the question. So was following him by car for the same reason. As the young man walked past, Harry decided to take the only available option and tackle him. Bring the man down and sit on him until Libby arrived.

He had to hope the man didn't have a knife.

You can do this, he told himself. *But you've got to commit, knife or no knife.*

As he hesitated, a freeze-frame picture of Lorraine drowning in the canal seared his vision. Her frantic movements, her fear and desperation. Was this young man connected to her killers?

Adrenaline surged.

Harry sprang out of his car and in four swift paces was behind the young man. He moved fast, tackling low, leading with his shoulder, driving it into the man's waist then wrapping his arms around the man's thighs. His momentum carried them both forward, Harry using his arms to squeeze the man to the ground with him.

He heard the man's *ooof* and then, 'What the...' as he scrabbled at the ground, but Harry had managed to grab his right arm and twist it into the base of his spine in an iron grip.

'Citizen's arrest,' Harry gasped. 'Stay down or I'll knock your head off.'

The man twisted his head around. The moment he saw Harry, he stilled. 'Shit,' he said. His skin paled.

'Harry!' Nicole shouted. 'Stop!'

'Jesus Christ.' A man's voice.

Footsteps hammered.

The next thing Harry knew he was being pulled off the young man and he was fighting to keep hold of him, stop him from escaping. 'Get the hell off me!' Harry roared. He didn't want to lose him a second time.

'If you want to take it out on someone, take it out on me!' Dave yelled back.

At that moment, the young man scrambled to his feet and bolted.

'He tried to knife me!' Harry pointed furiously at knife-man's greyhound form haring down the street. 'I was holding him for the police!'

Dave looked at the fleeing man then back at Harry. 'Oops,' he said. A glint came into his eye. 'Why don't you drive?'

He might detest Dave but right now, he needed him. Both men piled into Harry's car. Harry turned the ignition, shoved the stick into first gear and spun the steering wheel, tyres screeching. The instant the vehicle had turned around he rammed his foot on the accelerator. Midway along the street, he saw the young man tearing left, heading for the Warminster Road.

Hard on the power, Harry raced after him. As he came to the junction he hit the brakes and spun the wheel. Dave was hanging on to the roof handle, his feet braced in the foot well. Neither of them wore seat belts.

Just ahead, the young man was running full pelt. Chest out, arms and legs pumping, he was giving it everything he had. He had no choice but run dead ahead – there were no front gardens to hide in, no cut-throughs.

'Drop me,' Dave said. 'Then get in front of him.'

Harry stuck his foot on the brake, hauling the ancient Rover to a juddering halt. Dave barely waited for the car to come to a rest and leaped out, slamming the door behind him and chasing after the fleeing form.

Harry accelerated past his quarry. Barely ten yards on, he slewed the car half across the pavement, sprang out, and went for him.

The young man took one horrified look at Harry and swung round to charge back down the street, where Dave waited.

As he approached Dave, he tried to dodge past him but Dave blocked him. The young man spun to face Harry but Harry was going full tilt towards him so he spun back to Dave and Harry could see his old friend was focused on the tackle, concentrating on making it quick, simple and safe. He was on his toes, knees slightly bent and arms in front of him, ready to spring.

The young man's courage failed him and he turned around again but Harry was right there, running at him with short, choppy steps to close the gap, ready to change direction if the young man tried to feint.

He feinted left but Harry wasn't fooled and stepped towards him. The young man tried to get around Harry. Harry stepped right at him and tackled him from the side, throwing his shoulder into his gut and following up by throwing his momentum into his midsection, pushing with his legs, driving through the tackle for maximum power.

Go down! he yelled in his mind and then they were falling, tumbling and flailing to the ground.

Harry scrambled to sit on the man's legs while Dave whipped off his belt and secured the man's wrists behind his back. 'Consider yourself nicked,' Harry gasped.

Dave looked at Harry. A grin split his face.

Harry couldn't help but grin back.

Nor could he stop himself from giving his old friend a high-five.

Just like in the old days.

9

Nicole arrived at a trot, hair swinging, her face pink.

'What in heaven's name…' She peered into the young man's face. 'Ethan? Whatever's going on?'

'Yeah, Ethan,' drawled Harry. 'Why'd you try to knife me the day before yesterday?'

Nicole's eyes widened. 'He *what*?'

'He's wanted by the police, with a capital W. Libby's on her way.'

'I don't believe it.' Nicole looked astonished.

'Who is he?' Harry asked.

'He's our neighbour's son. Well, next street neighbours, to be precise. He's the son of Lord Stanning Jones.'

'Not *the* Lord Stanning Jones?' Harry said disbelievingly.

'The one and the same,' Dave said.

'Bloody hell.'

Mark Stanning Jones was Chancellor of the University of Bath and a member of the House of Lords Select Committee. He was what Harry would call a Big Cheese, with a string of letters after his name – lots of honorary somethings. He'd also written several books and was former chairman of a variety of mega companies. He'd also been a Conservative MP and what about his wife? She was also a Big Cheese, if he remembered correctly. A judge.

Harry clambered off Ethan's legs. Now he knew who the young man was and where his parents lived, he thought he could afford to be a little less forceful.

'Let's get him up,' he told Dave.

Together they manhandled Ethan to his feet. He'd scraped his cheek on the pavement and grazed his wrists, but otherwise looked okay. He was covered in sweat and trembling.

'So, Ethan, why did you attack me?'

'I didn't.'

'Yes, you did. There was a witness. Douglas King.'

A flash of defiance crossed Ethan's face. 'He saw you punching me. You went mad. I didn't do anything. He said so.'

Harry recalled Doug's words. *I didn't see a knife. I just saw you on the ground, hitting him.*

'You and I know what you did, or tried to do. I just want to know why.'

Ethan gave Harry a cold look. 'I don't understand why you've got it in for me. Maybe I look like someone you don't like?' He appealed to Nicole. 'I was just walking along the street minding my own business when he came at me...'

'Stop lying.' Harry lost patience. 'It really isn't doing you any favours and...' He paused to answer his phone. 'Libby, we're just around the corner.' He gave her directions.

'Why did you run just now?' Dave asked Ethan curiously. 'If you weren't guilty of something?'

'I didn't want to get hit again. He's got it in–'

'For you, yes,' Harry interrupted. 'I've got the gist of your defence.'

When Ethan saw the police car, he shuddered. Harry looked at him with interest.

'Never been arrested before?' he asked.

Ethan shook his head.

'Never been to a police station before?'

Another shake.

'What do you think your parents will do when they discover you've been arrested?'

Ethan blanched. Which gave Harry an idea.

'Hold him,' Harry told Dave. 'I'm going to have a word with Libby.'

Libby had parked alongside them. She had put on her cap and closed the car door behind her. Harry held up a hand and walked over.

'You got him.' She beamed. Libby was an old-school police officer. She liked nothing more than nicking bad guys. She already had her handcuffs out in readiness.

'Yes. But I've had an idea.' He filled Libby in on Ethan's parents. 'He'll deny everything until he's blue in the face, and since I don't have a witness, I'm on shaky ground.'

'A night in a police cell might help.'

'I don't think so. I think we could do better playing a longer game. What if Ethan's part of this knifing epidemic? What if he can help us find out what's going on?'

Libby looked sceptical. 'How do we get him to help us?'

Harry hastily outlined his plan.

'You think it might work?'

'It's worth a shot. Don't you think?'

Libby looked across at Ethan. She pulled a face. 'Posh nobs are the worst. They think they're so much better than everyone else.'

Harry waited.

'It's a shame.' She sighed. 'I would have loved to have banged him up, but if you're right...' She squared her shoulders.

'Let's do it.'

10

Harry took Libby's lead as she walked over to Ethan. He didn't want the young man to know it was his plan. He wanted him to think providence was playing a part.

'Hello, you little shit,' Libby said conversationally.

Ethan blinked in surprise. He obviously wasn't used to being called names by someone in authority.

'I've heard you attacked Dr Harry Hope two days ago. With a knife.'

'No, he attacked *me*. I've never done anything–'

'Shut up.' Her voice was like a slap. 'I've known Harry for years. I know he'd never attack a little shite like you. Why would he bother? I mean look at you, with your designer gear and hoity-toity accent. You think you can call Mummy and Daddy and they'll get you off scot-free but you're wrong. You'll have to climb over me first and I'm not going to stand for your "I'm innocent" crap because–'

'Libby…' It was Nicole, hands held high. 'Do you have to–'

'Piss off, Nicole,' Libby snapped. 'And take your drippy little lapdog with you.'

Nicole drew herself tall. 'There's no need to be like that.'

'Do it.' Libby's face was rigid, her body like board.

Harry could feel Nicole willing him to look at her but he kept his attention on Libby. Nor did he look at Dave as they walked away.

'Now, where were we?' Libby smiled but it didn't reach her eyes. 'Oh, yes. We were talking about what I'm going to do to you. How I'm going to bang you up and throw away the key. You see, we don't like people who carry knives in this city. We don't like them at all. So we want to set an example.'

'Libby...' Harry's voice held a warning. 'I don't think that's going to happen.'

'Why not?' She rounded on him so savagely he almost forgot they were play-acting.

'There wasn't a witness.'

He caught Ethan's look of surprise that he was defending him.

'You want him to get away with it?' She affected a look of dismay.

'Well, no... but I can't see I've got much of a case. It's his word against mine.'

'Hmm.' Libby jingled her handcuffs as she appeared to think. 'He'd only get community service anyway. Removing graffiti, clearing rubbish from wasteland. It's not very onerous.' Her face suddenly cleared. 'I know what. How about he does community service with you, Harry? That way you get the benefit and he gets punished.'

'What?' Harry pretended to be surprised.

'I think Ethan here should work for you, unpaid, for the next–'

'Hey, that's unethical,' Ethan interjected.

'So is knifing an innocent man,' Libby snapped.

'But I didn't–'

'Fine, have it your way.' She held out the handcuffs. 'Ethan

Stanning Jones, you are under arrest on suspicion of an attempted knife attack on Dr Harry Hope. You do not have to say anything, but it may harm–'

'Okay, okay,' he relented quickly, both hands raised. 'But I can't *work*. I'm at uni. I've got lectures and courses to attend.' His face turned desperate. 'I've got loads of studying to do.'

Libby watched him, expressionless. 'What days do you have free, for studying?'

'I don't, not really...' Ethan was pretending to think but Harry was pretty sure the lad would have his timetable off pat.

'Okay, let's say you work at Harry's every Tuesday and Thursday afternoon–'

'Not Tuesdays. Please.' Ethan was fraught. 'Mondays are better.'

'So, every Monday and Thursday–'

'Friday?' Ethan offered plaintively.

Libby took a breath. 'Every Monday and Friday you're Harry's until the first of June.'

'But that includes the vacation,' Ethan bleated.

Libby didn't say anything. Just looked at him.

A sick look came over Ethan's face.

'Great.' Libby clipped her handcuffs back onto her duty belt. 'I'll let you guys work out the hours, when you turn up, et cetera. Meanwhile, Mr Ethan Stanning Jones, if you're so much as one minute late or, God forbid, fail to attend your community service with Harry, I will be forced to take it up with your parents. Do you understand?'

'Yes.' It was a croak.

Libby strode for her car, climbed inside and drove away.

Harry brought out his phone. 'Ring me, so I've got your number.'

Ethan did as he was asked.

'I'll text you my office address later,' Harry told him. 'I'll expect you there this Friday at 2pm sharp, and for you to be there until five.'

Without another word, Harry headed down the street to where Nicole and Dave stood, but as he approached, Dave took Nicole's arm and led her away. It was a proprietorial gesture that told Harry that although Dave had just helped him apprehending Ethan, it didn't change anything.

Harry drove onto the Warminster Road and hit the accelerator.

11

Harry rang Jagoda on his way to work. 'I'm running late. Can you apologise to Susanna for me? Tell her I had an emergency but I'll see her at the end of the day if she's free.'

'Emergency?' Jagoda repeated anxiously. 'Are things okay?'

'I'll be with you in fifteen minutes. You can see for yourself.'

Fifteen minutes turned into thirty when Harry got stuck in traffic on The Paragon. To his alarm, his car's oil temperature gauge started to rise for no apparent reason, and he hurriedly made a mental note to take the car into the garage ASAP. The Rover was getting on a bit now, and Harry wondered if it was time to upgrade it, possibly for a 4X4 of some sort. It would make getting down Bannerdown, a steep hill between his house and the village, less hair-raising when it was icy if nothing else.

By the time he'd parked in his rented space on Harley Street, it was past two and various parts of his body were throbbing from having hit the pavement not just once, but twice, bringing Ethan down. From past experience on the rugby field he knew no real damage had been done, but it didn't help the pain much, and he ducked into the Co-op and bought a packet of paracetamol.

Jagoda's eyes went straight to his bruised knuckles. She pushed her keyboard away, all concern.

'I'm fine,' Harry insisted, and since nobody was in the waiting area he gave a heavily edited version of what had happened, which Jagoda seemed to take in her stride.

'Ethan's agreed to come and work here as punishment,' Harry told her. 'Redecorating the Centre. Are you okay with that?'

'For sure,' she said.

'If he makes you feel uncomfortable in any way, or behaves badly at all, let me know immediately.'

She nodded before saying crisply, 'Arnica. For your bruises. You would like some?'

He said yes to give Jagoda's nurturing spirit satisfaction. While she went to fetch the arnica, he picked through the pile of parcels on her desk. As usual, they were all for Doug. If he didn't know the man better, he'd think he was addicted to online shopping from the quantity of packages delivered.

Absently, he rubbed in some arnica lotion before he downed two paracetamol, and headed to his office. He had back-to-back clients until six o'clock, which was when he saw Susanna. His client didn't mention his rescheduling her appointment or seem to notice his bruised fists but launched straight in.

'He went away on business with her. To London. All last week. He's opening another dojo there.'

Susanna was an attractive woman in her early forties whose husband was conducting an affair with one of his staff – a younger woman. In itself, this wouldn't concern Harry overly, but the fact Susanna suffered from low self-esteem thanks to being the adult child of an alcoholic meant she took the blame on herself. *I'm a terrible wife*, she'd told Harry. *I'm a hideous, worthless old woman, no wonder he's gone elsewhere*. Susanna had originally come to Harry with an eating disorder problem but now her husband was playing away, she was having suicidal thoughts.

Harry didn't get tied in to her self-flagellation but concentrated on the thought patterns that were keeping her from feeling good about herself and her looks.

'Look at yourself in the mirror,' he instructed her. 'What words come into your head?'

'I'm ugly. Repulsive.'

'What do you see, in particular?'

'I've got blotchy skin. Wrinkles around my eyes. My neck's like a chicken's.'

Harry questioned whether the words she'd used were really accurate. Where were the blotches? The wrinkles? He encouraged her to rewrite her dialogues as though she were talking to her best friend, Amelia.

'Would you say those things to her?'

'Of course not.' She looked shocked.

'I'd like you to start talking to yourself like you would to Amelia.'

Even though he was absorbed with Susanna, Harry couldn't keep thoughts of Lorraine at bay, nor the wave of seemingly unrelated knife attacks, and when the session was over, he called Lorraine's husband Gavin, and asked if he could come over.

'Sure.' The man's voice was strained. 'I'm just getting supper together.'

Harry drove across town and parked outside the Prior Park Farm Shop. Walked back to Forefield Rise, a steep, narrow lane with no passing places and no parking. Halfway up, Harry paused outside a two-storey Victorian red-brick house to look at the view. Bath was spread below, starting to twinkle through the darkening sky. He could hear seagulls – a perennial problem in the city thanks to people dropping food on the ground – and smell onions cooking.

Even through his anxiety and sorrow he still managed to feel a rush of affection for the city. He'd been born here, gone to school and uni here, and after a stint in London, had worked here pretty much all his life. He was a bit of a homebody, he supposed, and he was lucky to have been so blessed to live somewhere so beautiful.

He unlatched an iron gate on his right and latched it again behind him. Terracotta pots stood on either side of the front door, filled with purple and red pansies.

Harry pressed the doorbell, gathering himself to say the right thing, to be a support. He couldn't imagine losing Nicole or Jessie to murder. Which emotion would dominate? he wondered. Rage would be near the top of the list, along with revenge.

From inside Harry heard Gavin call, 'Zara, get the door, would you?'

12

———

Seconds later, the door opened to reveal a plump woman with wavy chestnut hair and a harried expression.

'I'm Harry,' he said. 'Gavin said it was okay to come over.'

'Yes, he's expecting you.' She opened the door wide. 'I'm Gavin's sister, Zara.'

'I'm so sorry about Lorraine. I can't imagine what you must be going through.'

'Thanks. It's been...' Her eyes welled up. 'Pretty awful.'

'I can imagine.'

She led the way past a jumble of children's toys which included a hobby horse and a picnic set. Two bicycles were propped against the wall. Waterproofs and coats hung from hooks in the wall, below which lay a jumble of boots and running shoes.

'We're just washing up.'

Three children crowded around the sink clutching tea towels. Esme, Robert and George. Six, eight and ten respectively. As Harry stepped inside Gavin glanced around. His eyes were bloodshot, his skin pasty. 'Hey, look who's here.'

'Hi, Harry,' the children chorused.

'Hi, gang.'

Gavin turned back to the sink. 'Kids, why don't you go and watch TV. I want to talk to Harry for a bit. And take Bailey with you.'

All three pattered out, followed by the cockapoo, then Zara.

Gavin put down the washing-up brush. His head was bowed. 'I saw her today. I had to. I wouldn't have believed it otherwise.'

Harry crossed the kitchen to put his hand on Gavin's shoulder. 'I'm so sorry.'

'Jesus, man... why her? What did she ever do to anyone? She was the light of my life. What am I going to do without her?' He choked. Harry gripped his arm. They stood silently for a while. Then Gavin gave himself a shake. 'Kids don't know what's hit them. I'm trying for normal –' he gestured at the pots and pans of what looked like the remains of spaghetti bolognaise '– but it's weird. It's like it's happening to someone else.'

Gavin sank onto a chair. Put his head in his hands.

'I'm not surprised you're feeling dazed.' Harry gently began his second grief counselling session of the day. 'I'm glad your sister's here to help out.'

'That bloody dog. If she hadn't taken it for a walk...'

If, if, if. The perennial guilt-laden accusation.

Harry listened, calmed and empathised, but with Theo and the knifing attacks looming at the forefront of his mind, he finally turned the conversation to ask if Lorraine had had any enemies, or if she'd fallen out with anyone recently.

'Enemies? Don't make me laugh.'

'It could be as small as nicking someone's space in the super-market car park, or passing someone for promotion.'

Gavin had a think. 'She came home last week one night, really shaken up, but I don't think it's relevant. She told me a car had nearly knocked her over. Missed her by inches, apparently. It didn't stop. Just roared off. She didn't get its number.'

49

'When was this?'

'Last Tuesday.'

The day before the knife attacks started.

'Where?'

'Up at the university.'

Lorraine was a senior lecturer in creative writing, Harry remembered. Was the near-miss anything to do with uni student Ethan Stanning Jones? And what about the other attacks? Were the young men caught on CCTV filming Lorraine as she drowned also uni students? If so, then the university was definitely worth a look.

Harry felt exhausted when he arrived home. His bruised body was crying out for a hot bath, his mood a glass of whisky. Later he'd slump in front of the TV and try to forget about things for a while. His phone pinged as he climbed out of the car.

It was Jessie texting, asking if he was up for a visit.

You bet, he texted back. *And if you're hungry, I'll let you share my pie.*

It was then when he realised he hadn't eaten lunch. His stomach started to growl.

Yes, please x

He kicked off his shoes in the hallway and padded into the kitchen, checked the range was up to speed for the pie. He'd just poured a glass of whisky when the doorbell rang. He checked through the sitting-room window to see it was Theo.

'Beer?' he offered as the DI dumped his shoes next to Harry's in the hall.

'No Jessie?'

'She's on her way.'

Theo grunted and stalked to the kitchen and the supply of

Black Sheep beer. Helped himself. Came and joined Harry in the living room.

'Hell of a day.' He sighed.

Harry knew to remain silent. He'd known Theo for five years now. They'd met at a Neighbourhood Watch get-together. Talking afterwards, they discovered a mutual love of Formula 1, and when Harry mentioned he'd been given tickets to the British Grand Prix, he asked if Theo would like to join him. Theo's face had lit up. They'd had a cracking day, ending up at the White Horse, Silverstone, drinking real ale in surprisingly easy companionship. Theo had then invited Harry to a local wine-tasting evening and from there, their friendship had grown into one of mutual trust, which, considering the confidential nature of their professions, was as valuable as gold dust to them both.

'Which,' Theo continued, 'was nicely topped off by Libby telling me you're not going to press charges against your attacker.'

'He made a mistake.'

'Yeah, right.' Theo cradled his beer against his chest. 'You're too soft, Harry.'

'He's going to work for me, for free, as penance.'

'Doing what?'

'The Centre needs redecorating.'

'Nice one.' Theo yawned, showing a cavernous mouth and strong white teeth. 'In case you're wondering, I didn't come over just for your scintillating company, or your beer, but because we've found an interesting link between the attacks.'

Harry sat up. 'Which is?'

'You.'

13

Harry gaped at Theo. 'What do you mean, the attacks link to me?'

'You're the only common denominator we've found.'

'But I don't know any of them. Well, aside from Lorraine.'

'The first man to be attacked was Kevin Owen. His wife is Susanna Owen. Your client.'

Kevin Owen, who was cheating on his wife who in turn was beating herself up that it was her fault. Strange, that she hadn't mentioned her husband's attack.

When Theo kept his eyebrows raised, Harry admitted that Dave worked at the Chikara Martial Arts with Kevin Owen. 'Teaching judo. But that doesn't mean I'm the connection, surely–'

'The second man who escaped a knife attack was Philip Petty,' Theo interjected.

'My parents' neighbour?' Harry said disbelievingly.

'Yes.'

'And the third?'

'Junto Tanaka.'

Harry felt a rush of relief that he didn't recognise the name.

'Also known as John Tanaka.' Theo took another draught of beer. 'You met him at a car track day at Castle Combe Race Circuit.'

'I still don't know him.'

'He says he knows you. He took you round in his Aston Martin.'

Now that, Harry did remember. Tanaka had driven like a maniac, barely braking at each corner and leaving Harry somewhat weak-kneed afterwards.

'I met him *once*.'

'Still, it's a connection.'

Harry opened and closed his mouth. 'This is crazy.'

'But you can't deny you know all the victims. The five of you are connected.'

'Yes,' Harry agreed, 'but I'm sure if you dig a bit deeper you'll find we're all associated with other people in a similar way. We all live in the same city and it's not as if Bath's London.'

'That may well be. But right now, you're the only link, so we're going to have to start looking at you, Harry, and who else you know.'

'It's coincidence.' Harry was firm. 'A statistician would tell you the same thing.'

'Hmm.' Theo mulled for a moment. 'There is something very suspect going on here and I want to get to the bottom of it before someone else gets seriously hurt. I'd like you to list any interests or hobbies you all might share. Any courses you've been on, businesses involved in... Any links between you, no matter how tenuous.'

'You want me to do your donkey work,' Harry said wearily.

'You'll have far more success with your touchy-feely questions than a hairy-arsed sergeant, trust me.' Theo stretched before draining his glass. 'And please, Harry, go carefully with your free decorator. Don't turn your back on him.'

'I won't,' Harry agreed, and at that moment he heard the front door open and a woman's voice sang out, 'Get that pie in the oven! I'm starving!'

Theo rose. 'Later.'

Harry saw him out before heading for Jessie and supper eaten at the kitchen table. When he filled Jessie in on the day's events, she was shocked. 'Jesus, Harry. What the hell's it all about?'

'I don't know.' He mopped up the remainder of his gravy. 'But I'm going to do my best to find out.'

The next day, Harry went and saw his parents' neighbour, Philip Petty. He'd known him since he was a kid and could remember the party Phil had thrown when he got married for the third time. It had been his first experience of drinking wine – he'd sneaked a glass without anyone looking – and he'd found it so disgusting he'd spat it out in a pot plant.

Phil had looked fit to burst with pride with his new bride. 'Third time lucky,' he'd beamed, and it seemed luck had done her bit because he and Angela were still together twenty-five years later.

Harry had called ahead and when Phil opened the front door he was greeted by the sound of Blondie and the smell of freshly ground coffee beans.

'Harry, mate.' He put out a hand. 'Come in.'

He was in his seventies, whipcord thin with a strong hand-shake and a direct gaze. Harry had always liked the construction builder even though some people on the street had sneered, mostly out of jealousy once he'd made his first million. Harry liked Phil for keeping his feet on the ground and not turning into something he wasn't just because he was rich.

'Why would I live on the Royal Crescent for Pete's sake?' he'd once said. 'Surrounded by the upper classes and being forced to listen to opera? Here, I know who I am and I know who you lot are too.'

Harry drank a cup of the finest Columbian coffee before joining Phil in the garden, where he was tidying up the flower beds and borders. 'People always ask me why I don't get a gardener in but it's never done the way I like it.'

They talked over the improvements he'd made to the house over the years, from putting a self-contained flat into the attic to adding a huge conservatory and re-landscaping the entire garden. Then Harry turned the subject to Phil's knife attack. 'What happened?'

Phil put another handful of leaves and debris into his plastic tub. 'I'd come out of Everleigh's after a fry-up...' He looked around briefly before dropping his voice. 'Don't tell Ange. I'm on statins and she believes I'll drop dead of a heart attack if I even look at a fried egg.'

Harry chuckled. 'I've had far worse secrets to keep.'

'I bet.' Phil stood up, dusting his hands of dirt. 'There I was, minding my own business, putting on my helmet, when this guy comes out of nowhere and goes for me with a knife. He meant business, you know. He wanted to hurt me. He bloody nearly got me too except I managed to block him. Got my arm in the way.' He pulled his fleece sleeve back to show a livid red worm of a scar forming between a row of bristling stitches.

'I tried to grab his wrist, make him drop the knife. He didn't like that and ran away.' He pulled his sleeve down. 'I was lucky, I think. Made me glad I'd done some self-defence.'

'Do you know Kevin Owen?' Harry asked.

'I know of him, yes. He runs Chikara Martial Arts in town. His wife goes to Pilates with Angela.'

Harry felt a little surge of triumph. He wasn't the only link.

Susanna's husband was a judo instructor and then there was Dave, who also taught martial arts.

'What about David – Dave – Gardner?' Harry asked.

'No. Should I?'

'He's another martial arts instructor.'

Phil shook his head.

'What do you remember about your attacker?'

'Small and whippy. A bit feral-looking, if you know what I mean. Greasy hair. Jeans, sweatshirt, running shoes. Late teens, maybe early twenties.'

'The knife?'

'Huge.' Phil grinned briefly. 'Looked like an ordinary fighting knife to be honest. Eight inches long or so. Sharp as hell.'

Harry asked more questions. Phil pulled out more weeds. Harry ascertained they'd both been to the Forum, a music venue in Southgate, eaten at Noya's Kitchen and gone hot-air ballooning. They had lots in common just living in the same city, but no other definite link that Harry could uncover.

As Harry left, a woman arrived. Flashing smile, long legs, lots of honey-gold, bouncy hair. Harry recognised her as the estate agent who'd found him his practice rooms. After she'd gone inside, Harry turned to Phil. 'Not selling up, are you?'

'Do me a favour, mate?' Phil's voice was calm, but his expression was cold. 'Don't tell anyone she's been here, okay? And if you so much as breathe a word to Angela, I'll rip your balls off.'

14
___

Harry drove to Harley Street deep in thought. He knew he should tell Theo about Phil and the estate agent – he couldn't for the life of him remember her name – but he also didn't want to bring destruction to what had appeared to be a rock-solid marriage.

He had to admit he was surprised. He hadn't thought of Phil being a philanderer, he'd seemed too moral, too decent, especially considering each time he fell for a woman, he married her. What had changed? Harry wondered. Did he feel unloved or unappreciated? Perhaps he was lacking excitement? If so, it could explain him bringing his lover into the marital home. Nothing like making love with the risk of the wife catching them in flagrante at any moment.

As he drove past the Approach Golf Course, dotted with cheerful clumps of daffodils as well as the odd golfer, he wondered whether Nicole had brought Dave into their home. Made love to him in their bed. She'd said she hadn't, but since she knew Harry would go berserk if she had, she'd probably lied.

He was glad his home was now filled with Jessie. Marital

ghosts laid to rest. He drank less, made love more. Laughed more too. He was a lucky man, he admitted. Even if he won the lottery tomorrow, he didn't think he could be happier.

Before he saw his first client, Harry did some work on a presentation he'd agreed to give next week. He'd learned over time it was best to rewrite and practise, practise, practise, and since he'd be speaking to his peers, he wanted his talk to have real impact. It had been a fellow psychologist who'd roped him in to perform at the Swiss Psychological Association's Congress which, this year, was being held in London rather than Zurich to coincide with the tenth British Psychoanalytic Film Festival.

Doug had attended the congress multiple times thanks to dividing his time between his practice in Bath and his work at the University of Zurich, where he was a psychosexual therapist and clinical traumatologist. Because Doug was a previous congress award winner he was giving the keynote address. He hadn't had anything to do with Harry being invited to speak and when Harry mentioned it, had looked startled.

'I'm not treading on your toes, am I?' Harry had asked.

Doug had opened and closed his mouth and for one horrible moment, Harry thought he was going to say *yes*, but then he grinned.

'It'll be great to have you there. I can introduce you around. Give you the inside track.'

Harry had arranged to stay in London for two nights before heading back to Bath first thing on Thursday. He was rather looking forward to it all.

He'd rewritten the first two paragraphs when Doug tapped on his door and popped his head inside.

'You and Jessie still on for dinner tonight?'

'Absolutely. What can we bring?'

'Just yourselves. Catherine's got it all sorted.'

Harry was glad Doug had invited them to supper, a gesture

that he hoped meant that their friendship was back on track. He'd obviously touched a nerve recently because when he'd questioned Doug about his last trip to Zurich, pointing out that the flight times hadn't matched up to the agenda Doug had given Jagoda and giving him an unaccounted day who knew where, he'd flown off the handle.

How dare you pry into my affairs. Do I ask where you are for every second of every day? Do I demand to know where you've been when you're late in, in the morning? What next? You want to install a punch card system in the Centre? Or would you prefer to put a geolocator on my phone so you can see where I am at any time?

Harry had immediately backed off but even though he'd apologised profusely it had taken Doug a while to calm down. Eventually Doug had apologised too, muttering he'd had to go to hospital on the day in question and hadn't wanted anyone to find out, but when Harry, concerned, had wanted to know more, Doug had held up a hand.

Stop. Leave me some privacy, please.

Ever since then, Harry had felt as though he'd been treading on eggshells and when the invitation came for dinner, he'd been inordinately relieved.

Now, Harry gestured at his computer screen. 'Rewriting my speech.'

'You don't have to do it, you know.'

Harry had confessed to Doug that when he was first asked, he'd been in two minds thanks to an already heavy workload.

'I can always fill in for you,' Doug insisted. 'I'd do it in a heartbeat.'

'You're a sucker for punishment.' Harry chuckled. 'But thanks anyway.'

Doug hesitated, looking as though he was going to say something more, but then Jagoda buzzed Harry to let him know his client had arrived and Doug vanished. Harry spent the rest of the day absorbed in counselling, and the anxieties, frustrations and mind-wanderings that went with it. Once he'd written up his notes and cleared his desk, it was past six, and he found himself half-walking, half-jogging to his car, not wanting to be late in collecting Jessie.

He was aware he hadn't walked up Gloucester Street since Ethan had tried to knife him. Not that he thought the young man would try a second time after he'd had his nose broken. And what about that look of loathing he'd caught? What was all that about? It was something personal, but since Harry didn't know Ethan, he couldn't begin to imagine what it might be. Maybe he'd find out tomorrow, when Ethan started 'work'.

Showered and changed, Harry drove to Jessie's cottage, which she shared with another Aussie. Perched above Box on Box Hill, just five miles east along the valley from Batheaston, it had stone roof tiles and a conservatory with far-reaching views all the way back to Bath. Across the valley stood Colerne, and if asked, Harry could have rattled off the names of all the villages that surrounded Bath as well as their pubs thanks to having walked their interconnecting footpaths since he was a child, sometimes with his parents and their dog, sometimes with a girlfriend.

He'd barely parked when Jessie trotted outside, wearing a pretty dress and clutching a bottle of, surprise, surprise, Aussie Shiraz.

'My favourite,' he said.

'Only because I've been educating you that there's more to red wine than Rioja and Bordeaux.'

'True.'

Harry drove along Bloomfield Rise and parked outside Doug's home, an end-of-terrace house dressed in Bath stone.

'I still can't get over the fact they've lived here for so long.' Jessie shook her head.

'Why?'

'I would have thought Doug would have moved somewhere larger. I mean he can afford it, right?'

'Oh, yes.' Harry unclipped his seat belt. 'He can afford it all right. We've been ribbing him about it for years. While we've all upgraded our houses, the Kings have stayed put. Doug doesn't see the need to follow the crowd. He carves his own furrow.'

He watched Jessie looking at the house. 'What does Catherine say? The kids?'

'She'd like a bigger place for the family but Doug insists there's no point. He harks on about when the kids leave home, they'll just have to downsize again, so they may as well save the money they'd spend moving, on other things.'

'Like what?'

They climbed out of the car. Harry glanced at an airliner droning above, heading to Bristol. 'His work in Zurich, for a start. He puts a lot of money into research on trauma victims.'

'A philanthropist, then.'

'It's what makes him tick.'

15

As they approached the house, the door opened and Doug ushered them inside. It was the usual chaos, with bicycles in the hallway, piles of shoes, and wall hooks weighed down with bulging rows of scarves and coats.

'Kids!' Doug yelled up the stairs. 'Come and say hi to Harry!'

'Hi, Harry,' voices chorused. A thunder of feet followed. Identical twins Mia and Paton came and kissed his cheek before greeting Jessie. 'I like your dress,' Mia said.

'Why, thank you.' Jessie fluttered a little curtsey.

'You missed a bit,' Paton told Harry, pointing at his cheek.

Harry touched the area to feel bristles. 'I didn't miss them, I left them just for you so you could have the pleasure of pointing them out.'

Paton giggled.

The six of them squeezed into the kitchen while Doug poured the wine and Catherine served a bubbling lasagne and plates of crusty garlic bread. Jessie hadn't met the twins before and Harry saw her sneaking glances at them, obviously fascinated by their likeness. Same curly brown hair, quick brown eyes and serious expressions. Even the spread of freckles across their noses were almost identical.

'How long have I known you?' he asked them.

'All our lives,' answered Mia.

'Which is eight years and three months,' added Paton.

'You're Mia, right?' He looked at Paton.

They both collapsed into giggles.

'Oh.' He pretended to be crestfallen. 'I really thought I'd got it taped.'

He knew they loved it when he got them mixed up.

'I gather you're giving a talk at Doug's congress,' Catherine said to Harry.

'It's not my congress,' Doug protested.

'Well, since you're its president, I'd say it was.'

Harry raised his eyebrows at Doug. 'You never said.'

Doug shrugged, looking uncomfortable. 'I don't like making a big deal of it.'

'You need to update your website,' Harry told him. 'It still says that Nieder-someone's president.'

'Niederhouser,' Doug supplied helpfully. 'I'll tell them but trust me, it won't happen overnight. The organisation itself may run like clockwork but the web guys are a law unto themselves. Now, what's your presentation about? Didn't you say it was about organisational culture?'

Harry looked at the twins. 'That's like you two dressing alike and interacting the same within the family. You're an organisational culture of two.'

The twins grinned.

'How's the book coming along?' Harry asked Doug. He'd started a novel recently. A modern international thriller that, Doug joked, could become a bestseller and make him enough money to retire. When he'd told Harry the plot, even to Harry's, albeit inexpert, ear, it had sounded rather good.

'It's not.' Doug was curt.

Belatedly Harry took in the shadows around his friend's eyes, the way the grooves on his cheeks had deepened. The last time he remembered Doug looking so tired was when Paton had been hospitalised with meningitis. Doug was stressed about something. Harry elected to try to find out what it might be in case he could help.

'What a shame.' Harry strove to be neutral. 'I have to say I liked the idea.'

Doug nodded but didn't say any more.

After pudding, the twins were allowed to go back upstairs, leaving the adults to coffee and a huge box of hand-finished Swiss chocolates from Doug's last Zurich visit. When Catherine took Jessie into the sitting room to show her the Aboriginal carving of a goanna a friend had brought her from Sydney, Harry turned to Doug.

'Talk to me, Doug. What's wrong?' He used his counsellor's voice, dispassionate, non-judgemental.

Doug gave a wry smile. 'Remind me never to have you over when I'm trying to keep up a facade.'

'Am I allowed to know?'

'What, aside from the fact my parents are having to go into a home?'

Harry had met Neil and Marjory a few times. Neil was a landscape gardener, Marjory a nurse. Nice people, reliable and straightforward, but now very elderly.

'I'm sorry.'

'I've found a good place for them, but it's not exactly cheap.'

'They rarely are.' Harry studied his friend. 'There's more, isn't there?'

Doug sighed. 'Bad things never come one at a time, do they?'

Harry waited.

'I got a bit of a shock this week when I heard my creative writing teacher died. She drowned.'

Harry felt his jaw soften. 'Not Lorraine Brown?'

Doug nodded.

'Did you know Lorraine was a friend of Nicole's?'

'No.' Doug looked startled. 'I had no idea.'

'Nicole is Esme's godmother.'

Doug passed a hand over his face. 'That poor family.'

'And you?'

'I miss her,' he said simply. 'We used to go out for a drink, talk about writing. Not often, but enough for Catherine to question our relationship.'

'Which was?'

'Get your mind out of the gutter, Harry.'

'There's something else, then.'

'Isn't that enough?' Doug said wearily. 'My parents, then Lorraine?'

'No.' Harry topped up their glasses. 'It's *me*, Doug. Come on. Tell me.'

Long silence.

Doug sighed. 'I suppose someone ought to know.'

Harry waited.

When Doug finally met Harry's eyes he looked ten years older. 'I have cancer.'

16

After Harry had dropped Jessie back to her cottage, he went home and poured himself a brandy. Doug had told him that he had follicular lymphoma, a type of cancer that wasn't necessarily an immediate death sentence, but it was still a disease that was incurable. At least now Harry knew why Doug looked so tired.

'I'm told I can live a normal life for years,' Doug said. 'They're not advocating treatment until the symptoms become particularly painful.' His mouth twisted. 'It's like living with a time bomb that one day could destroy me, I just don't know when.'

He'd sworn Harry to secrecy.

'Catherine doesn't need to know. And the twins certainly don't. Not unless I need treatment, that is. I'll cross that bridge when I come to it. Promise me you won't tell Catherine. Not *anyone*.' He was fierce.

If Catherine found out that Harry knew and he hadn't told her, he doubted she'd forgive him. And she'd be right.

'Swear it,' Doug hissed.

Against his will, Harry promised to keep Doug's secret but

when he eventually went to bed, he lay in the dark, thinking about mortality and murder, and when he finally fell asleep, it was to dream he was drowning.

First thing in the morning, Harry dropped Theo an email, telling him he'd found another connection, this time between Doug and Lorraine. Theo rang him ten minutes later.

'There's been another attack on Philip Petty.'

Harry put a hand on the wall. 'What happened? Is he okay?'

'A car ran him down when he was coming back from the Old Crown last night. He's in intensive care. I've been told he may not make it. Serious head injuries.'

Jesus Christ.

'No witnesses,' Theo went on. 'He might have died in the road if it wasn't for a quick-thinking pub goer.'

'Lorraine told her husband she nearly got run down by a car ten days ago.'

'Where was this?' Theo's voice was sharp.

'Up at the uni. After she'd finished teaching.'

'Did she get the make of car, a number plate?'

'Gavin said not.'

'Knives, now cars.' Theo was ruminative. 'What does that say to you, Harry?'

'Desperation. Honestly, Theo, do you really still believe they're connected?'

'I've never had any truck with police officers who have hunches, but this time my alarm bells are ringing. Four knife attacks, one murder and another attempted murder in ten days? It's out of hand, Harry. Something nasty's going on.'

Put like that, Harry admitted Theo could be right. He told Theo that Doug had been on Lorraine's creative writing course before reiterating that Phil's wife went to Pilates with Kevin Owen's wife. 'Everyone knows everyone, it seems. Any luck with the Halloween horror masks?'

'No. You can buy them on eBay, Amazon, anywhere.' Theo's frustration was clear in his tone. 'You seen Kevin Owen yet?'

'It's not something I'm comfortable with. His wife is my client.'

'You'd rather let Lorraine's murderers get away with it?'

'That's unfair.'

'See him.'

'Okay.' Harry sighed. 'I'll try to do it today.'

'Let me know how you go. But in the meantime, eyes in the back of your head, Harry. I don't want you to be the victim of another hit and run.'

With Theo's words ringing in his ears, Harry walked to work feeling jumpy. He watched the traffic, the people, trying to look for tension, anything out of place. But how would he see it? He wasn't experienced at this kind of thing. He was a psychotherapist for heaven's sake.

He arrived at the Wellbeing Centre to find Ethan towering over Jagoda in the miniature reception area. He was smiling, oozing charm, which vanished when Harry appeared.

'Harry,' Jagoda greeted him. 'You have two calls.' She passed him a pink slip where she'd made a note of the names and numbers.

'Thanks.' He turned to Ethan, studied the swellings hanging beneath his eyes like purple plums. 'Looking better already,' he said cheerfully.

'No thanks to you,' Ethan spat. Hatred poured off him in waves.

Jagoda looked between them, shocked.

'Did you tell Jagoda why you're here?' Harry asked.

Ethan dug the toe of his trainer against the leg of Jagoda's desk. 'Work experience.'

'And how did you explain your smashed face to her?'

He bit his lip before muttering, 'Car accident.'

'Right.' Harry strode to the corridor. 'My office. Now.'

When they were both in the therapy room, Harry closed the door behind them. Ethan slouched against the wall by the window. He was trying hard to look nonchalant but Harry could see the young man's nerves were strung tight by the way his pulse was jumping in his neck.

'There is one thing I like less than people who carry knives,' Harry said, 'and that's liars.'

'What about paedos?' The loathing was back.

Harry's psychotherapy antennae began quivering.

'What about them?'

Ethan turned his head. 'Nothing.'

If this had been a normal conversation or therapy session, Harry would have taken a different tack, but as it was, he turned brisk. 'Well, I can't say I like them much either, but I'm not going to get distracted, okay? Lying is one thing I will not tolerate in this building. Do you understand?'

Ethan nodded. He looked sulky.

Harry folded his arms. Rocked back on his heels. 'Seen your parents lately?'

'Yesterday,' he said warily. 'Why?'

'Tell me what story you gave them about your broken nose.'

Ethan gave an exaggerated sigh, as though he was bored. 'I said I got it playing basketball. That I ran my nose into another player's head.'

'And they believed you.'

A nod.

'Are you usually believed, even when you lie?'

He shuffled his feet briefly. 'Yes.'

'Ever thought of going into the security services? They'd love you. Tall, not too ugly. Ability to lie convincingly. They pay pretty well, you know. Good pension scheme too.'

'How would you know?' Derision warred with curiosity.

Harry kept his face perfectly neutral.

'No way!' Ethan looked outraged. 'You're a shrink, not a fucking spy!'

'Who says it's not a cover?'

Ethan blinked.

'I travel all over the world to mental health symposiums. Sydney, Singapore, Moscow. I speak Spanish, a little Japanese. I have strong interpersonal skills. I'm flexible. I can be subjective as well as objective. I can read upside down. I know how to disable a car and fire a Glock 23. I can also sling a decent right hook. As you know.'

'You're lying,' he said. He was staring at Harry as though Harry had just grown another head.

Harry stepped across the office, invading Ethan's space and forcing him backwards. 'I haven't spoken a single word that isn't true. I may not work for the security forces but there's no reason why I couldn't. Don't judge people too quickly, Ethan. You never know who they might be.'

17

E than gulped. The pulse in his neck was pounding.
'Do we understand each other?' Harry pressed.
'Yes.' It was strangled.

'In that case,' Harry said smartly, 'let's get you painting.'

Having already bought the equipment needed to paint the Wellbeing Centre a while ago – Harry had planned on spending the Easter holiday redecorating – he thrust a set of coveralls at Ethan and told him to start with the reception ceiling.

'White,' he added. He'd planned on the walls being a calming blue colour.

The rest of Harry's morning was spent with two clients. One, a man suffering from agoraphobia, the other a teenage girl with anorexia who, he was delighted to see, had made some serious progress. When he'd written up his notes, he walked into town to meet the third knife victim – Kevin Owen, married to Susanna and the subject of the headline: *Victim describes 'terrifying knife attack' outside judo school.*

Normally he wouldn't meet the spouse of a client of his, but this was an extraordinary situation. Theo seemed convinced the knifings were related, and if Harry could confirm it or disabuse him, then it had to help clarify the case in some way. At least he hoped so. Gavin and his children needed closure at some point, as well as Nicole.

He'd called Susanna to let her know, and that he wouldn't talk about her or her therapy to her husband, just the knifing attack.

'I understand,' she'd said simply.

When he asked why she hadn't mentioned her husband's knife attack, she said, 'I was ashamed.'

He heard her sigh.

'Because for a moment I wished the attackers had succeeded, and that he was dead.'

Which wasn't an abnormal reaction to being continually bullied over the years but Harry didn't say so. It could wait until their next session.

Chikara Martial Arts was on James Street West, a brand new two-storey building with a red and blue logo featuring two inter-locked figures. He'd called ahead, and when he arrived he found Susanna's husband behind the reception desk talking with two other men. All wore white judo uniforms but their belts were different colours. Owen's was black. Harry recognised him from his picture in the newspaper. Although all three men looked fit, Owen appeared the most muscular. He wore designer sunglasses perched on his head even though it was raining.

'Harry Hope for Mr Owen,' Harry announced.

Owen turned around. Smiled warmly and put out a hand for Harry to shake. Although the man's grip was good and strong, his face seemingly open, Harry took an instant dislike to him. He had a cocky, I'm-so-good-looking-I-can-get-away-with-anything air about him that instantly made Harry bristle. Plus, he'd always had a good instinct for people and he wouldn't trust the judo instructor as far as he could throw him. Which he wouldn't be able to do. Not without years of training. Harry would have to be ultra-cunning to get one over on Mr Owen.

'Kevin, please.'

'Kevin,' Harry repeated.

'Let's give you a tour.' He snapped a finger at one of the men. 'You, cover for me.'

Kevin led the way through a door, down a corridor and into a large room with lots of light and a floor lined with blue spongy mats. A large orange square sat in the centre.

'The dojo.'

It was an impressive space but Harry didn't remark on it. He didn't want to waste time on small talk. 'DI McCannon told me you were attacked by three men on April the first.'

'DI McCannon,' Kevin mused, 'told me I had to see you. I didn't have a choice – Dr Harry Hope was part of the investigative team into the Bath knife attacks and I couldn't say no.'

Harry hadn't realised Theo had strong-armed the judo instructor into seeing him. 'I see,' he said neutrally.

Kevin ran his eyes up and down Harry's body as though calculating his fighting form. 'It's thanks to you, you fuck, that Susanna tells me she's thinking of having a trial separation.'

18

Susanna *was thinking of a trial separation?* You could have knocked Harry over with a flick of Owen's black judo belt. He decided to keep quiet. See where this led.

'Since she's been seeing you, she's become hard. Self-centred.'

She's standing up for herself, you mean.

'She was happy before. She loved her life, taking care of the kids, looking after our home. She's the best organiser, the best cook... I adore her. I don't know what I'd do without her.'

Harry couldn't miss the subtext: *my wife gives me the freedom to live my life the way I like. When I come home it's to a hot meal. My cupboards are full of clean shirts. The kids are looked after. She's my cook, my nanny, my domestic help all in one. And although I have a mistress, there's no way I'm going to leave my wife for her.*

'You've been filling her head with crap. She's even started talking to herself in the mirror, for Chrissake.'

Still Harry remained silent. He'd been on the receiving end of angry husbands before and didn't want to rile Kevin into doing something he might regret. Like practising his latest killing blow.

'How do you sleep at night?' Kevin widened his stance, crossing his arms and tucking his fists beneath his biceps to make them appear larger. 'Knowing you're destroying families?'

And saving the children's mother from suicide.

'To think it's my money too.' His eyes were as hard as polished marble. 'Paying you to separate me from my wife.'

Harry kept his body language loose and unthreatening but he didn't drop his gaze.

Kevin thrust his jaw forward. 'Is this what it's like when people sit on your couch? You just stand there and don't say fuck?'

Move on, would you?

'Jesus…' Kevin rolled his eyes. 'No wonder someone attacked you. They were probably trying to get some kind of response from you.'

'There were three of them,' Harry stated calmly. 'How did they interact between themselves?'

'Why should I talk to you about it? You're not a cop.'

'Did they act as a team? Say anything to one another? How did they work together? Was it planned or spur of the moment? Was there a leader? If so, how did you know?'

A spark of interest rose in the instructor's eyes. 'They weren't trained, if that's what you mean.'

Harry nodded encouragingly.

'They didn't know fuck about fighting. They were by my car when I finished work. One of them was peering inside. I thought they were going to break into it. I challenged them. They came for me.'

'And you fought them off.'

'I snapped the first one's wrist. He screamed like buggery. It scared the hell out of the others and they ran away.'

Kevin relented to answer more questions. Harry ascertained it had been 8pm, that each man had a knife, and each wore the perennial uniform of jeans, hoodies and trainers. Unlike Lorraine's attackers, they hadn't worn masks, but then there was no CCTV on this particular street.

'Would you say the attack was against you, personally?'

Owen was about to say something but stopped. Seemed to change his mind. 'I don't know.'

Harry had an inkling that Kevin wasn't telling the whole truth.

'Do you normally work that late?'

He shrugged. 'Sometimes.'

'Alone?'

Another shrug but this time a tiny smirk appeared as he accessed his memory of 'working late'. *Aha*, thought Harry. *I thought so.*

'Who else was with you?'

'No one,' he said quickly. 'Everyone had gone home.'

'Please don't lie,' Harry said calmly.

The judo instructor unfolded his arms and took a step back.

'If there's another witness,' Harry continued, 'we need to speak to them. Another pair of eyes could be vital.'

'There wasn't anyone.' He turned aggressive. 'So you can fuck off, okay?'

Harry didn't think it worth staying for more abuse and without another word, walked out of the martial arts studio. Outside, it was still raining. Car tyres hissed along the street as Harry headed back to Margaret Buildings. En route, he passed Queen Square, where he'd played boules, where he and Nicole had dined at the infamous Le Beaujolais Bistro – now sadly closed – and where he'd taken a girlfriend to a talk at the Bath Geological Society which had been so screamingly dull they'd left early and ended up having an endless snog on the corner.

God, he loved Bath, he suddenly thought. And all those memories that wrapped him close, layer upon layer. And now, more memories were being created. Not so nice ones. Harry pulled out his phone and rang Theo. He talked to him as he walked.

'I think there was someone with Kevin when he was attacked. Probably a woman. Probably younger than him. It might be worth putting a bit of pressure on his female staff and seeing what you come up with.'

'He's having an affair?'

'I didn't say that.'

'That's great,' Theo said brightly. 'I knew you'd get us another lead.'

19

After checking Ethan's decorating skills – average – and sending him away until after the weekend, Harry saw two more clients before he wound up for the day. It being Friday, he'd normally have a beer with Doug at The Chequers before going home, but Doug was apparently spending the weekend in Bristol, talking to a professor of policy studies about the impact of potentially revising the 2003 Sexual Offences Act.

How Doug managed to fit it all in, Harry didn't know, but at least he now knew why Doug's client list – never particularly large – had dwindled to virtually nothing. He was simply too busy elsewhere and his therapy room at the Centre was now used as little more than an office. Harry wondered how Doug was coping after his cancer diagnosis, and hoped he was keeping it together.

Harry did a big shop at Waitrose before he headed to pick up the boys for the weekend. Pizzas, ice cream and huge boxes of cereal. Both Ben and Tim had chosen weekly boarding at Kingswood in Bath: Tim for his GCSE and Ben his sixth-form years. It bumped up the cost but Harry had agreed with Nicole that it was a good idea, enabling them to concentrate better on their studies.

'Where's Lottie?' Ben asked as he piled into the car having nipped just ahead of Tim to grab the front seat.

'Your mum's dropping her round later.'

'Cool. I haven't seen her in ages.'

Lottie, when she arrived, fell onto the boys with shrieks of excitement. 'You've got to come with me! Gigi's had puppies!'

Gigi was a poodle who'd been mated with next door's Labrador.

'Awww, cute,' Ben said.

'Mum will drive us,' Lottie announced.

'No she won't,' Nicole said. 'Because Mum wants to have a word with your father.'

'Ben can drive Dad's car, can't he?' Lottie begged Harry with her eyes. 'I really, *really* want to see them.'

'Your brother,' Harry responded, 'said he'd rather drive a mobility scooter, he's so embarrassed by my car.'

'Sorry, Dad,' Ben said, not looking sorry at all. 'But it is a bit of a rust bucket, you have to admit. I bet you wouldn't even get fifty quid for it on eBay.'

'How old is it, anyway?' Nicole said.

'I bought it in 1998,' Harry said stoutly.

'It's older than me.' Ben looked shocked.

'I don't care how old it is. Ben can still drive it, can't he, Dad?' Lottie begged some more. All three kids were looking at him.

Ben had passed his driving test six months ago and although Harry thought he drove pretty well, he wasn't sure about having all three children in the same car with him at the wheel.

'Oh, let them go, Harry,' Nicole said, surprising him. 'It's only around the corner.'

'No,' Harry said. He knew all too well how teenagers could egg one another on, sometimes with disastrous results. And, if he was honest, he would have felt a lot more confident if they were in a newer car with newer airbags and top-of-the-range safety features. He really *had* to get a new car, he realised. He had the money, he just had to pull his finger out and buy one.

Nicole looked surprised.

'As you said, it's only around the corner,' Harry said reasonably. 'And the exercise will do them good.'

All three kids groaned and moaned but only for about thirty seconds because the instant they were outside, they raced each other to the gate. Ben won, but only by a whisker.

'How are you bearing up?' Harry asked Nicole.

'Wobbly.' She took a breath. 'I wanted to let you know Lorraine's funeral's a week on Thursday. The day before Easter.'

He'd forgotten Easter was looming. Nicole was having the kids over the holidays, which meant he and Jessie would have Easter together. He wondered if they might go somewhere, like Dorset, and do some walking.

'I'll be there,' he assured Nicole.

'That would be good.'

He turned to look at her. She wore a caramel-coloured dress that rode above her knees and showed off her narrow waist and the tilt of her breasts. He'd thought he was immune to her beauty after the horrors of the divorce, but as she licked her lips he couldn't deny the desire that rose in him. Nicole seemed to feel it too.

'Harry...' It was a whisper.

He held up both hands. 'Stop right there.'

'We've still got it, haven't we?' Nicole gave a small smile.

Harry decided not to get into a discussion about their sexual chemistry. She was with Dave, and he was with Jessie. Full stop.

'I'll drop the kids off as we arranged earlier.' His tone was formal.

He watched her walk to her smart BMW – something she'd

always longed for but he'd never done anything about – and drive away.

The weekend passed in a flurry of cooking, talking, watching Netflix and, for the boys, homework. Jessie dropped in once, joining them for Sunday brunch, but she didn't stay over.

'It's their house,' she told Harry as she kissed him goodbye. 'And although I know they like me, which is great, they don't need me hanging around. They want their dad.'

He'd hugged her close. 'Thank you.'

He drove them back to school first thing on Monday, and after he'd dropped Lottie at Nicole's, he took a call from Theo.

'Harry, my man.' He sounded inordinately cheerful.

'Good weekend?'

'You came up trumps. Kevin *was* with someone the night he was attacked. She's young and pretty and deeply sorry she didn't come forward earlier...'

'She was scared of being found out.'

'Yup. Thing is, she saw a fourth man. He was on the opposite side of the street. She reckons he was either taking photos, or he was filming the whole thing.'

'Description?'

'Tall and skinny, jeans, hoody.'

'Same as with Lorraine.' Harry thought further. 'Were the other attacks filmed, do you think?'

'I'm beginning to wonder. I've got our tech team on it, trying to see if anything's been posted online but it's like asking them to find a single blade of grass in a hundred-acre field. How's your own personal attacker? Did he have a film crew with him?'

'Not that I remember.'

After they'd hung up, Harry walked to work, his mind on

Ethan and how to get him to open up. A breeze flurried with blossom petals greeted him as he turned the corner into Catherine Place. A woman was walking towards him, long legs, lots of blonde hair. When their eyes met, he raised a hand in greeting.

'Harry.' She paused amiably. 'How are you? How's the Centre? Need upgrading yet? More space?'

He smiled. 'Not for a while, but thanks.'

'Anything I can do for you...'

'I'll let you know.' He looked past her then back. 'I'm sorry about Phil.'

'Phil?' She looked blank.

'Philip Petty.'

She frowned for a moment, then her brow cleared. 'Ah, that's where I saw you. I was doing a valuation for him. Why do you say you're sorry?'

'He's in hospital. Hit and run driver.'

'Gosh, poor man. Is he going to be okay?'

Unless the woman was a superlative actor, Harry could see no reason to believe she was anything but an estate agent to Phil. He could have kicked himself for assuming they were having an affair. Top rule of psychotherapy: never assume.

'He's still in a coma.' Harry had rung the hospital over the weekend.

'His poor wife.' Her face suddenly creased with concern. 'You won't tell her I valued their house, will you? Phil was adamant she shouldn't find out.'

'Sure.'

Harry watched her walk away, hair bouncing in the brisk spring breeze, and wondered why Phil was so concerned about keeping the house valuation from his wife.

20

Harry arrived at the Centre to find Ethan had finished the ceiling and was prepping the walls.

'Good weekend?' Harry asked generally.

Jagoda pulled a face.

'Boyfriend trouble?' Harry asked sympathetically.

'He is no good.'

Since Jagoda and her boyfriend broke up and got back together again with monotonous regularity, Harry didn't take it too seriously.

'Ethan?'

When the young man looked across, Harry saw the plum-like bruises were fading fast, the swelling around his nose almost gone. He looked at Harry with such dislike, Harry thought he was going to say something along the lines of *get lost* but instead he said curtly, 'Fine.'

Harry left them to catch up on emails. He raised his head when someone knocked on the door. Ethan.

'Yes?'

'I want to decorate the whole place in one go, rather than twice weekly.'

No pleasantries. Just a demand.

'Why?'

'I can finish it faster.'

Harry waited.

Ethan shifted from foot to foot. 'I guess it will be less disruptive for you guys too.'

Harry considered. 'I think that would be fine.'

Ethan gave a nod but he didn't leave.

'What is it?' Harry asked.

He dithered a moment, then took the plunge.

'What was wrong with that young girl you saw last week?'

'I'm sorry, but I can't say.'

'Client confidentiality.' Ethan practically spat out the words.

'But I can say a lot of the girls I work with come to me for help with depression, anxiety and eating disorders. I try to help them, when I can.'

Ethan gave Harry a long look that he couldn't figure out before he withdrew.

Small steps, Harry told himself. You may not have much time, so you'd better make every second count.

The day eased past, the smell of paint battling with the scents of aromatherapy oil. Since it was a mild spring day, Harry opened his window, Jagoda the front door, allowing a fresh breeze to flow through. No clients complained.

Harry left work early to head for the Royal United Hospital to see Phil, who was still in the Critical Care Department. Harry sat with him for a while, talking to him about the weather, the new traffic calming system along Julian Road – nothing too stressful for a patient in a coma to listen to – until another visitor turned up. Small, with wavy brown hair and skin that looked faintly tanned.

Angela. Phil's wife.

'I'm so sorry,' Harry said.

Her lips quivered. Her eyes were red and looked sore. She went to Phil and gently kissed his forehead. 'Hi, love. It's just me.'

As Harry watched her tend her husband with care, he felt a knot of anger form beneath his breastbone. He hoped Theo would catch the bastard who'd done this.

And I will do everything I can to help, he silently promised.

After a little while, Harry rose. 'I'm going to get a coffee. Would you like one?'

'I'll join you.'

Together, they walked to the Atrium Coffee Bar. Harry opted for a cappuccino, Angela a latte. They stood to one side, sipping slowly.

'Do you mind if I ask a question or two?' Harry asked.

'Go ahead. The DI who I spoke to told me you were working with him.'

'Yes.' Harry turned his cup around in his hands. 'I wanted to know if everything was all right before the hit and run. Or if there was anything bothering Phil. Or you, for that matter.'

She shook her head. 'The police already asked me.'

'No thoughts on moving house?'

'Whatever for? We love it where we are.'

Harry asked several more questions before asking if Phil had any enemies.

'I'm not sure enemies is the right word.' Her gaze grew distant. 'A lot of people are jealous of what we can afford, but to run him down like that? I don't think so.'

'Has anyone approached you wanting a loan, or help financially, and you refused them?'

'Charities are always door-stepping us.' She was rueful. 'We ended up giving the responsibility for all that to our investment manager. Hugh's been brilliant, by the way. Thanks so much for introducing us.'

Harry tipped up the cup to get the last of his coffee. 'Hugh who?'

'Hugh Lamont.' She looked at him as though he was being slow. 'He's your investment manager too.'

'I don't have an investment manager.'

Her eyebrows arched. 'You don't?'

'No.'

'But he *knows* you.'

'What does he look like?'

'Same age as you. Same height, I guess. Grey hair. Ordinary-looking. Moustache.'

'You've got a number for him?'

'It'll be on Phil's phone. I'll text it to you later.'

But when Harry tried the number, it had been disconnected.

21

Harry had been home for half an hour when the doorbell rang. He'd been packing for the congress tomorrow and he walked to the door with nothing on his mind but which jacket he should wear for his presentation. He assumed it was Theo dropping by for a decompression session over a Black Sheep beer and was totally unprepared when the door swung inward hard, pushed by a towering man in black. He rammed a fist into Harry's diaphragm and as Harry bent forward, belted the back of his neck with both fists.

Harry slammed to his knees. Coughing and gasping he tried to scramble up but another terrible thump between his shoulder blades felled him to the floor.

Another man appeared. Younger, but just as big. He shut the door behind him with a brown-booted foot. He was swinging a baseball bat.

'Paedo,' he said. His voice was filled with hate and at the same time, he brought the bat down on Harry's back. The older man began kicking him systematically. Another belting from the bat made Harry wonder if they wanted to kill him. He tried to fight them but each time he managed to kick or punch one, the other would land a solid blow where it caused maximum pain. Harry managed to lash backwards, hitting the older man's knee with enough force to make him curse and lean over and give Harry a sickening rabbit punch in the kidneys.

He wanted to tell them to stop, ask why they were doing this, but the only sounds he made were grunts as any air in his body was beaten out of him.

They'd done this before, Harry realised. They knew where and how to hit and leave his head alone. He tried to curl into a ball at one point, desperate to protect his intestines being ruptured, but the older man hauled him upright and let the younger one break a couple of ribs.

When they let go Harry crumpled onto the flagstones. One of them gave him a final kick.

Harry heard the door open and then close behind them. He didn't move. He wasn't sure if he could, even if he wanted to. Pain flowed through him, as hot as lava. He closed his eyes, concentrating on the cool of the stone floor against his cheek, trying to ride it out, trying to slow his breathing which was coming in choppy gasps.

He didn't know how long he lay there for, minutes or hours, but eventually he began taking stock. His limbs seemed to be working even if his ribs shrieked when he tried to move. With fierce determination, Harry made it to the hall chair. Sat there staring at his feet, shuddering, breathing shallowly, trying his best not to be sick.

Don't move and it will go away.

It took a long time until the nausea passed. The light from outside softened into gloom. He guessed it was after 8pm He would have to move eventually. Just not right now.

He heard the doorbell ring and glanced up in panic. Had they returned to finish the job? He hauled himself to his feet as it rang again.

Must get to the phone. Should have done it before.

The fear of another beating forced Harry to stagger along the corridor, pain howling.

He heard the door open.

He hadn't locked it. He felt like weeping at his stupidity.

'Harry? You in?'

'Theo,' Harry croaked. 'Thank God.'

'Been on the sauce already?' Theo sounded amused. 'It's only Monday, Harry.'

Harry put his hand on the wall, fighting not to collapse. Waves of pain crashed over him.

'What the hell...' Theo came and was about to put an arm around him, bolster him, when Harry said, 'Don't.'

Theo reared back.

'Ribs. Broken.'

'Christ, Harry.'

'I need to... lie down.'

Leaning on Theo, he made it into the sitting room and levered himself carefully onto the sofa. Closed his eyes. He heard Theo calling an ambulance and wanted to say no, he didn't need one, but he had no energy.

'What happened?' Theo's voice was urgent. He was squatting next to Harry.

'Two of them. One baseball bat. Called me... a paedo.'

Theo scowled. 'Mistaken identity?'

Only last month a paediatrician had been attacked for being a paedophile. Nothing like confusing a doctor who cares for children with someone who abuses them.

'Maybe.' But Harry wasn't so sure. Not after Ethan's look of loathing and his using the same word.

Theo peppered Harry with questions but he found it hard to describe his attackers beyond Older and Younger. No masks though. Hard faces. Men, not youths. One in his fifties, the other his thirties.

When the ambulance arrived, Harry tried to say he didn't need to go to hospital but they weren't having it, using words like internal bleeding, concussion, pneumothorax, pulmonary contusion and the like. With infinite gentleness they transported him across town and to the Royal United Hospital, where he was scanned and scrutinised before finally being allocated a bed in a ward and allowed to sleep. He wasn't allowed to go home. They wanted to keep an eye on him for a while. 'Just in case.'

22

If it hadn't been for some super-strength painkillers Harry doubted he would have slept a wink and, in the morning, when they'd worn off, he was so stiff and sore it took an immense effort of will to get to the bathroom. On his way back to bed, the nurse gave him two tablets which, thankfully, kicked in within minutes, making life just about bearable.

While waiting for the duty doctor to discharge him, Harry rang Jagoda and asked her to put his clients off for the morning. 'I've fallen over,' he told her. 'I'm okay. Just a bit sore, that's all.'

He thought about the congress starting that evening, and although he reckoned he'd be able to give the presentation a fair go the following morning, the thought of lugging his suitcase through train stations with four broken ribs was another matter. He felt nauseous just thinking about it. Harry rang Doug, filled him in.

'A second attack?' Doug sounded shocked. 'Whatever's going on?'

'I'm not sure. But I'm going to do my best to find out.'

'Good for you, but be careful, Harry. It sounds as though they mean business. Now, I'll call the congress and explain, and get them to put me in your place. You don't have to do a thing. Just get better soon.'

The next call was to Jessie, who didn't panic, didn't turn it into a drama but simply said she'd be there in a flash, what could she bring?

'I'll be thrown out by lunchtime, there's no point in–'

'See you in half an hour.'

He then rang Nicole and texted the kids. He didn't want any of them finding out he'd been hospitalised without knowing he was okay. Nicole delicately asked if she could help, to which he replied that Jessie was on her way. Ben sent him an emoji of a sad face with a head bandage while Tim simply told him to get better soon. Lottie sent him a long message about puppies and getting well, signing off with a row of emojis of puppies and *can I have one????!!!*

Jessie arrived in a flurry of colourful scarves and clouds of fresh, flowery scent. 'Hmm,' he murmured as she bent to kiss his lips. 'You smell lovely.'

'Wild bluebell.'

She'd also brought him a cappuccino and a chocolate crois-sant. 'So, what do you mean, you were in a bit of an altercation?' She perched on his bed, shifting the mattress which in turn pressured his ribs which ferociously stabbed back. Jessie looked at him in horror. 'My God, Harry. What happened?'

'Just bust a couple of ribs.' Harry decided to play it down. He gave a sigh. Big mistake. More pain.

Her horrified expression remained. 'What did you do, have a punch-up with Mike Tyson?'

'Not exactly...' He went on to tell her what had happened.

Raw apprehension twisted her face. 'They think you're a paedophile?'

'Maybe.'

'This is sick. Why on earth do they think that?' She frowned. 'Unless someone's out to get you?'

Harry wondered about the other attacks. Were they also cases of mistaken identity, or had the victims been misrepresented in another way? He slowly ate his croissant wanting to think about connections and knife attacks but his head was woozy and when he finished his pastry, he closed his eyes.

When he opened them, Jessie had gone, and in her place stood Dave.

'Seen you looking better.'

'I've been better,' Harry managed.

Dave stepped outside for a moment, came back with a chair. Set it next to Harry's bed.

'Come to gloat?' Harry said.

'Not at all. I simply thought it too good an opportunity to talk to you with no one else around.'

Harry watched a patient with a plastered leg hobble outside.

Dave cleared his throat. 'Nicole said you were attacked again.'

'A case of mistaken identity.'

'How do you know that?'

'I just do, okay?'

Harry flicked a tiny flake of croissant off his bedsheet.

'She also tells me you're trying to find Lorraine's killer.' Dave leaned forward, hands between his knees. 'That you think the Bath knife attacks might be linked. What do the police think? Or rather, what do the police *know*?'

'You knew Lorraine, didn't you?'

Dave's gaze slid to one side. 'Not really. She and Nicole would have girls' evenings out. I never saw her on her own. Seriously, Harry, what do the cops think is going on?'

'You work with Kevin Owen.'

'Yes. So?'

With a little chill, Harry suddenly realised that Dave could be the common denominator between all the victims. Dave had met Phil at a barbecue Harry had held two years ago and he'd also been at the track day at Castle Combe and met John Tanaka.

'What about Hugh Lamont?' Harry asked. 'Know him too?'

Dave leaned back, slowly, away from Harry. 'Who?'

'Investment manager.'

'Why would I need an investment manager?'

'I didn't say you *needed* one. I asked if you knew this one. Hugh Lamont.'

'No, I don't.' His voice was calm but something was wrong. Harry couldn't put his finger on it.

Dave stretched. 'If you get any news from the police about the investigation–'

'I'll ring Nicole.'

After a long moment Dave got to his feet, looked down at Harry.

'I'm sorry,' he said. 'For everything.'

'Fuck off,' said Harry. His tone was weary.

23

———————

Harry was discharged late morning with a packet of painkillers and instructions to keep breathing and coughing normally to prevent chest infections. At home, Jessie pottered around without being overbearing, which was a relief. He ended up on the sofa, sleeping for most of the afternoon, inordinately grateful he'd made the decision not to go to the congress.

He texted Doug, who texted back telling him he'd been given the go-ahead to fill his slot. After a simple pasta supper, Jessie checked all the doors and windows were secure.

'Don't answer the door to anyone unless you know who it is,' she said fiercely.

'Promise.'

He double bolted the door when she'd gone. Staggered to bed.

Having cleared two days for the congress, Harry decided to use the time convalescing and catching up on piles of admin. On Thursday he headed into the office to find Ethan halfway through decorating his office. White ceiling, teal blue walls. Very restful.

'Nice job,' Harry remarked.

'Slave labour,' he said, but there was less rancour in his tone than Harry expected.

'I wanted to ask you something,' Harry said.

A guarded look came to the young man's face.

'I wanted to know why you mentioned paedophiles when I talked to you about lying.'

Harry saw his gaze turn inwards.

'It seems to me it means something personal to you.'

Ethan's face went blank, telling Harry this was an area where he didn't want to go.

'I understand,' he added gently. 'It's a difficult subject.'

No response.

Knowing there was no point in pushing it any further, Harry took his laptop into Doug's office. Settled on Doug's visitor's chair by the window. Turning to the internet he typed in *Hugh Lamont, Investment Manager, Bath.*

Immediately a website popped up.

Hugh Lamont & Co is one of the most respected firms on the London Stock Exchange.

We specialise in private client investment management. Your dedicated investment manager will create a portfolio which is tailored to you and your individual circumstances.

The hallmark for our firm is an enduring commitment to excellent client care.

Harry searched the site extensively but found no photographs of the CEO or professional advisors. No address either. The telephone number was different from the one Angela had given him, so Harry rang it.

'Hugh Lamont & Co,' a bright female voice sang.

'Can I speak to Hugh, please?'

'I'm sorry, he's not here right now. Can I ask him to call you?'

'I just wanted to know what his firm's address is.'

'I'll get him to ring you straight back.' She was firm. 'Your number?'

'Look, I'm working with the police on a murder case and I don't have time to mess about. What's your address?'

'Good heavens.' She sounded shocked. 'I'm sorry. It's, er... well, it's not actually Hugh Lamont & Co's address because it's mine. I'm a virtual receptionist. I answer calls for over a hundred small businesses.'

'Where are you?'

'Freshford.'

Which, if he took the toll road over the river, was just over six miles dead south. It was one of his favourite places not just because it was in a conservation area with great walking, but it had an excellent pub too. Not that he'd have time to stop by for a pint, he sighed, but it would make a pretty drive.

'Can I come and see you?'

She gave him her address.

'And your name?' he asked.

'Odell.'

He checked his watch. 'I'll be there in twenty minutes.'

Odell was in her late twenties, dressed in faded jeans, and worked out of a converted barn on the edge of the village. Spacious and airy, the office held an enormous curved desk, a wall of filing cabinets, another of what looked like technical manuals, and a black Labrador called Olly.

Harry petted Olly while Odell made a cafetière of coffee. By the time it had brewed she'd answered three calls and made two appointments. She showed Harry her computer software.

'When the phone rings it flashes a customer's information onto my screen so I know who the call is for and what information to give for the company. I do diary management as well as admin support.'

'Clever. Can I see Hugh Lamont & Co's information?'

It showed the same website that Harry had visited earlier, but nothing else. Odell pushed back her chair and walked to a filing cabinet. Fished around, and returned with a glossy brochure. 'Sometimes I send one of these out with his business card attached.'

The brochure showed a variety of investment bonds, from green forestry with a fixed return of 8% per annum to renewable energy boasting up to 48% over four years. Scams? Harry wondered, or were they genuine? He checked the business card to see Hugh Lamont's name, the name of the company, and a mobile number.

'Do you keep a diary for him?'

She shook her head. 'He makes his own appointments. I just take the calls.'

'How many?'

'Very few. Say, two or three a month. He's probably my smallest client.'

'You've met him?'

'I see him every six months or so.'

'What does he look like?'

'Probably the same age as you? Tall-ish. Sort of average-looking. He's nice, though. Pays on time and is always grateful for anything I do.'

'Hair colour? Is he bearded?'

Her face lit up. 'Moustache. Grey hair, but not old grey, if you know what I mean. More like silver. It makes him quite attractive.'

'How does he pay you?'

For the first time, she looked uncomfortable.

'I'm not with the Inland Revenue,' he assured her.

'He pays cash. Up front. Five hundred pounds every six months.'

'Is that usual?'

She nibbled her lip. 'Not really. He's the only one. He said it was the easiest way for him, so I made an exception.'

Harry didn't ask if she declared it. It wasn't any of his business. Thanking her for her help, Harry took his protesting bruises back to the office.

24

Thursday morphed into Friday, Friday into the weekend. Harry's bruises were slow to fade. Jessie applied arnica and let him make love to her in a comfortable if less conventional way.

He watched Alvin the pastry chef on YouTube and after downloading the recipe, decided to give making a venison and ale pie a go. The venison was from Toby Haynes in Corsham – Harry's favourite butcher – the ale from Theo's supply. Harry found the whole process utterly absorbing, which in turn had a restful effect. No thoughts of thugs or killers. His mind was taken up with nothing but browning the meat, rubbing salt into flour, adding liquids and binding to a dough.

He was surprised that creating such a pie was, as Alvin said, surprisingly easy. While it baked in the oven, he settled on the sofa. Theo had sent him a set of computer files of mug shots for him to look at, in case his attackers were already known to the law, and he scrolled through the pages without any real enthusiasm until he came to a photograph taken two years ago.

His towering attacker, the older man who'd been dressed in black, stared out at him through a pair of small, mean eyes.

For a moment he couldn't believe it. It was him. The man who'd held him while his pal broke his ribs. Harry immediately rang Theo. 'I've got one. Number two hundred and sixty-one.'

'Hang on, let me check...'

Harry heard the clicking of a keyboard. 'Are you at work?'

'No rest for a detective trying to solve a murder case... Ah, here he is... Oh.'

'What?'

'His name is Clive Farmer. He's a self-styled paedophile hunter. A vigilante. We've arrested him three times for assault and public order violations.'

'Bloody hell. He thinks I'm a paedophile?'

'I'll bring him in. Find out what's going on.'

'I'd like to see him.'

'I'll let you know when I've picked him up. Hopefully by the end of the day.'

It took Theo longer than that thanks to Clive Farmer being out of town and that evening Harry and Jessie ate the pie, accompanied with spring greens, mashed potatoes and gravy.

'You *made* this?' Jessie looked astonished.

'Yup.' He felt an inordinate rush of pride.

'I don't believe you.'

He grinned.

'Not just great in the sack,' she announced, shaking her head in mock-wonder, 'but he can cook too.'

It wasn't until Tuesday when Theo called him to tell him that they had, at last, arrested Clive Farmer, who needless to say was denying ever having been to Batheaston, let alone beating up Dr Harry Hope.

When Harry arrived at the police station, Theo showed him

into one of the interview rooms. One table, four chairs, all bolted to the floor. The air smelled of disinfectant and stale sweat. Clive Farmer sat on one side of the table with his brief, a thin woman of around forty, while Theo and Harry took the other. Harry had wondered if his memory had exaggerated Clive Farmer's size but no, the man was just as large as he remembered. He had acne marks on his upper cheeks which Harry hadn't taken in before. Too busy trying to prevent his organs from getting burst open.

Theo activated the recorder and stated the date, time and who was present, then he leaned back and said, 'Go ahead, Dr Hope.'

'Hello, Clive,' Harry said.

The man's face showed nothing. No interest in him. No curiosity.

'You'll be pleased to hear I'm off the painkillers at last. You and your friend did a good job, you know. Four broken ribs.'

A gleam of pleasure entered the man's eyes.

'Otherwise, I'm fine.' Harry tapped the table with his fingers. 'Which is lucky for you, because if I wasn't, I might not be here talking to you and willing to offer you a deal.'

No interest.

'You see, I'm not a paedophile,' Harry went on. 'Which is why you came to my home, wasn't it? To teach me a lesson.'

The gleam was back.

'The trouble is, you and your friend were fed a lie. Someone wanted me beaten up and they used you to do it for them. I want to know who that someone is. In return for their name, I won't press charges.'

Clive Farmer folded his arms and leaned back in his chair.

Harry leaned forward. 'How do you feel about being used?'

Stony silence.

'What did they say?' Harry pressed. 'That I used my psychotherapy practice to lure children to my office?'

A tiny flicker of Clive's eyelid confirmed Harry had got it right.

'I have two child clients at the moment,' Harry went on. 'In total I have counselled forty-five. The youngest was eleven, the oldest eighteen. I could call on each one to come and see you and tell you I haven't touched them, but I can't do that because of client confidentiality.'

Somewhere a metal door banged. Nobody moved.

'In my profession, you can probably understand that I occasionally get harassed.' Harry leaned forward again. 'I don't suppose you checked my property for CCTV before you pushed open my front door?'

A blink of surprise.

'Ah.' Harry nodded. 'So whoever set you up didn't tell you about the cameras.'

Clive's solicitor glanced at her client who was gazing at Harry, seemingly unmoved.

'Your funeral.' Harry got to his feet, looked at Theo. 'Throw the book at him.'

25

'CCTV?' Theo spluttered later. 'I thought people in your profession weren't supposed to lie?'

'I didn't,' Harry protested. 'I asked him if he'd checked, that's all.'

'Sneaky.' Theo gave him an approving look. 'He doesn't believe you, you know. That he's been used. He's convinced you're the real deal, a child abuser one hundred per cent.'

Harry mulled it over. 'I don't get it. How? What's his evidence?'

'I'll see if we can do a deal of some sort. See if we can get to the bottom of it.'

'Is he married?' Harry asked. 'Can I see his wife?'

'You won't get very far. She's a tough one.' Still, Theo gave Harry an address.

The Farmers lived in Bedminster, which was once a separate town in Somerset before it became part of Bristol. On the south side of the city, it was yet another area that would soon start to fight gentrification thanks to Bristol being crowned the 'Best Place to Live in the UK' by *The Times* recently. Not just because it was apparently cool, charming and cosmopolitan, but it had plenty of affordable housing. However, as Harry looked at the cracks in the walls of buildings, scarred with pollution, and the weeds growing out of gutters, he thought it still had a long way to go.

As soon as Mrs Farmer opened her door, Harry could see what Theo meant. It wasn't just her size – she was a true behemoth with wild red hair like a Viking – but her expression appeared to be permanently angry. Even though he knew he was probably on a hiding to nothing, Harry persevered. He explained he wasn't a paedophile, that her husband had been hoodwinked into believing he was, and that he was going to go to jail unless Harry found out who was telling lies about him.

Mrs Farmer heard him out, then slammed the door in his face.

Great.

He knocked on the door again. Called through the letterbox. 'If you help me, I'll help Clive. He beat up an innocent man, okay? A psychotherapist who *helps* kids. The judge won't take kindly to that. He'll get six months, at least.'

The door was yanked open. 'If you're so innocent, explain this.'

She shoved a handful of computer printouts at him.

Harry looked at the first image. She saw the deep shock in his face and smiled in satisfaction.

'You perverts think you can get away with anything. I hope Clive hurt you really badly.'

Harry unstuck his tongue from the roof of his mouth. 'This isn't me.'

'Yeah, right. You want these pictures posted further afield? You want your wife to see them? Your kids? If you don't drop your accusations against Clive, I'll put them on the internet, send them to your work, all those therapists around the country, your friends.'

Harry flicked through the other images. He felt sick.

'You deserve everything you get,' she spat.

'They're fake.' He pointed to the second image. 'That's not even my hand.'

'If Clive isn't home by eight tonight, I'll post these into the public domain and your life will never be the same again.'

Before Harry could move, she snatched the pictures back, turned around and slammed the door shut.

Harry's mind galloped around and around like a horse on a merry-go-round but nothing useful came out. Who on earth was doing this to him? Setting him up in such an appalling way? He knew if the pictures were posted he could be ruined. People invariably believed there was no smoke without fire and fighting his innocence would be an uphill battle.

Feeling as though his head had become separated from his body, Harry walked jerkily back to his car. Called Theo.

'She *what*?'

Harry said, 'Let him go. I'm retracting my accusation.'

'Jesus, Harry.'

'I have to find out who's after me.'

'Wait there,' Theo told him. 'I'm on my way.'

Harry took Theo at his word but when an hour had passed, he decided he couldn't wait any longer and rang him.

'Ten minutes,' Theo promised. 'I had to get authorisation.'

'For what?' Harry asked but he'd disconnected.

Half an hour later Theo arrived, accompanied by another policeman, a beanpole in plain clothes. 'Techie,' Theo said. He turned as a patrol car arrived with two uniformed officers. Both donned their caps as they climbed outside.

'The authorisation I wanted,' Theo told Harry, 'was so we can tear the place apart. Okay?'

Harry swallowed. He didn't see that he had a choice, which was probably why Theo was bulldozing him.

Theo took in Harry's tension. 'I'm not letting them get away with it,' he said fiercely.

'It's not your reputation on the line.'

'If we don't stop them, they'll—'

'It's okay, Theo,' Harry interrupted. 'I get it. I just needed a moment to get my head around it.'

Theo nodded before gesturing to the three officers to follow him. All four of them strode to Mrs Farmer's front door. When she opened it, Theo showed her his warrant card and some papers and then the uniforms firmly moved her aside and they, Theo and the techie, vanished inside.

Thirty-five minutes passed before the techie appeared with a laptop computer in a clear plastic bag, and another bag that seemed to hold scraps of paper, Post-it notes and printouts. He put them in the back of the car. A little later, the police officers appeared with Mrs Farmer. They put her in the back of their car as well and drove away.

Theo came and stood next to Harry and watched them go.

'That's my job done,' he said. 'What's next for you?'

Harry didn't have to think about it for long.

'I'm going to see a student.'

26

'Why can't you do it?' Nicole complained.

'Because I don't want to tip him off.'

She sighed. 'All right. Give me his number and I'll call you back if I get something.'

Five minutes later Harry put Ethan's address in his phone to see he lived on the south-west side of Bath, past Bear Flat and towards the village of Englishcombe.

'How did you get it?' he asked, curious.

'I pretended I was from Parcelforce,' she admitted. 'Everyone wants their parcel delivered, don't they?'

The sun was lowering towards the horizon as Harry pulled off Englishcombe Lane and down an unmarked road into a densely wooded area. He passed a couple of large houses, and then the road narrowed, the ancient beech trees looming over-head, leaves fluttering a vivid spring green. When he came to the stone gateposts at the end of the lane, and read the brass plate, *Combe House*, he wondered if he'd come to the wrong place. This didn't look like student living. Cautiously, Harry eased his car up the drive – smooth gravel with lawns on either side – and parked outside a beautifully renovated Georgian house. Three storeys, with sash windows painted white and a front door the colour of pale jade.

The only indication students might live here were the vehicles scattered around: a Vauxhall Corsa, a Ford Ka and a black VW Golf. However, where two of the vehicles were obviously second-hand, with faded paintwork and a variety of dents in their bodywork, the Golf was brand spanking new.

Harry parked his ancient Rover with the tattier cars, climbing out just as a flock of goldfinches passed overhead, their calls sounding like a bunch of tiny trembling bells. He could smell damp earth and freshly cut grass. He walked up the stone steps to the front door. Drew the brass pull doorbell a couple of times. Heard it echoing deep inside the house.

The door opened to reveal a petite young woman with soft fair hair and hazel eyes.

'I'm Harry Hope,' he told her. 'I'm here to see Ethan.'

'He's in the front room.' She stepped back, letting him into the hall while she closed the door behind him. 'This way.'

Her footsteps were light, her movements smooth and elegant, almost balletic. Harry felt clumsy and graceless as he followed her, his shoes tapping loudly on the floor tiles and echoing through the vast, airy space.

He wasn't sure how to play this out. He'd wanted to take it gently with Ethan, let the young man open up to him at his own pace, but with his ribs throbbing at every movement, the thought of those hideous photographs being on the net, Harry didn't feel he had time on his side any more.

'Ethan,' the young woman announced as she walked through a doorway. 'Someone's here to see you.'

Harry allowed the images to wash over him. Ceiling roses, shutters folded back from the windows, pink and green wallpaper swirling with boughs and peacocks. China vases, old school photographs on the walls, bookshelves crammed with law journals and legal literature. A young man was stretched out on one of the sofas with what appeared to be a technical book of some sort – lots of diagrams and charts – and on the floor, within arm's reach, sat a bottle of craft beer. Wavy blond hair framed an angular face with over-sized features that wasn't handsome so much as arresting. He didn't look up, or give any indication he'd heard them enter.

Ethan sat in a wing-backed chair next to the fireplace. He was holding a glass of red wine and gazing at the piles of ash in the grate, expression thoughtful, but the instant he saw Harry, the muscles in his face contracted, as though he'd sucked on a lemon.

'Harry!' He affected pleasure, but Harry could tell the effort it took. 'Guys, meet Dr Harry Hope, psychologist extraordinaire.'

'Hello, shrink,' drawled the young man on the sofa.

'Hello, student,' responded Harry, which made the young man smile. He didn't get up, though, but remained on the sofa. His eyes returned to the pages of his book.

'That's Cabe,' said Ethan, putting down his wine and getting to his feet. 'You've already met Wren, of course. Not that that's her real name. She refuses to use Winifred, don't you, sweetheart? Too mundane and old-fashioned for an up-and-coming fashionista like yourself.'

Wren pulled a face at Ethan who pretended he hadn't seen.

'Wren suits you,' Harry told her, earning him a smile.

'Don't compliment her,' Ethan said with a groan. 'She gets enough adoration as it is, trust me. Now, shall we go and get you a glass of wine? There's an open bottle in the kitchen and–'

'I'm not here to socialise.' Harry's voice was polite but cool. 'I'm here to talk about the recent knife attacks that have occurred across the city.'

27

The three students stilled, reminding Harry of a group of hares who'd just sighted a fox on the horizon.

Ethan raised his eyebrows in an exaggerated version of looking surprised. Harry would bet his last bottle of Black Sheep beer that the young man hadn't told his housemates anything about attacking Harry, let alone his atonement at the Wellbeing Centre.

'I didn't say before.' Harry held Ethan's eyes. 'But I'm working with the police on Lorraine Brown's murder.'

At that, Cabe put down his book and twisted round to look at him. He was frowning. 'What brings you here, then? We're not murderers.'

Harry didn't drop his gaze from Ethan. 'I'm concerned that each victim has been misrepresented in some way. For example, one victim was attacked because his attacker thought he was a paedophile, but he wasn't. A week ago, this man was attacked again but this time by two thugs – one of whom held him while the other beat him with a baseball bat, breaking four ribs. They also thought he was a paedophile.'

'That's sick.' Wren scrunched up her face.

'Yes,' Harry agreed, watching Ethan, who was watching him back. Ethan's face was alabaster smooth. Harry could have been talking about the city traffic for all the emotion on the young man's face. 'What I want to know is where the attackers got their information from, because it's wrong. And I'm concerned the other knife attacks may have been undertaken for the wrong reasons too.'

Long silence. Nobody fidgeted. They all stayed quite still, seemingly lost in their own thoughts.

'Did you know Lorraine Brown?' Harry asked them.

Another wave of tension swept through the room.

'No,' said Ethan at the same time that Cabe said, 'Nope.'

'No,' added Wren, but it lacked conviction.

When Harry fixed Wren with his don't-mess-with-me gaze she squirmed. 'No!' she said hotly. 'I didn't know her!'

Harry folded his arms. 'How come I don't believe you?'

'Because you're wrong,' she snapped.

'For God's sake just tell him,' Cabe said, sounding irritated. 'It's not as though you were there, were you? It was your *friend*, not *you*. Don't make such a big deal out of it.'

Wren shrank. 'Really?'

'Just do it, will you?' This was from Ethan, sounding exasperated.

'Well, okay...' She took a breath. 'It's just that... well, this friend of mine said her tutor got nothing she didn't deserve.'

'Why's that?' Harry asked.

'Lorraine Brown accused her of cheating.'

'In what way?'

Wren thought for a moment. 'She told her that the first chapters of the book she was working on wasn't her work at all. She said something like "I'm just wondering if you've had any help with this?" and then went on to say it was nothing like her previous work and did she have anything to say about it?'

Wren nibbled her lower lip. 'She did this in class, in front of *everyone*, utterly humiliating my friend. She hadn't cheated. She was really angry but Lorraine Brown refused to countenance the fact that her writing had improved thanks to her tutelage, and that what she'd written was actually very good. We reckon she always had something against her. We don't know why.'

'What's the name of your friend?'

Wren paused. Ethan was watching her with an interested expression. Cabe too.

Eventually she cleared her throat. Said, 'Vera Wang.'

'Do you think Vera could have been involved in Lorraine's attack?'

Wren looked blank.

'She couldn't have been, could she?' Ethan said with a frown. 'Isn't she in Hong Kong?'

At that, Wren's face cleared. 'I'd forgotten. Yes, she's overseas, so she couldn't be involved.'

'You're forgetting social media,' Harry said. 'The internet. She could have encouraged others. Spurred them on.'

Wren suddenly looked anxious. 'I don't know.'

'What about the other victims? Did you know any of them?'

They all shook their heads.

'Any of you do judo?' Harry prompted.

More head shaking.

'Do any of you know a man called Philip Petty?'

'Only what I saw on the news,' said Cabe. 'He was attacked and then someone ran him over, putting him in hospital.'

'What about Kevin Owen?'

'Same.' Cabe yawned. 'On the news.'

'Hugh Lamont?'

'Who?' asked Ethan.

When Harry repeated the name, all three frowned. It was the first time each face showed genuine perplexity, making Harry realise that he couldn't trust anything any of them had said since he'd arrived. Did Vera Wang exist? he wondered. And what about the story Wren had spun him about Lorraine accusing Vera Wang of cheating? Was it true?

Harry turned to Ethan. 'I'd quite like that glass of wine you offered earlier.'

'Before you toddle off,' said Cabe, 'I'd like to know what brought you here. How you know Ethan, for a start, since you came to visit him. You're not his shrink, are you?'

Harry looked at Ethan. 'Yes, how do we know each other, Ethan? Do you want to tell them, or shall I?'

28

To Harry's surprise Ethan didn't baulk or look concerned in any way. He simply said, 'My sister.' He didn't weigh the words heavily or put any emotion into his tone, but the other two immediately backed off.

'See you around then, shrink,' said Cabe, and with a flap of a hand, went back to his book.

Wren gave him a small smile and walked to an occasional table in one corner and picked up a tome, brought it to Ethan's wing-backed chair and she curled up inside it.

Ethan picked his wine glass up off the floor and walked past Harry, saying curtly, 'With me.'

He brought Harry to an ultra-modern white-tiled kitchen with brushed chrome appliances and sleek surfaces. Eight chairs were scattered around an oblong island.

'How many of you live here?' Harry asked.

'None of your business.'

Ethan picked up an open bottle of red wine and topped up his glass. He didn't offer Harry one.

'Who owns the house?'

'I don't have to tell you anything.' The loathing was back. 'Time for you to go, don't you think?'

Harry turned and marched outside, Ethan following. Ethan obviously thought Harry was heading for the front door because when he turned right for the living room, he tried to stop him. 'Hey, wait a minute...'

Both Cabe and Wren looked up when Harry entered.

'How many of you live here?'

'Er, four,' said Cabe. 'Why?'

'Sometimes it's eight,' added Wren.

'Eight?' Harry queried.

'Cabe, Wren, Filipa and I live here. Our various boy- and girlfriends live elsewhere but come and stay from time to time.'

'Who owns the house?'

'Okay, okay.' Ethan gave an exaggerated sigh and looked at the ceiling. 'My parents own it.'

Harry folded his arms and tapped his foot, waiting. Cabe and Wren sat watching them warily.

'Dad bought this house ages ago for the family to use as a kind of holiday pad. We lived in London until Dad retired last year. We used to come here for Christmas occasionally, or a couple of weeks in the summer. In between times he'd rent it out for house parties. It sleeps nine. In between block rentals he'd fill it with people wanting a B&B, but when I got a place at Bath Uni, he suggested I use it while I'm here.'

'Nice,' said Harry.

Ethan didn't like that and reached out to take Harry's arm, perhaps to try to usher him outside.

'Do not touch me,' Harry said. His voice was cold.

Ethan snatched his hand back.

'Kitchen,' Harry ordered.

Ethan looked as though he wanted to object, but when Harry walked out of the room, he followed.

This time, Harry helped himself to a glass of red wine. He didn't drink though. Left it on the counter. 'Now, where were we? Oh, yes. I was making conversation. Trying to get a picture of you and your housemates. Do they pay much rent?'

Ethan leaned towards Harry. 'I can't help it if my parents have money.'

In return, Harry mirrored Ethan, leaning into the student's space.

'And I can't help wanting to know why you sodding well came at me with a knife.'

'You know why.' The muscles in Ethan's jaw were bulging with rage. He wasn't faking. He was filled with hate for Harry. 'An eye for an eye,' he hissed.

'Who told you I was a paedophile?'

'No one,' he said quickly.

'Was it something you saw online?'

Ethan's eyes narrowed for a moment as though he was accessing a memory.

Harry was about to tell him he should know better than to believe anything online when a door banged nearby and a woman's voice sang out, 'Grocery delivery!'

Ethan reacted as though he'd been shot. His eyes widened, his jaw dropped. He looked at Harry in what could only be termed horror. 'Stay here,' he ordered. He bolted outside.

Curious, Harry followed Ethan down the hallway to the back door, where a young woman stood, clutching several shopping bags.

Ethan was blocking her from entering and she was looking fed up.

'Why can't I come in?'

'Trust me, okay?' Ethan's voice was urgent. 'You don't want to meet this guy...'

'The ice cream's defrosting! Let me in, Ethan, for fuck's sake.'

'Hello,' Harry called out. 'I'm Harry. Can I help with the shopping?'

Ethan spun round, hands open, as though he'd like to herd Harry away.

'Yes, you can.' The woman was disgruntled. 'Here.' She thrust out a bag. Harry stepped to take it.

'Heavy,' he remarked.

'Potatoes,' she responded. 'Thanks.'

She followed him into the kitchen where she dumped her bags on the island and proceeded to unpack them. She was tall and extremely pretty, with a striking heart-shaped face and the most vivid blue eyes Harry thought he'd ever seen. They were framed by thick, dark lashes and appeared almost luminous. Her hair was bright steel silver and seemed to radiate light. Harry found it hard not to stare and forced his gaze to Ethan, who was standing just inside the kitchen door, looking as though he didn't know where to put himself.

'So,' she said, 'what do you do, Harry, that makes my brother anxious for me not to meet you?'

'I'm a psychotherapist.'

She stopped at that. Looked him in the eye. 'He always said he didn't need one.'

'People usually only see us when they've tried every other avenue.'

'I'm Filipa,' she told him. 'Ethan's sister.'

'I guessed.'

She smiled. 'Has he told you about me?'

'No.'

She looked at Ethan. 'Perhaps he'd better.'

Harry looked at Ethan too. 'He knows where to find me.' His tone was cool.

29

Since he passed Bloomfield Rise on his way home, Harry decided to drop in on the Kings. He could thank Doug for arranging cover for his absence at the congress as well as see how he was bearing up with his cancer diagnosis. He dropped his colleague a text saying he was on his way round but didn't get a reply. He'd play it by ear when he got there, he decided.

When he rang the doorbell, he heard for the first time, barking. High-pitched barking from what sounded like an extremely small dog. 'Wait while I catch her!' Harry heard Catherine yell.

'Okay!' the twins chorused.

Half a minute passed and then the door was flung open.

'Harry!' shouted Paton.

'It's Harry!' Mia called.

'Yes, I heard.'

Catherine appeared, cradling a tiny black and white puppy against her chest. Tiny black eyes, black nose, a tiny pink tongue trying to lick Catherine's face. A Jack Russell. It couldn't have been more than eight weeks old.

'I don't believe it,' Harry said. Doug had always refused to allow the twins a dog saying, *over my dead body*.

'I know.' Catherine was smiling. 'He finally caved in. I don't know why. He came home with her the day before yesterday. The girls are incandescent with joy.'

'What's incandistant?' Mia asked.

'Glowing. Beaming. Shiny. Come in, Harry. Have a glass of wine.'

'She's called Daisy,' Paton said proudly.

'I wanted to call her Bella but I wasn't allowed,' Mia added.

'You only thought of that name *after* she'd been named.'

The twins chattered as Harry walked into the kitchen with Catherine.

'I was passing,' Harry said. 'Thought I'd drop in. I tried to ring Doug to let him know but he didn't pick up.'

'Oh.' She looked surprised. 'Didn't he tell you? He's in Edinburgh for the next couple of days. Some conference or other. Back Thursday.'

'That's okay. It's good to see you.'

He sat at the table while Catherine popped the puppy on the floor before pulling out a bottle of white wine from the fridge. Poured them both a glass. Came and sat next to him.

'I still can't believe it.' She was gazing at the puppy snuffling around its water bowl.

'Me neither.'

They chinked glasses.

'And he's taking us away for Easter.'

'Good grief,' Harry said. 'Where to?'

'Wales.' Catherine reached across the table for the laptop sitting on top of a magazine. Brought it over and opened the lid. She tapped on the keyboard before turning the screen to Harry. 'That's the house he's rented.'

Seabreeze was an apparently stunning seaside home that was perfectly located to embrace the beach lifestyle with an outside terrace, a wood burner and open-plan living.

'Wow.'

'No neighbours either, which means we can make as much noise as we like. The kids are almost sick with excitement. It's been five years since we last went away. *Five years*. It feels like a lifetime.'

Being diagnosed with cancer wasn't great for Doug, Harry thought, but it seemed to be giving the family a shot in the arm, and by the time Harry had downed his glass of wine and held the puppy while the twins talked him through the animal's routine of sleeping, eating, peeing and pooing, he felt quite buoyed up on their behalf. Perhaps Doug had started believing that charity should start at home. Which couldn't be a bad thing. He hadn't seen Catherine looking so happy in ages.

It was dark when he got home, but the lights were on, his house looking welcoming and warm thanks to Jessie letting herself in earlier. She stir-fried them both some chicken and vegetables, lots of chilli and garlic, which they ate in front of the TV. When they went to bed, Jessie checked his bruises, which were losing their black and purple bloom and turning yellow and grey. She gently stroked on some more arnica which in turn led to more stroking and, wary of his ribs, Harry made love to her slowly and carefully, which she seemed to like.

'Nice,' she murmured later, tucked against his chest, eyes closed, her breathing already deepening into sleep.

'Hmm.' He kissed her forehead and fell asleep wondering if he could ask her to move in with him.

The next morning, Jessie left at her usual time of eight o'clock to make sure she was at Eddie's Farm in time for the eight-thirty meeting that set out the agenda for the day. Jessie was now communications manager, but despite the smart title she also pitched in where she could, helping with the lambing and mucking out the horses. Although Eddie himself was no longer there, it was, Jessie said, still a great place to work.

After they'd kissed goodbye, Harry took his bruises to work. Ethan had yet to turn up but since it was the first time he'd been late, Harry wasn't going to bust his balls over it. After he'd seen one client, he was preparing to see the second when Jagoda buzzed through to say they'd cancelled.

'Is okay,' Jagoda added. 'You have a new client. She is here already, waiting to see you. You have room for her, yes?'

Harry's client list was full, but rather than reject the woman outright via Jagoda, he said, 'I'll be there in a minute.' It could take an enormous amount of courage for some people to come to a psychotherapist's office, and he'd rather explain his reasons why he couldn't take on a new client face to face than knock them back via a third person.

His surprise when he saw who it was made him blink several times. Filipa Stanning Jones laughed.

'Surprise!' she said.

'Hello.'

As he walked over to her she got to her feet. 'I'm sorry I didn't call ahead. I just wanted a quick word. I mean a *very* quick word.'

'What kind of word?' Harry asked cautiously. 'It's just that my client list is–'

'Oh, God no. Not as a client.' She looked shocked. 'I just wanted to have a word about Ethan.'

Jagoda had busied herself on her computer, pretending to be absorbed in what she was doing and not listening, but Filipa didn't even flick a look at her. It was as though Jagoda didn't exist.

'Ethan's not a client,' Harry told Filipa.

'Oh.' Her face fell. 'I rather hoped he was. I mean, last night he admitted he'd been coming here. I thought that meant he was getting therapy.'

Harry shook his head. 'Even if he was, I really couldn't discuss him with you.'

She digested that, vivid eyes thoughtful. 'But if he isn't a client...' She brightened. 'We can talk about him, right?'

'I'm not sure if it's appropriate. I'm sorry.'

'Why is he coming here if he's not getting therapy?' She was frowning.

'You'd better ask him.'

For the first time, she looked irritated. 'God, you're annoying.'

'It's not the first time someone's said that.' Harry smiled.

She didn't smile back but to his shock, gave him a look of dislike. She was used to getting her own way, he realised, and didn't like the fact he wasn't susceptible to her looks or her charm.

'It was good of you to drop by anyway,' he told her evenly. 'Can I tell Ethan you were here?'

'I wouldn't if I were you.' She watched him, expressionless.

He wanted to ask why, but he didn't want to give her the satisfaction so he nodded and said, 'If you'll excuse me,' and walked away. He could feel her gaze burning resentfully between his shoulder blades. She wouldn't like him turning his back on her.

30

Taking advantage of his client's cancellation, Harry rang Theo and when he heard he was at Bath University, asked if he could join him.

'Come on up. You can be the good cop to my bad.'

'Who are you interviewing?'

'Lorraine Brown's students. It's been a bit like herding cats but we've got most of them together.'

Theo handed Harry a list of all the students Lorraine had taught. 'Any familiar to you?' Harry looked at the lists of names once, then he read through them a second time.

'There's no Vera Wang here.' He explained what Wren had told him.

'She might be protecting someone,' Theo suggested.

Harry thought back to his conversation with Wren, and Ethan and Cabe listening. His realising he couldn't trust anything they said. 'I'll talk to her again.'

'And I'll check to see if Vera Wang is a registered student here.'

Lorraine had had around forty students who she taught en masse in a lecture hall but her tutorials and workshops were given to smaller groups, with a maximum of twelve attending at any one time. Harry joined Theo part-way through his talking with the second group in one of the classrooms. The tables were nicer than the ones Harry remembered from his uni days here, with beech tops and lacquered bullnose edges. The hard-wearing blue and grey carpet looked the same, as did the poly-carbonate chairs, but the twin screens were new along with the audio-visual equipment.

He'd met Dave at Bath Uni, but where Harry had taken his psychology degree into a therapy role, Dave had moved into sports psychology, and now worked in the university's Sports Training Village with some of the top athletes in the UK. They'd shared a house on St Kilda's Road with three other students, all male, and when Harry remembered those days they were a happy blur of parties and pub crawls, endless nights of caffeine-fuelled study and meals of baked beans on toast.

Even when Harry started going out with Nicole, he and Dave would still go to the pub, watch TV, go to the rugby together. Until Nicole organised a picnic one summer's day. She'd packed a basket with food and wine, and when Dave had joked about his missing out on a spiritual experience – Solsbury Hill wasn't just a place near Bath, but a song by Peter Gabriel – she'd invited him. The three of them had traipsed to the top of Solsbury Hill where Nicole had spread the picnic blanket and they'd spent the afternoon looking over Bath, getting drunk on cheap rosé and discussing everything between Jung and Freud's differing conceptions of the unconscious to whether Galaxy Minstrel chocolates were better than Maltesers. It had been a defining moment for the three of them, and in their last semester, they became pretty much inseparable.

Now, Harry put his memories aside to listen to Lorraine's students. Nobody had seen Lorraine nearly getting run down three weeks ago. Nobody had any idea if she had any enemies.

Eventually, having watched Theo question the last group, Harry's curiosity grew.

'Nobody seems to have a bad thing to say about Lorraine,' he mused out loud.

'So?' a young woman remarked. 'She was really nice.'

The students nodded. They were a mixed bag, their ages ranging from early twenties to fifties. All were doing an MA designed to help them write a novel that they hoped would eventually be published.

'She accused one student of cheating,' Harry said. 'I heard it caused a bit of an upset. Apparently Lorraine publicly humiliated them. That wouldn't have endeared her to her student, would it?'

'Cheating's a stupid thing to do,' the young woman snorted. 'Nobody's going to publish your novel if you've plagiarised it.'

'Were there any rumours you heard about Lorraine?' Harry pressed the group. 'Anything nasty?'

'Like what?' This time a man spoke up. Around Doug's age, in his late thirties, he was apparently writing a historical crime novel.

'Like anything,' Theo said, looking at each student in turn. Most held his eye, but the young woman fixed her gaze on her feet.

'Gemma?' Theo prompted the young woman.

'There was something,' she admitted.

Theo and Harry waited.

'But it's so horrible, and so obviously untrue, I'd rather tell you privately.'

31

After Theo had wound up the meeting, handing the students to a team of officers to ask where each had been the night Lorraine had drowned, Harry joined Theo and Gemma standing outside The Edge, an arts space next to the Sports Training Village. The air was soft and filled with birdsong, the sun warm on Harry's shoulders, reminding him that summer was on its way.

'What did you hear?' Theo prompted Gemma.

'That she was charged with cruelty to children but got off.'

Harry was opening his mouth to protest but Theo held up a hand, stalling him.

'What children?' Theo asked.

'Hers. The rumour said she beat them, but she never hit their heads or faces so you couldn't tell. I heard that she burned them too. Cut them. That she poured boiling oil over her daughter's arm because she was late down for supper one evening. She got off, the story says, because she's got rich parents.'

It was so patently untrue – Lorraine's parents weren't rich by a long shot for a start – that Harry was momentarily silenced.

'Where did you hear this rumour?'

Gemma frowned. 'I'm pretty sure it started on social media, but I can't really remember. It's just been around, like a bad smell, you know?'

'How long ago did you hear it?'

'Two or three weeks back, I guess.' She looked at Theo suddenly, horror dawning. 'Do you think she was killed because of it? The rumour?'

'It's possible.'

'God, how awful.'

'Who talked to you about it?'

She screwed up her face as she thought. 'It was in the café. There were a whole bunch of us. We didn't take it seriously.'

'If you could send me a list of who was there, that would be great.' Theo gave her his email address. 'And if anyone can remember the social media site...'

'Sure.'

After Gemma had left, Theo said, 'I'll have to check with the courts as well as Lorraine's husband. And her kids. Just in case. But if it's untrue, like your accusation of paedophilia, then we'd better start looking at rumours put out about Phil Petty and Kevin Owen, and find where they came from. We're already checking the university social media sites. Oh, and Libby and I will be at Lorraine's funeral tomorrow, keeping an eye out.'

Harry wasn't looking forward to it. Not that anyone actually looked forward to funerals, but Lorraine had been so *young*. And being taken away from her kids and Gavin... A rush of anger filled his heart at the youths who'd killed her. He had to help Theo find the bastards. Bring them to justice.

They both turned their heads as a group of female students passed, deep in conversation and looking fearsomely earnest.

'I've got a date on Saturday,' Theo suddenly said.

Harry knew Theo had been single for a long time after he'd split up with his previous partner. *Too difficult*, he'd said when

Harry questioned him. *And she never asked my opinion about things. Like getting another dog. She'd already got two and she got a third – a sodding great mastiff – without asking how I felt about it. I didn't mind the dog as much as not being part of the decision. When I realised that I mattered less than the dog, well, it was game over.*

'That's good,' said Harry.

'She's a landscape gardener.'

'Interesting.' Harry put an encouraging tone in his voice but when Theo didn't say any more, Harry knew it was time to move on.

'Any luck with Clive Farmer's computer?' Harry asked, and immediately his broken ribs gave a twinge at the thought of the big man holding him while his baseball-bat-wielding pal did his worst.

'Lots of nasty stuff,' said Theo. 'The CPS are throwing the book at them.'

Nice one, Harry thought.

He was filling Theo in on the elusive Hugh Lamont, the financial advisor who'd lied to Phil Petty about knowing Harry, when he caught sight of a familiar figure heading his way. The man was carrying a gym bag and in his wake were half a dozen students, all vying for his attention. Four men and two women, one of whom was looking up and into his eyes, apparently entranced.

Dave.

Harry watched as Dave said something that made the group laugh. He'd forgotten how charming his old friend could be. Charismatic. Good company. Out of nowhere Harry realised he hadn't just been mourning Nicole when she'd dumped him, but Dave too. Talk about a double whammy.

At that moment, as though he'd heard Harry's thoughts, Dave turned his head and looked straight at him. For the first time Harry saw him separately from the divorce and the betrayal, and his own pain. Dave was super-fit and although he wasn't handsome, exactly, there was something about his face, the way he quirked an eyebrow and lifted the corners of his mouth that made you want to look at him twice. No wonder his students were in thrall.

After a long moment, Dave's shoulders dropped infinitesimally and Harry saw his gaze turn inwards, his mind moving through various options, and then he came to a decision and turned his head back to the young woman, ignoring Harry completely.

Dave wasn't a wimp, Harry realised. He'd gone after Ethan that day without hesitation. He'd only hidden from Harry because he knew what a shit he'd been. Harry realised it was time for him to move on. Not that he'd be having a pint with Dave like he used to, but it was time he began to be civil.

As he watched Dave and his entourage disappear into the training village, he heard Theo answer his phone. Harry didn't listen to the conversation because he was still thinking about Dave, but finally Theo's excitement broke through his introspection.

'That's fantastic news, Libby. We'll be there as soon as we can.'

Theo hung up and looked at Harry. Harry could almost feel the crackle of energy buzzing through the policeman. It was like standing next to an electricity pylon.

'You're cancelling your afternoon appointments,' Theo told him, 'because our techies have had a major breakthrough.'

32

Harry didn't endear himself to Theo when he refused to turn his back on his clients and when he eventually arrived at the MIR in Bristol later in the day, the DI didn't make an issue of it. Simply took him into a side room where the same techie who'd been at Mrs Farmer's house – the beanpole – was working on a laptop.

'Adam.' Theo introduced them. 'Talk Harry through what you've found.'

Adam pushed back from the desk a fraction before turning the laptop so Harry could see.

The image was an animated illustration in semi-realistic style. It showed a judge in full court dress with a robe of black damask embellished with gold. He wore a traditional white wig and a pair of gold half-moon glasses. He appeared to be in his sixties. He looked like the quintessential judge you'd see in cartoons. A plaque sat before him: CHIEF LORD JUSTICE.

Harry looked at the website address: ExecutorOfJustice.

'It doesn't have that much traffic yet,' Adam said, 'because I think it's pretty new. But it's gaining traction.' He tapped on the keyboard. Another page came up.

THE BATTLE WITH BOREDOM ENDS HERE!
BECOME A QUALIFIED EXECUTOR OF JUSTICE!

Adam clicked through several more pages. The site appeared to be directed towards late teens or students. Harry knew that curious youngsters had Google at their fingertips and could search for anything they could think of. He also knew that not much – not even the most extreme content from porn or IS beheadings – shocked them. The website promised to give them real excitement and euphoria as they faced real danger, culminating in a real sense of fulfilment that they would never forget.

UNFORGETTABLE! the site screamed over and over.

The words *real* and *reality* were used prolifically. Further text was cleverly written, leading the viewer to believe they'd been hoodwinked by other entertainments online, and that other sites were conning them when there was so much on offer if you were interested in truth, honour and righteousness.

THE HALLS OF JUSTICE NEED YOU!

Adam clicked to another page where an array of videos became available to play. Harry's skin tightened. One of them was of Lorraine drowning. Another of Kevin Owen being attacked outside his judo school. Phil Petty's attack was also there, albeit in shaky form, but Harry's wasn't. Had Ethan been acting alone? Or had Harry's punching Ethan made it too ignominious to have been posted?

'You pay a nominal fee to join.' Adam took Harry through the site, quoting verbatim. 'You become a Qualified Executor of Justice, meting out harsh punishments to people whose grave crimes have gone unpunished.'

Another couple of clicks and over a dozen portrait photographs filled the screen. Phil Petty was there, along with Kevin Owen, Lorraine and Harry, and another man he didn't recognise.

'Who's that?'

'Richard Johnston. He died six months ago. We thought it was an accident, but it's not. Show him, Adam.'

The video showed a man up a three-section extension ladder, trimming some wisteria around the top storey of a handsome red-brick house. He was on the fifth rung from the top, concentrating on the job in hand, when a figure strode into view and without pausing, kicked the ladder from beneath him.

'Christ.' Harry felt his breathing stop as the man was flung twenty-odd feet onto the stone driveway below.

The man who kicked the ladder vanished. The video ended.

'His daughter found him an hour later,' Theo told him. 'He'd broken both arms and a leg. He might have survived if he hadn't had an open fracture. He died of sepsis two weeks later.'

Another click.

RAPIST RICHARD JOHNSTON GOT HIS COMEUP-PANCE AND THE POLICE DIDN'T HAVE A CLUE!

YOU CAN GET AWAY WITH IT TOO!

Adam clicked the page back to the portraits. Harry felt dizzy and unbalanced as he stared at his own picture. It had been taken outside, at least five years ago, because he hadn't worn that particular fleece since he'd accidently spilled creosote over it.

'Do you know anyone else pictured here?' Theo asked.

They were all strangers to Harry, except one. He pointed at a photograph of a man in his early eighties. 'That's Catherine King's father. Doug's father-in-law. He's a widower. He lives in a cottage, in Monkton Farleigh.'

'I'll send Libby to talk to him. Talk him through security.'

'What's Vince been accused of? Do we know?'

'When you click on a portrait,' Adam explained, 'the supposed crime is shown.'

'Do mine,' Harry ordered.

Adam clicked.

The photographs that Mrs Farmer had shown Harry

appeared below a headline: ONE OF BRITAIN'S MOST PROLIFIC PAEDOPHILES. HE AVOIDED JAIL BECAUSE HE KNOWS THE RIGHT PEOPLE, IN THE RIGHT PLACES. DON'T LET HIM GET AWAY WITH IT.

'Bloody hell,' said Harry.

'Show him Lorraine's,' Theo bade Adam.

A page of heart-rending pictures of a little girl nursing raw and weeping burns on her arms and legs appeared. She looked very like Esme, but it definitely wasn't Lorraine's daughter. MOTHER BURNED FIVE-YEAR OLD FOR NOT DOING HOMEWORK. SHE THINKS SHE'S SO CLEVER BEING A UNIVERISTY LECTURER BUT WE KNOW WHAT SHE DOES BEHIND CLOSED DOORS. DON'T LET HER GET AWAY WITH IT.

'What's Phil supposed to have done?' Harry asked.

His old neighbour was accused of stealing from charities. HE'S NOT A SELF-MADE MAN. HE'S A THIEF. HE STEALS FROM THE DISADVANTAGED, THE POOR.

Kevin Owen was accused of raping a toddler. Doug's father-in-law of committing years of torture on his grandchildren.

'People bid for a "job",' Adam explained to Harry. 'The highest wins, which is maybe why we get three people attacking one person, because they've pooled resources.'

'How much?'

'Lorraine's reached six hundred and fifty pounds. Yours, on the other hand, has only had one bid of a hundred pounds.'

'I don't understand.' Harry was frowning. 'If it's one bid, then how come I was attacked twice? First by Ethan, then by Clive Farmer?'

'We don't know,' Theo answered. 'But we're concerned there might be another site out there.'

'God, I hope not,' Harry said feelingly. 'I don't want another brace of vigilantes on my doorstep.'

Theo leaned past Adam and tapped on the keyboard. 'Our main concern is that it's inciting murder.'

Another page appeared.

DO THESE PEOPLE DESERVE TO LIVE?

Below the headline was a picture of an ancient Roman gladiatorial fight, and an emoji of an emperor inviting the viewer to vote thumbs up, the accused lived, or thumbs down – they died.

Nobody had clicked on the thumbs-up emoji. Over fifty people had voted for him and Lorraine, Phil and the other four supposed defendants, to die.

Harry's mouth turned dry. 'Can you find out who's running the site?' Harry asked. 'Who's taking the money?'

'Not yet. But one thing I will say is that whoever it is, wants to raise the stakes. They started by suggesting five thousand pounds per attack but the attackers so far – aside from Clive Farmer, of course – have been students. They can't afford that much.'

'Then they're given our addresses?'

'That's how it seems to work.' Theo cleared his throat. 'We've taken the site down, but I still want you to be vigilant. We're trying to find the members through their IP addresses but it's bloody difficult. Computers can be routed through ISPs, proxy servers and the like. It's an uphill battle at the moment.'

Harry stared at the computer screen. He'd never been on anyone's hit list before. It scared the hell out of him.

33

Back in the MIR, Harry looked at the rows of desks and computer terminals, the officers busy working to find Lorraine's killers. Above the white board, in capital letters, Theo had written OPERATION ARMOUR. He could tell it was Theo's writing because it slanted upwards, and the N wasn't a capital letter but lower case. A little quirk that Harry had always found rather endearing in a man always so in command.

'We need to talk to Ethan,' Theo said. 'See how he got put onto the site.'

'Yes.' Harry glanced at his watch. 'He should still be at the Centre, but I'll check with him first.'

Ethan said yes, he'd still be there when Harry got back, and agreed to wait for him if he ran late. He sounded oddly troubled, almost upset, and Harry asked if he was okay.

'I... well, I'll tell you when I see you.'

Harry didn't mention he'd be bringing a DI with him.

Jagoda was still there, chatting to Ethan, when he and Theo turned up. Ethan had shed his overalls and tidied up, ready to head home. His face tightened when Harry introduced him to Theo.

'There weren't any witnesses,' Ethan told Theo stiffly. '*He* attacked *me*. He broke my nose.'

His bruises had almost faded, Harry noticed, and he'd nearly finished Libby's off-the-cuff community service. He just had Doug's office to do.

'Let's talk in Harry's office,' Theo said, all congeniality.

Ethan looked as though he might object until Theo brought out his warrant card and said quietly, 'Please, don't be difficult.'

As Harry closed his office door behind them, Theo went to stand by the window while Ethan stood uneasily beside the small round table that was placed between two easy chairs.

'Do I need a lawyer?' Ethan asked.

'It depends on what you think you've done.' Theo cocked his head to one side.

'Look.' Harry took a step towards Ethan. 'We need your help. We're trying to find the people who killed Lorraine Brown, and–'

'I had nothing to do with that.' Ethan reared backwards. 'You can't pin that on me.'

'Just listen,' Theo snapped.

Ethan bridled, but he kept quiet as Harry sketched out the Executor of Justice website and its role of meting out justice to people who'd supposedly committed heinous crimes.

'Who put you onto it?'

Ethan stared at Harry. 'I've never heard of it.'

Even Theo blinked at his seemingly genuine response. Was Ethan that good a liar? Harry wondered.

'My picture is on the site,' Harry told him. 'With doctored photographs of children and... me.'

Ethan spread his hands in apparent bafflement. 'Seriously, I have no idea what you're talking about.'

Theo brought out his phone and showed Ethan the home page but Ethan shook his head. 'This is the first time I've seen it. Honest to God.'

'So why did you attack me?' Harry asked.

Ethan glanced at Theo. Harry knew he wouldn't get any joy with the policeman there. He asked Theo the question with his eyes.

Theo sighed. 'You've got five minutes,' he told them. 'Make it snappy.' He let himself out.

'Sit,' Harry told Ethan.

He did as he was told and Harry took up the chair opposite. Adopted a neutral pose.

'Talk,' Harry said.

Ethan fidgeted, crossing and recrossing his legs, leaning forward, then back.

'Spit it out,' Harry said gently.

'Shit.' The young man's long legs started jiggling nervously. 'Well... it's just that...' He scrunched his eyes closed for an instant. 'I've really fucked up.'

Harry waited.

'I mean *really* fucked up.' He faltered. His legs continued to jiggle. 'Because the thing is...'

He lost his nerve and fell quiet.

'Ethan – you were saying?' Harry prompted.

When the young man looked at him, his gaze was a desperate plea.

'It's just that... I got things wrong about you. It was only when Filipa saw you...'

He fell silent.

Normally Harry wouldn't feed Ethan a question at this moment but with Theo hovering outside and waiting to pounce, he didn't see he had a choice.

'Why didn't you want her to see me?'

Ethan groaned. Put his head in his hands. 'I thought you were...'

Harry leaned forward. 'I was what?'

At that, Ethan closed his eyes as though he couldn't bear to look at Harry. 'When she was thirteen, Filipa was raped. By her child psychologist. She made me swear not to tell our parents. She was terrified they'd blame her. She was also really worried he'd get struck off. She really liked him, you see. She didn't want him to go to jail. It wasn't until later, when she grew up a bit more, when she realised how sick that was. Mum and Dad still don't know...'

'How old were you?'

'Fifteen. I went mad. I wanted to kill him but I didn't know how to find him and Filipa wouldn't tell me. She stopped seeing him, of course, but the damage was done. She's never been quite right since, a bit off the wall, a bit crazy. She does weird things. She says she can't help it. She changed that day. Irrevocably.'

Ethan opened his eyes. Drew a long breath. 'It's only recently she's been saying she'd feel so much better if she knew he was dead. That she'd feel more secure, more able to be herself again.'

Harry struggled to keep his composure. 'You thought I was her rapist.'

Ethan gave a jerky nod.

'You wanted to kill me.'

The young man suddenly looked incredibly tired. 'I told you I fucked up.'

At least that explained the looks of loathing Ethan hadn't been able to disguise.

'But I didn't know I'd made a mistake until Filipa saw you,' Ethan blurted. 'It was obvious she hadn't met you before.'

'Does Filipa know you attacked me?'

'No.' He hung his head.

After a moment, Harry said, 'We – that is the police and me – need to know how you came to think I was your sister's rapist.'

Ethan twisted in the chair and brought out his phone. 'I was sent this.'

It was a mug shot of Harry. It was his passport photo, taken nine years ago against the wall of the kitchen by Nicole, in which he wore an open shirt and a short stubble beard which he'd shaved off eighteen months later. On the bottom right-hand corner was the Avon and Somerset logo with its red velvet crown and the red dragon holding scales of justice.

Below the mug shot were the words, *The police didn't have enough evidence to lock him up. He's still out there, preying on little girls. What are you going to do about it?*

The link attached went straight to the Wellbeing Centre's website, where there were photos of all the staff along with their biographies.

A fist of anger buried itself in Harry's stomach. 'Didn't it cross your mind you were being manipulated?'

Ethan appeared to give his question some thought. 'Actually, no it didn't, because I showed this picture to Filipa. She was really shocked. She said that the man in this picture was her rapist. She asked me to take it to the police.' He swallowed. 'But I didn't.'

Harry studied the photograph. 'Do I look that different today?'

'A bit. You're older. You don't have a beard.'

Jesus Christ. I nearly got knifed because I used to have a beard?

'Send me a copy of that message, please.'

Harry's phone pinged as it arrived. He stared at it. Neither of them spoke.

Ethan jumped when the phone on Harry's desk rang. Jagoda whispered hurriedly, 'Your friend is going to come in to see you any moment.'

Harry turned to Ethan. 'You do realise you're going to have to tell DI McCannon what you've told me.'

'Yes.' Ethan looked up as Theo entered. He put his hands out in a parody of offering his wrists to be handcuffed, trying to act nonchalant, but his mouth was twisted and Harry could tell all he wanted to do was curl into a ball and cry.

34

Theo didn't arrest Ethan, but he took his phone and told him to wait outside because the young man was going to accompany him to the station where he would make a statement. Ethan traipsed outside looking like a man about to be hung.

Harry showed Theo the message Ethan had received.

'How did our suspect get their hands on your picture?'

'Nicole took loads. I got eight printed online, if I remember correctly. I've used a couple since, for a library ID, one for a talk in London.'

'It's possible your photograph was hacked online, but if not, it would mean someone closer to home nicked one.' Theo seemed to ignore Harry's sick look. 'If you used two photos for your passport application, and have used two since, that leaves four.'

Harry opened his desk drawer and had a rummage. Found two, tucked in an envelope. 'The others will be at home.'

'Let me know if you find them.'

After Theo had left, Harry headed home. He checked the drawer in the spare room cum office where passport photos and the like were kept, but they weren't there. Had he taken them all to the Centre? He couldn't remember.

Although Jessie came around, he was quiet that evening. Introspective. Who in the world wanted him dead? Who was using students like assassins? He tried to work out the psychological pathology behind such a person and why they were using such an extraordinarily complex scheme to affect their plan. A plan that had a pretty poor success rate with two deaths out of four attacks and two hit and runs. And even then, both Lorraine's and Richard Johnston's deaths had been more by accident than design. If Richard hadn't got sepsis after his ladder had been kicked from beneath him, if the canal hadn't been so deep at that point, if Lorraine hadn't been wearing that tweed coat. If, if, if.

Was it about creating fear? Or was it just about giving the originator of the website a thrill that he could destroy lives? Terrify people? Perhaps he was a control freak and enjoyed sending students to do his bidding. Harry doubted a woman was behind this. Women could be vicious, vindictive and cruel, but for some reason this smacked of being created by a man. But why? He couldn't work it out. What did the perpetrator want to achieve?

Harry had spoken to Doug about his father-in-law, who was on the portrait page of the Executor of Justice website. Doug sounded deeply shocked and kept repeating, 'But who would want to kill Vince?'

Harry couldn't answer. He felt as though he was in some kind of living nightmare with visions of falsified photographs of himself doing unspeakable things to children searing his mind. He double-checked the latches on the windows and locks on the doors, and then went online and ordered a burglar alarm, to be delivered into his recycling bin tomorrow. He'd install it tomorrow night.

'Perhaps I should get a guard dog,' he mused. He and Jessie were eating lamb chops at the kitchen table. A seasonal choice by Jessie that had surprised Harry, considering Eddie's Farm would be awash with cute little spring lambs. But Jessie was country born and bred and had a practical streak the size of the Murray River. She'd muttered about turning vegan for the planet but so far that's all it had been: talk.

'A dog won't stop someone trying to run you over.' Jessie took his hand and turned it over, kissed his palm. 'Have you thought of going away for a bit, while all this is going on?'

'I couldn't–'

'Leave your clients, I know.' Her green eyes held his steadily. 'But are you really willing to die for them?'

He was going to tell her she was being over-dramatic, but then he saw her point. He'd feel pretty bloody stupid if he got killed tomorrow.

'What do you suggest?'

'Let's go to France!' Her face lit up. 'Normandy? Brittany? I've never been, and you know how I love cheese.'

'I think France is a bit OTT.'

'Easter's only two days away.'

Harry had forgotten Easter was late this year and for a moment he had to remember what he'd organised and then he remembered – the kids would be with Nicole, which was why he'd had them earlier in the month.

'Everything will be booked up.'

'Spoilsport.' She pulled a face. 'I just want to keep you safe, Okay?'

'Understood, but I was thinking more of staying somewhere different every other night, parking somewhere different, and approaching the Centre from a different direction each day.'

'What, like a spy?'

'I guess so.'

'It's not such a bad idea. If they don't know where you're sleeping, and you don't park up Harley Street, then they won't know where to lie in wait for you.'

'That's what I was thinking.' And hang the expense, he thought. I can't spend any money if I'm dead.

35

The next morning Harry had singularly failed to find a B&B to stay in locally, so he switched to Airbnb. He was checking out a place in Box that described itself as *sparkling clean* when Nicole rang.

'Just wanted to let you know the school has just gated your son.'

Whenever one of the kids got into trouble, they always became his responsibility.

'I take it you're talking about Tim?' Ben, being the older brother, was usually the more responsible.

'Who else would it be? He's only been caught driving the school's ride-on mower.'

'Someone left the keys in it?'

'Apparently, yes. He's mown down a whole row of daffodils. The ones on the way to the chapel.'

'Oh dear.' He tried to keep his tone neutral but Nicole obviously picked up on something because she snapped, 'It's not funny, Harry.'

He sobered immediately. 'No, it's not. Sorry.'

'Don't you dare encourage him.'

'I won't!' he protested. 'I'm just glad he wasn't caught dealing cocaine and heroin, that's all.'

Nicole sighed. 'You're right. It could be worse.'

'I'll call him in a minute. And I won't express anything but deep displeasure, I promise.'

'Thanks, Harry.' Another sigh. 'It'll be pretty awful having Easter without him, but I suppose he's got to be punished.'

'Absolutely.'

A small silence fell.

He heard Nicole draw a breath. 'I'm dreading this afternoon.'

Lorraine's funeral.

'I know,' Harry said gently. 'Lean on Dave.'

'And you'll lean on Jessie.'

'Yes.'

Another pause.

'What are you up to?' Nicole asked. 'You're not at work, are you?'

'Looking online for an Airbnb in Box.'

'Whatever for?'

When he told her, she sounded horrified. 'You're on a death list?'

'I wouldn't have told you, except I thought you'd better be aware.'

'Jesus, Harry.'

'Hence staying somewhere else.'

'Why don't you stay with friends of mine? They run Lorne House, it's fabulous.'

'They'll be booked.'

'Leave it with me.' She was brisk. 'And if they can't have you, they'll know someone who can.'

With Nicole on the case of his accommodation, Harry rang Tim.

'You idiot,' he said. He tried to sound cross but it came out sounding far too amused.

'It was too tempting, Dad. The engine was running and nobody, I mean *nobody* was about and there was this huge stretch of lawn just waiting to be driven down, it was *sooooo* inviting, I can't tell you.'

'And now you're going to miss Easter with your brother and sister.'

'I know.' He sounded glum.

'Anyone else there with you?'

'No,' he said miserably. 'I'm here all on my own.'

'For every action,' Harry said gently, 'there has to be a consequence. Get it?'

'Yeah. But it still sucks.'

After they'd hung up, Harry's phone gave a *ting*. A message from Nicole.

Lorne House say they can have you as a favour to me. All booked in. Stay safe, Harry x

Harry looked the place up to see it was a large Victorian villa in the village of Box and a stone's throw not just from Jessie, but his favourite curry house, the Bengal Bear. As he scanned the online brochure he learned it had been converted into a small hotel which, he read, was also available to rent as a whole house. He was immediately reminded of Ethan, and his parents allowing him and his student friends to stay at the very grand, very luxurious Combe House at what he guessed would be minimal rent.

Lucky Ethan, but not so lucky having been tormented by his sister's rape. At fifteen, he would have felt the full weight of adult responsibility on his young shoulders, and by not telling their parents, they'd created their own sibling circle of dysfunction.

Although Jessie hadn't met Lorraine, she'd said she wanted to come to her funeral. Harry's daughter Lottie would be there,

Jessie said, and besides, she wanted to support Harry. He didn't dissuade her. He knew he'd endure it far better with her at his side.

The funeral was held at St John the Baptist Church in the village of Colerne, seven miles from Bath and across the valley from Box. Harry hadn't known that Lorraine had been brought up there, nor that she, Gavin and the kids attended the church most Sundays before having lunch with Lorraine's parents, who lived on Watergates – a street just behind the church. It made him think about how well he thought he knew people, but of course you couldn't know everything about everyone, even if you lived with them.

How well did he know Dave, for example? Doug or Catherine, or Theo? He drove up Bannerdown reflecting on the subject, glad that Jessie was empathetic to his mood and didn't chat.

36

It was drizzling when they arrived, the sky heavy with grey clouds. Apt weather for a funeral. He saw Theo and Libby standing by the church gates beneath their umbrellas, watching the arrivals. They gave Harry a nod. Later, during the service, he spotted them sitting in the rear pews. Dave was in one of the front pews with Nicole and Lottie. Doug was there too, but no Catherine.

Harry was surprised to see Ethan's sister, Filipa, and after the graveside service, he asked Jessie if she was okay on her own for a minute.

'Of course. I'll see you by the gates when you're done.'

Harry gave Jessie his umbrella and strode after Filipa. Fell into step with her. Rain dampened his head and the shoulders of his coat but even though she was tall enough to share her umbrella, she didn't make any move to do so. Still smarting from him turning his back on her, no doubt.

'I didn't know you knew Lorraine,' Harry said blandly.

She turned her vivid blue eyes to him. 'She was my tutor at Bath Uni.'

'You were on the creative writing course?' He couldn't

remember her being on any of Theo's lists.

'I was considering it. She invited me to come along and see if it might suit.'

'Did it?'

'I wasn't convinced. You see, I was thinking of writing my story. I've had some... difficult times, and I thought I might help people who'd been through the same sort of thing.'

'Like a self-help book?'

'More a memoir.'

'It could be really useful.'

She brightened at that. 'Do you think so?' She moved the umbrella to encompass them both.

'In my experience, books written by people who've had a certain experience and recovered can help inspire others who've been in the same situation. It helps them see there's life beyond what's happened to them.'

Filipa glanced sharply across at him. 'Ethan's been talking, hasn't he?'

'If he had, would it bother you?'

She lifted a hand and brushed back a tendril of silver hair. 'It's no big secret.'

He remembered the way the housemates had backed off the instant Ethan had said *my sister* when they'd asked how Ethan knew Harry. Ethan had lied, but the lie had served him well, shutting them down from asking anything more. Harry found Filipa's apparent dispassion about her rape interesting. It was his understanding that a lot of people who'd suffered rape kept it quiet, not wanting to be demarcated or defined by it.

'But your parents still don't know.'

She moved away from him at that, removing the shelter of her umbrella. 'Sometimes,' she said, her voice perfectly even, 'I wish Ethan would keep his trap shut.'

'Would you mind looking at something for me?'

She stopped for an instant, caution rippling over her face. 'Like what?'

Harry brought out his phone and, expanding it to exclude the police logo and text, showed her his old passport photograph.

A tiny spasm tightened the skin around her eyes and lips. 'Where did you get this?' Her voice was cold.

'You know who it is?'

For a second her eyelids flickered and then her face turned perfectly blank. Just like Ethan's did when he was confronted with something emotionally difficult.

'You obviously do,' she snapped, 'so don't rub it in.'

'It's me.'

The blank look remained. 'What?'

'It's my passport photograph. Taken nine years ago. When I had a beard.'

She stared at him. He couldn't think what might be going on in her mind. Finally, she licked her lips. Looked at the picture again. 'It's you?'

'Yes.'

She reached out a hand. Harry let her take his phone. She studied it at length, then she looked at him. 'Good God. It *is* you.'

'Did Ethan tell you how he came by this photograph?'

'No. I told him to take it to the police.' Her eyes slid to Libby and Theo, standing at their posts by the church gate. 'Which I guess he did, since you're apparently working with that DI.'

'You should ask Ethan about that,' Harry suggested. 'And get him to tell you why he's been at the Wellbeing Centre for the last couple of weeks while you're at it.'

She evaluated him briefly. 'Okay. I will.'

Filipa moved off without saying another word. Harry stood watching her walk around the market square to a blazing-red, brand new sporty little Mazda MX-5. She slipped inside. He wasn't surprised she'd double-parked, she had beauty and the arrogance of youth on her side, but he was surprised when Doug appeared at a trot and hopped in the passenger seat.

Although Harry knew they'd probably met on Lorraine's course, there was something disconcerting about seeing them together. Harry watched them drive away. He stood watching the space where the MX-5 had turned out of sight for a long time.

37

'I see you met the Ice Queen.' Gavin came and poured Harry another glass of sparkling water. Gavin was drinking whisky, along with his father. Everyone else was on wine, or water.

The wake was well attended, with a mix of students and family and friends. Over a hundred people. Jessie had gone to use the loo, leaving Harry to admire the view from the living room, which reached over the Box Valley, bursting green with flashes of pink and white blossom. He'd been incarcerated in a WWII pill box down there last year. Locked up in sub-zero degrees and left to die. Part of him still couldn't believe he'd escaped.

'Ice Queen?' Harry repeated with a frown.

'One of Lorraine's students. Well, sort of. Miz Stanning Jones didn't like her work being criticised so she quit.'

If you'd been traumatised and wrote about the experience, the critique would have to be incredibly sensitive not to cause real pain. Harry couldn't blame Filipa for leaving.

Gavin took a gulp of whisky. 'Lorraine said she had the emotions of a tea towel.'

When Gavin took in Harry's startled response he quickly

added, 'Not to *her*, you idiot. She said that to *me*. God, she'd never be that unsympathetic to a student. But she would offload to me from time to time. Let her frustrations out.'

Filipa could appear emotionless, Harry guessed, because she'd be hiding her issues behind a carapace of cool dispassion. Survivors of trauma used all kinds of different behaviours to help them survive.

'How are you bearing up?' Harry asked him.

'Shit.'

'I'm not surprised.'

Gavin's normally healthy ruddy glow had been replaced by pasty skin and haunted eyes. 'It's been made worse because... Oh, God.' He closed his eyes briefly.

'Worse because...?' Harry prompted.

'I haven't told her mum and dad.'

'I won't tell anyone.'

'I know.' He gave a twisted smile. 'You're like a priest, Harry. You never seem shocked or flustered. You just listen. No judgements.'

'I'm not imperturbable,' Harry responded. 'Some days my hair goes up in flames.'

'You know what I mean.'

'Yes.'

Gavin took another gulp of whisky. Turned his gaze outside. 'You probably don't know, but Lorraine was left some money by her gran when she died last year. Over fifty grand. She put it aside in a separate account. For the kids, you know?'

'I didn't know. But it sounds eminently sensible.'

'Well, unbeknownst to me, she withdrew the whole amount eighteen months ago. This didn't freak me out as much as you might think, because I do okay for money, but I'm just a bit stunned by it.'

'I'm not surprised. It's a lot of money.' Harry watched a crow flapping around a bird feeder in an attempt to eat the fat balls. 'Do you know what she did with the money?'

'No idea. I can't find it anywhere.'

'I'm sorry.' Harry put a hand on Gavin's shoulder. 'It must be incredibly frustrating not being able to ask her.'

'Damn right.' A spasm of pain crossed his face. 'God, Harry. It's all so fucking awful.'

'Come and see me,' Harry told him. 'When you're next in town. And if that's too difficult, I'll nip up to you. Talking about it can really help. Especially over a pint or two.'

Gavin's mouth twisted but there was no humour there. 'Thanks, Harry.'

As Gavin moved away, Jessie came to stand by Harry, slipping her arm through his. 'The poor bugger.'

'Yes.' Harry sighed.

'Are you okay?' She was looking at him with a concerned expression.

'Nothing a double whisky won't fix,' he said feelingly.

'Then let's go and–'

'Hello,' a man said smoothly. 'You must be the lovely Jessie. Sorry we haven't met before, and sorry it's not at a more cheerful event.'

Urbane, eyes warm, that quirky eyebrow in place, he was holding a glass of red wine.

Dave.

Jessie withdrew her hand from Harry's arm to shake his hand.

'I'm sorry too,' she said. Her tone was warm.

Dave held her hand a little too long for Harry's liking. *Be civil, be civil*, he chanted.

'This is Dave,' Harry said, tone brittle. 'Nicole's partner.'

'Oh,' said Jessie. Her expression had closed. Even Harry didn't know what she was thinking.

'I hope Harry hasn't maligned me too heavily.' Dave's eyes twinkled, inviting her to collude with him. 'I'm not so bad once you get to know me.'

He made to chink his glass with hers but Jessie stepped aside so he missed, slopping wine onto the carpet.

'Oops,' she said.

Dave eyed her warily, all bonhomie gone.

'We'd better get a cloth,' Jessie said. 'So it doesn't stain.'

Taking Harry's arm, she steered them briskly through the room. As they stepped into the hallway, Harry shot a look over his shoulder to see Dave gazing after them with an expression that made his steps falter.

Regret overlaid with something else. Something Harry couldn't identify.

Harry thought suddenly of the picnic on Solsbury Hill. The three of them lying on the prickly picnic blanket and squirting wine straight out of the box into their mouths. Eating strawberries and chocolate and arguing whether nice people could make great music. Nicole sitting between Harry's knees, making a daisy chain while Dave pointed out the swallows darting above.

They'd all loved one another in that careless way of youth, taking it for granted, assuming that it would be there for ever. But Dave had taken their friendship and torn it up into tiny pieces, chucked it into the wind.

Harry felt out of sorts for the rest of the day, but finally, after he'd eaten, brushed his teeth, and turned out the bedside light in his Victorian villa hotel, he recognised what the second emotion in Dave's face had been, because it echoed what had been in his own soul.

Bitterness.

38

Harry woke late on Friday. For a moment he couldn't work out where he was. He could hear traffic and somewhere, a church bell was pealing.

Lorraine's funeral.

Memories rushed in. He was in Lorne House. He sat up, rubbing his eyes. It was Good Friday. A holiday. He was supposed to be meeting Jessie for lunch.

Harry checked his phone for messages. One from Tim, saying he was so bored he wouldn't joyride anything ever again even if it was a skateboard. Another from Jessie sent last night, after he'd gone to sleep, rather raunchy, which made him smile. He'd enjoyed her reaction to Dave yesterday. She had firmly planted her flag with Harry and let him and Dave know it. He loved her loyalty.

A quick look at his emails showed nothing urgent, so he got up and showered, pattered down to breakfast. He'd just finished an excellent scrambled egg on toast when Jessie rang.

'Harry, I'm sorry, but I'm going to have to cancel today. We're two staff down and there's nobody else to fill in.'

After rearranging their lunch for the next day, Harry drank

another cup of coffee while reading the news online. Climate change dominated, followed by more trouble in the Middle East. He looked outside to see sunshine and a blue sky. He felt oddly adrift being here, having an enforced holiday, and he realised he didn't like it. He wanted to be at home. He had things to do, like mow the lawn and install the burglar alarm.

Sod it, he thought. I'm not staying here any longer.

After he'd paid the bill, apologising for only staying the one night, Harry walked to his car and slung his bag in the back. Looked up and down the A4, thinking. Doug's father-in-law Vince lived in Monkton Farleigh, just over the hill and barely three miles from where he stood. Harry had been there before on several occasions, usually to help celebrate Catherine's and the twins' birthdays over the years.

Although Theo had said he'd sent Libby to talk to Vince about security, Harry thought it prudent he spoke to him too. Plus, he wondered if between them they could find a link to help Theo and the murder team.

Harry tried to ring Vince but there was no reply. Would he mind Harry dropping in? From what he remembered of the man, he didn't think so. And if he was busy, or had people staying, Harry could leave him be.

Vince lived just outside the village, below the manor house and with sweeping views over green fields that reached to a line of hills on the horizon. Harry could just make out the pale smudge of the Westbury White Horse. Low-slung, ancient, the cottage seemed to grow out of the ground. It reminded Harry of somewhere a hobbit might live.

As he approached the layby next to the cottage, he put his

foot on the brake. It felt mushy, so he pushed his foot down harder and came to a slow stop behind two cars already there.

Sorry, old girl, he thought, *but it's definitely time to trade you in*.

Harry climbed outside and walked to the side of the cottage. A lone Hereford bull watched him pass.

'Hello, fellow,' Harry greeted it.

The bull made a huffing sound, flapping its ears in reply.

He rang the doorbell. No response. He knocked loudly, and when nothing happened, rang Vince's mobile. When he heard it ringing inside the cottage, he moved to the front and the door that overlooked the lawn. Nobody answered the phone. Nobody seemed to be around.

Harry went to peer into the kitchen. A buzzing noise made him look up. Honey bees were flying in and out of an air brick set in the chimney. He hoped it was defunct or they'd get one heck of a shock when the fire was lit. He tried Vince's mobile again. As he listened to it ring, he walked back to the side door. Someone was standing there with a carrier bag in one arm, the other outstretched as they pressed the doorbell. Someone familiar.

'Harry?' Catherine looked startled.

'Hi. Hope you don't mind but I was in Box, and thought I'd drop by and have a word with your dad. He's not answering his phone.'

'He didn't answer when I rang earlier either.' Anxiety rose. 'I hope he's all right.' She delved into her handbag. Pulled out a key and fitted it in the keyhole and turned it. Opened the door.

'Dad?' she called. 'Dad, it's me. Are you there?'

Harry pushed his phone at Catherine. 'Stay here. If anything happens call Libby Harding. She's a cop. Tell her what's going on.'

Horror pinched her face. 'Dad told me he was on some crazy list, you can't think...'

'Stay here,' Harry repeated.

He moved swiftly through the utility room, the open-plan kitchen and into the little living room. He could smell cold ash and something else. Something unpleasant.

Please God, no.

He rounded the corner. His stomach hollowed.

Vince lay at the bottom of the stairs. He was dressed in striped pyjamas and his feet were bare. From the catastrophic angle between his head and neck, Harry knew he was dead. Even so, he still squatted down and pressed his fingers against the man's carotid artery. Nothing. No pulse. He'd died only recently as his skin still held some warmth. Harry rocked back on his heels, shuddering inside. He knew that Vince could have fallen but every instinct told him that he'd been pushed.

'Dad?' Catherine's voice was a whisper.

'I am so sorry,' Harry said. He rose, reached out a hand. She took it. She was trembling.

'He's dead?'

'Yes.'

She made a keening sound deep in her throat. 'Oh, Dad.'

'Sorry, love,' Harry said. 'Can I have my phone?'

Catherine fumbled to return it. Her eyes remained on the fallen form of her father.

'Dad,' she whispered. She dropped to the ground. Picked up his hand, held it to her mouth. Kissed it. Tears began to fall. 'I love you so much,' she choked. 'I baked you a cake, you know. Double chocolate. Your favourite. I had to save half for Paton and Mia or they'd never have forgiven me. They're demons for chocolate too.'

Harry withdrew to call Libby, giving Catherine the privacy to say goodbye to her father.

39

'What the hell, Harry?' Libby stared at the dead man.

Catherine was in the kitchen with Doug, who had raced over the minute she'd called him. Harry could hear her weeping, Doug's soft words of comfort. The twins were in next door's cottage, with Vince's neighbour, who knew them well enough to look after them for a while.

'I don't think it's an accident,' Harry said.

'No kidding.' Libby took Harry through the precise timings of his phone calls to Vince and when he arrived. 'Did you see anyone?'

He shook his head.

'Cars?'

'There were two parked ahead of mine. I can't remember what they were. But wouldn't the killer be long gone by now?'

'You never know if they're hanging around, watching.' Libby scribbled in her pocket book. 'Getting a thrill seeing us turn up.'

This propelled Harry outside but he couldn't see anyone. The Hereford bull surveyed him steadily through tiny eyes.

'I wish you could talk,' he told it. 'Tell us who turned up earlier.'

The bull shook its head, dislodging some flies feeding in the corner of its eyes.

When Harry turned he saw that Libby was gently ushering Catherine and Doug outside, explaining they couldn't stay indoors because the cottage would have to be processed by the police.

They came and stood next to Harry. Doug had his arm around Catherine's waist. She looked as if she'd fall if he withdrew his support. Her skin had gone linen white.

'What the hell's going on, Harry?' Doug hissed.

Knowing it would eventually come out in the press, Harry gave them both a rough overview of the case, culminating in the list of names on the Executor of Justice website. Doug's face contracted into a look of horror. 'That's crazy,' he said. 'You can't think Vince has been murdered, surely?'

'That's for the police to decide.'

Over Doug's shoulder, Harry watched Theo arrive, along with a forensic van and the SOCO, Scene of Crimes Officer.

'He was buying a second home,' Catherine said dully. 'He was looking forward to it so much.'

'Really?' Harry was surprised. He would have thought running a second home might have been a bit of a challenge at Vince's age.

'It's not your normal second home,' Doug said. 'It's on a cruise ship. A residential yacht, you could say.'

'He'll never see Namibia now.' Catherine scrabbled for a tissue. Blew her nose. 'Or Cape Town.'

Doug drew her closer and kissed the top of her head. 'I'm so sorry, darling.'

Harry watched Theo pattering down the stone steps and when the DI met his eyes, he beckoned Harry over. Theo asked the same questions as Libby, made pretty much the same remarks but peppered with a lot of swearing. Theo only swore under duress so Harry didn't mention it.

'Still warm, you say?'

'Not totally cold, no.'

'It takes around twelve hours for a human body to be cool to the touch...' Theo stood aside as the forensic team moved into the cottage. 'But twenty-four hours to cool to the core. We'll know more when the boys and girls have done their stuff. In the meantime, Harry, you should know that things have gone crazy on social media. Facebook, Instagram, Twitter, you name it, the videos of Lorraine's drowning, the stabbings, have gone viral.'

Harry closed his eyes. 'Christ.'

'A copy of the Executor of Justice website went up yesterday. We took it down as soon as we realised, but the content has already been copied a thousand, a million times over. Worldwide.'

Theo dragged a hand over his face. 'Everyone's going insane wanting to know who the Chief Lord Justice is. Some people think what he's doing is a great idea, meting out justice where it's deserved, but of course they're taking it at face value and not looking any further or doing any research. They're just believing this shit as it happens.'

'Those photos of me are out there?' Harry's voice was hoarse.

'I'm sorry, Harry.'

Harry closed his eyes. Suddenly, a trip to France with Jessie was looking very attractive.

'We've got to *find him*.' Harry opened his eyes. He was filled with impotent rage. 'And sodding well *shut him down*.'

'We will. But in the meantime, eyes in the back of your head, okay?'

40

———

Harry walked with Doug and Catherine to their car. With Catherine inside, looking dully ahead, emotionally shattered, Harry took Doug aside.

'I saw you got a lift with Filipa yesterday.'

Doug didn't respond. He clasped his hands in front of him and gazed down the ride of beech trees. Behind him the Hereford bull swished its tail.

'Yes,' he said eventually. 'She came and collected me.'

'Do you know her well?'

Doug sighed. 'Yes and no. She was doing psychotherapy at university but decided it wasn't for her. She joined Lorraine's classes because she'd had some life difficulties. She wanted to write about it, and maybe help others.'

'She was raped.'

Doug looked appalled. 'How the hell do you know that?'

Harry debated whether to tell Doug about Ethan and decided to keep his own counsel for the moment. 'I just do, Doug. Who else knows? I mean, if she was writing about it, did the rest of the writing class know?'

'Yes. She was really open about it, actually. When she

learned I was a psychotherapist, we talked. She wasn't a client, but I hope I helped her a little.'

He glanced at Catherine, then away.

'Between you and me, she wanted to know how she could find joy in sex and romance again. Her last relationship broke down because of her inability to give and receive affection.'

'It's not uncommon.'

Doug ran a hand down his face. 'I'm sorry about this Executor of Justice situation. It must be awful for you.'

'Understatement of the year,' Harry said on a sigh. He had a slightly sick sensation in his stomach and knew it wouldn't go away until everything had been resolved, the perpetrators caught. He resolved to talk to Ben and Tim about it. He didn't want them stumbling on something on social media unprepared.

Doug touched him on the arm in a silent, empathetic gesture before he returned to his car. As Harry watched them drive away he saw Libby appear from the cottage.

'I'm heading home,' he told her. 'Got a burglar alarm to put in.'

'Hope it comes with a panic alarm.'

'No, and I'm not going to install a panic room either. If they gain access into the house the alarm will be creating such a din even Theo will hear it down the hill.'

'You're joking. He sleeps like the dead, that one.'

He raised his eyebrows.

'Your mind, Harry,' she scolded him, but she didn't look cross. 'If you want to know, we were on a team-building exercise together. Bloody awful. We both agreed.'

She stretched and gave a yawn that showed her tongue, small and pink, like a cat's. 'He wanted you to know that there's no Vera Wang at Bath Uni. And when he asked Ethan, the lad shut down. Went into a "no comment" funk, apparently.'

Interesting, Harry thought. What were the students protecting? Were they the instigators of the Executor of Justice? He wouldn't have thought so, but with such a peculiar modus operandi he'd be wise to keep an open mind.

Libby stretched again. 'Theo's sending me back to base. More alibi and number crunching to be done.'

They walked to their cars. Libby followed him through the village in her Astra towards Bathford, but just after they'd passed the King's Arms pub she pulled over, Harry guessed to take a phone call. Harry followed another car out of the village, continuing along Farleigh Rise which soon narrowed into Prospect Place, a steep lane through the woods with a sharp bend at the bottom. Harry dropped a gear as his father had taught him. *Let the engine do the work.* It was an old-fashioned way of driving but then he had an old-fashioned car.

As the car ahead flared its brakes before the corner then swung right and out of view, Harry tried to think what kind of person would kill a vulnerable elderly man like Vince. Someone callous. Cold-hearted and pitiless. It appeared obvious that Vince hadn't thrown himself down the stairs on purpose, not with his plan of buying a second home on a cruise liner to look forward to.

When he saw a little red car come into view near the bottom of the hill, climbing out of the hairpin bend from Bathford, he put his foot on the brake, wanting to pull over in the designated passing place just ahead.

Nothing happened.

The Rover didn't slow down.

Dear God, stop!

He tried it one more time, thrusting his foot flat to the floor.

Nothing.

The brakes had failed.

41

The Rover kept going, flashing past the passing place and increasing speed as the hill steepened. The engine was screaming now, the revs in the red.

Harry yanked on the handbrake with all his strength. The rear wheels locked, squealing over the tarmac. He slammed his hand on to the hazard light button on the dashboard, praying the driver below would get the message and *get the hell out of the way!*

The Rover shrieked straight down the hill with Harry hauling on the handbrake and yelling, 'Stop! For Chrissake, stop!'

He was heading straight for the little red car. Behind it was a driveway with a garage dead ahead and a grassy bank on the left which, if the red car got out of the way, he might be able to swing into and take some speed off before he crashed. Because he had no doubt that was what was going to happen.

Teeth gritted, eyes squinting, he aimed for the driveway, screaming at the red car in his mind: *Get out of the way!*

The Rover screamed downwards, a hot cloud of stinking rubber smoking behind it.

As Harry neared, the little red car suddenly seemed to realise the danger it was in and sharply reversed. But it was too late.

Harry clipped the front of the red car which immediately snapped around, its rear flank hitting the rear of the Rover and making it spin.

There was a horrendous sound of tearing metal as the cars crunched and spun on the corner. Harry's airbag deployed and then suddenly, the Rover slammed backwards into a lamppost, flattening the road sign behind it and coming to a rest against a stone wall.

He was now facing up the hill with the little red car slewed across his bonnet. It was, he saw, a Skoda Fabia hatchback.

He felt pain stabbing through his ribs each time he breathed in and for a moment he sank into a pool of dark reflection, wondering why the hell he hadn't bought a new car earlier. Was it because he was stubborn? Economical with his money? Whatever his reasons, he felt pretty stupid at the moment.

With a shaking hand, he switched off the engine. He left on the hazard lights.

Get out, he told himself. *You've got to check the other driver*.

Carefully, Harry tried to open his door, but it was smashed shut so he had to scramble over the central console and push himself outside through the passenger door. Every movement sent agonising stabbing pains through his ribs.

Putting a hand on the car bonnet, he staggered around his car to the Skoda. Someone was standing there, already opening the driver's door. Someone familiar.

'Harry.' It was Libby. 'You okay?'

'Yeah. Think so.'

'You, sir?'

A man in his twenties climbed out of his crumpled Skoda. He looked shaken, but no broken bones that Harry could see.

'Yeah.' He looked at Harry. 'What the fuck?'

'Brake failure.'

'Shit.'

'That's why I had my hazards on.'

'Yeah. Sure.' He ran a hand over his head and back. Said *fuck* a few more times then, 'You insured?'

'Yes.'

Harry looked at the crumpled cars. The Skoda's front panel, where he'd clipped it, was folded inwards and over the wheel.

'Neither are drivable,' Libby declared. 'I'll call a breakdown truck. I know someone who'll be here within the hour if I push it.'

'That would be great,' Harry said.

The young man nodded.

Libby moved back to take photographs of the scene, waving away any traffic that appeared while the young man and Harry also took some photos before swapping information and exchanging insurance details.

To his surprise, Libby waited until the breakdown truck turned up. She spoke at length to the driver, who nodded several times before loading the vehicles on board. The young man's girlfriend came and picked him up. As he watched the truck with its shattered load inch its way down the hill, Harry carefully rubbed the side of his head. It was aching after smacking into the window as the Rover spun.

Libby came over. Reaching up, she took his chin in her hands. Twisted his head from side to side, peering into his eyes.

'Headache?' she asked.

'A bit.'

'Blurred vision?'

'No.'

'Drowsiness? Nausea?'

'No and no.'

She dropped her hands. 'I'm still taking you to A&E.'

'Libby, I'm fine.'

'I'm not having it on my conscience if you suddenly drop dead. Jessie will eviscerate me.'

'Drop me home,' Harry said. 'Please.'

'Not until you've seen a doctor.'

42

For the second time in ten days Harry found himself in A&E. Libby didn't wait with him but high-tailed it to the police station. She said she didn't want to miss out on anything the murder squad might find.

Harry was given a neurocognitive test followed by a CT scan, after which he was given the all-clear. Since he was in the hospital, he went to see how Phil Petty was doing.

Not good, Harry decided, as he looked down on his old neighbour. The man's eyes were shut, his mouth slack. Harry went to the end of the bed and picked up Phil's chart, checked the continuing assessment record. With an overall score on the Glasgow Coma Scale of six out of fifteen today, it wasn't great, but at least he seemed to be improving from Monday's score of four.

'Hello, Harry.'

He turned to see Angela approaching. She'd lost weight and her skin was pale and stretched taut over her bones. Her eyes had lost their sparkle, her hair its lustrous shine. She looked every inch of her sixty-six years.

'I just nipped out to get a coffee,' she told him. 'Can I fetch you one?'

'No, thanks.' He looked down at the diminished figure in the bed. 'I'm sorry this happened to you both.'

She put her coffee cup on the table tray, next to a handful of get well cards. 'I can't seem to do anything but sit with him. I keep waiting for him to wake up.'

'That's understandable.'

'I talk to him all the time.' She gave a hollow laugh. 'I don't know if he can hear me or not, but I do it anyway.'

'That's good. Coma patients who regain consciousness sometimes say they hear everything and that it helps them get better.'

She looked down at her husband. 'I hope he didn't hear me earlier.' Her voice hitched. 'I was horrible.'

Harry half-watched a woman in a pale green tunic start to mop the floor at the far end of the ward.

'I was really angry, actually.' She took a breath. 'I still am, if I'm to be honest.'

She was trembling, Harry saw. Whatever had made her angry was distressing her too.

'You can tell me, if you like,' Harry said. 'I can be bound by client confidentiality if that helps.'

A brief smile flashed over her face. 'Are you always on duty, like a policeman?'

'Sometimes.' He smiled ruefully.

'I haven't told anyone else yet.'

'And you don't have to either.'

Another flash of a smile, which was good.

'The thing is...' She hesitated briefly. 'Well, it's just that I discovered Phil had had our house valued recently, with a view to selling. It unsettled me, to be honest, as we've never considered moving. Not *ever*. We love it where we are. The neighbourhood, our friends... We always say we'll be carried out of our beautiful house in boxes rather than ever live anywhere else.

'And then I discovered our nest egg, the one that we never touch because it's our back-up, our *security*, is gone. All eighty-six thousand pounds of it.'

What felt like a horde of ants scurried over Harry's skin.

Lorraine's fifty thousand was missing, and now Phil and Angela's nest egg had gone?

'He couldn't have put it somewhere safe?' Harry suggested. The cleaner had moved to mop between the two beds opposite. She was humming beneath her breath.

'It was on deposit at our private bank. We agreed we wouldn't risk it, not like our financial portfolio which has stocks and shares.'

'And that money's okay? Your portfolio, I mean.'

A look of alarm seared her features. 'I have no idea.'

Harry didn't want to worry her further, but an alarm bell was ringing at the back of his mind. 'I think it's worth checking.'

'I'll ring Hugh later.'

Harry pondered briefly.

'Can I ask how you met Hugh Lamont?'

'He came to the house. He said he was your investment manager and that he'd like to talk to us about our finances. He was really nice, and everything he said made sense. We gave him a small amount of money and the returns were fantastic, so we gave him some more. He's been terrific, actually...' She trailed off, anxiety suddenly cloaking her features. 'But you said you didn't know him.'

'That's right.'

'Then why did he say he knew you?'

'To gain your trust?'

'But...' Her eyes started to skitter. 'He's looked after us for ages now. Over three years.'

'Could you check your investments?' Harry suggested. 'Not by taking Hugh Lamont's word for it, but by visiting the sites where your stocks and shares are held, certificates and the like. I'm sure everything's fine –' *like hell, you liar* '– but I think it's worth knowing exactly where things stand.'

'Yes. I'll do that.' Her voice was faint. She picked up her cup of coffee but she didn't drink. Just put it back down again.

Harry left her sitting by Phil's bedside, her body small and diminished and broken, as sad as a discarded doll.

43

By the time Harry stumbled out of the hospital, it was late afternoon and all he wanted was to go home. He took a taxi to Batheaston and collected the burglar alarm from where it had been delivered in the recycling bin. Over a restorative cup of tea, which Harry considered the cure-all for all Brits, he read the installation manual.

It took longer to install than he expected. He'd chosen a wireless system to avoid the alarm going down when there was a power cut, something the area suffered two or three times a year. He placed sensors and motion detectors throughout the house and, lastly, tested it.

'I've stuck a bloody great siren bell box outside too,' he told Jessie when she rang. 'A blind person couldn't miss it. It flashes police blue at you when it goes off.'

'Still, if you even hear a mouse crossing the room, call 999,' she insisted.

'I will. I have no intention of joining poor Vince.'

Jessie had been inveigled into staying at the farm for the following night, which gave Harry the opportunity to do some thinking. Although Theo had said the team hadn't found any signs of foul play, with Vince's name on a killer's list, Harry didn't reckon there was much doubt he'd been murdered. What he couldn't get his mind around was: why?

Vince was a retired RAF officer whose wife had died three years ago, of cancer. He played golf and went flying with a friend of his, who'd built his own aeroplane. He was active, energetic, and a thoroughly decent man. Why had he been targeted?

After making another cup of tea, Harry rang the Kings' number, wanting to speak to Catherine. Paton picked up. When she heard Harry's voice she said, 'Grandpa died.'

'Yes, I know. I'm really sorry.'

'Will I die when I grow up?'

'Everyone dies someday,' Harry told her.

'What, even you?'

'Even me. But I expect to go on living for ages yet. The same goes for your mum and dad.'

'And Daisy.'

'Yes, Daisy too.'

'Do you want to speak to Daddy?'

'Actually, is your mum able to come to the phone?'

'Hang on... Mum! It's Harry!'

There was a clatter as the phone was put down, and then someone picked it up.

'Harry.' Catherine's voice was bled of emotion. 'Thanks for being there today.'

'I'm so sorry it happened.'

'Yes.'

'I need to ask you something. I'm sorry to ask you this at such a difficult time, but did your father know someone called Hugh Lamont?'

'I have no idea. Certainly, I've never heard the name before, not that I know of, anyway. Shall I ask Doug?'

'Would you mind?'

He heard the phone being put down again and then a brief silence followed.

'He says not, Harry.' She sounded exhausted.

Harry let her go.

The next morning, Harry took a bus into Bath where he hired a car, a silver Ford Fiesta that felt strangely tinny and cheap compared to his clunky old Rover. He'd wanted to rent a 4X4 but the cost had been prohibitive. He would, he decided, test drive a selection another time.

Bath was busy at the start of the Easter holidays, the streets filling up with foreign tourists as well as school kids. Although he couldn't be sure that anyone was in, he still headed for Combe House; he wanted to taste the atmosphere. See if he could glean anything from being in their territory.

He arrived to find two vehicles parked on the gravel drive. A builder's van and a bright red sporty little Mazda MX-5. The van had *A. D. Bubb Builders* on its side, the Mazda a personalised number plate, *BD5M*.

Harry parked next to the Mazda. Walked to the front door. Rang the brass pull doorbell.

He didn't have long to wait before the door was flung open.

'Why, if it isn't Dr Harry Hope himself.' She sounded delighted.

Filipa stood in resplendent, what Harry could only term post-sex, glory. Her hair was tousled, her mouth swollen and slightly bruised. She wore a turquoise silk robe that made her eyes even more luminous, her hair even more silver. It barely covered her sex.

'Is Wren here?' Harry asked. 'I just wanted a quick word.'

'She's away.' Filipa opened the door wide, inviting him in. 'You'll have to put up with me.'

Behind her, halfway down the stairs, stood a muscular man with nothing but a towel around his waist. 'Filipa?' The word came out as a low growl.

'This is important, Andy. Go back to bed. I'll join you in a minute.'

Harry couldn't see Andy's features thanks to him being backlit by the sunlight pouring through the windows behind him, but he had the impression the man wasn't sure about being dismissed by the way he hesitated. But then, with a grunt, he turned and padded back up the stairs.

'He's my bit of rough trade,' Filipa whispered to Harry. 'He's dreadfully thick but I don't mind. He's got a huge dick.'

Harry decided not to comment.

'He did a job for Ethan a while back,' she said airily. 'Fixing the roof. He looked dreadfully sexy in his leather pads.'

Still, Harry refused to be drawn.

Filipa gave an elegant shrug as if to suggest she didn't care he wasn't reacting. 'Come to the kitchen with me. I need wine.'

Harry followed her lithe form through the hallway, keeping his eyes firmly on her shoulder blades and not on the arch of her buttocks moving sensually beneath silk. He knew she was being purposely provocative, and pasted on his calmest, most neutral expression.

You are unaffected by her sexuality, he told himself. *She is vulnerable and troubled. Keep your professional distance at all costs.*

Despite his resolve to be steadfast and retain control, he still felt as though he was walking into the lair of a tigress.

44

Filipa moved soundlessly to the fridge and plucked out two glasses, which immediately clouded at the change in temperature. She poured a pale white wine, and passed Harry his glass. He took it but when she chinked her glass against his, he didn't drink. Just put it down on the island. Her eyes narrowed. She took a long sip from her glass, put it next to his.

'Why do you want to see our little Wren?'

'Because she lied.'

The aqua eyes opened wide. 'Did she? What on earth about?'

'She said that Vera Wang was a student of Lorraine's. That Lorraine accused Vera of cheating.'

'Did she? What a little sweetie she is.'

Harry didn't ask why Wren was a sweetie for lying. Being a therapist had taught him how to play a waiting game.

Filipa took another sip of wine, watching him over the rim of her glass. Slowly, she put the glass down, and then she spun around and bent over, lifting her robe to expose her buttocks.

Lightly tanned, they were as smooth and round as a pair of sweet persimmons, except for the stripes of vivid red weals. The skin had split on one wound which was weeping blood and bruises were already forming on the others.

'Andy is a real gentleman, except when he's not.'

She stood up straight, dropping her robe back into place and twisting around to face him.

'When I opened the door to him he grabbed me and marched me into the sitting room where he wrapped my hair around his fist and pushed my head into the sofa, where I could barely breathe. He then sat on my legs and beat me with a riding crop. What do you say to that, doctor?'

'I don't give free therapy sessions, I'm afraid. But if you call my office and make an appointment, I'll be happy to talk to you.'

She put her head on one side, surveying him. 'Not like your pal, Doug, are you?'

Harry didn't reply.

'Doug's fascinated by those who engage in high-impact play as part of BDSM and those engaged in non-suicidal self-injury behaviours.'

Is he indeed? Harry knew about NSSI behaviour – people who wanted to hurt themselves but who weren't suicidal. Was Filipa one of those? He wasn't an expert in the area but he found her involvement in BDSM worrying considering her sexual assault. He hadn't seen any scars from cutting on Filipa, but that didn't mean she didn't have any hidden out of sight.

'He thinks that turning to BDSM reduces self-harming episodes.'

Harry wasn't going to get into a psychological discussion with her, especially if she was already talking to Doug, who specialised in sexual trauma.

'He says that because I've never known what to do with my own pain, I like putting my pain in someone else's hands. He thinks it's because I can stop any BDSM session with single word.'

It made sense, but Harry still didn't like the idea in case she met the wrong partner who could retraumatise her, and potentially lock her in that trauma for eternity.

She topped up her glass. 'Why aren't you drinking, Harry Hope?'

'I'm driving.'

'You can have *one*, surely.'

'Maybe another time. Thank you.'

She locked gazes with him. Her aqua eyes seemed to darken. Why did he feel as if it was a contest? He didn't drop his gaze. He didn't blink. Nor did she.

'I wish I'd met you before I met Doug,' she murmured. 'You are much more fun.'

'When's Wren due back?' he asked. He continued to hold her gaze, refusing to be manipulated.

At the mention of Wren, Filipa lifted her chin. Finally, she let her eyes slip from his, to his mouth. Slowly, she licked her lips.

'Little Wren won't be back until the first of May,' she said. Her voice was husky. 'She's gone to see Mummy and Daddy up in Yorkshire.'

'If you could please tell her–'

'Wren lied for me.'

Harry couldn't help his blink of surprise.

Filipa studied her wine as she swirled it around her glass. 'Darling little Wren. She didn't want me to get into trouble. The story she told you of Lorraine Brown accusing Vera Wang of cheating was a hundred per cent correct. Except it wasn't Vera she accused. It was me.'

'I see.'

'Do you?' She arched both eyebrows high. 'Tell me, Harry Hope. What is it you see?'

A minefield opened up in front of him. He tried to take the least explosive route. 'I think it could take an enormous amount of courage for someone to write about a traumatic experience. And if that writing was evaluated in a less than loving or accepting way, how very hurtful it could be.'

She remained quite still for a moment. Then she put down her glass. Her breasts rose and fell as she took several deep breaths and he suddenly realised she was trying to keep control of herself. Tears had filled her eyes. She angrily brushed them away.

'I didn't mean to distress you.' His voice was soft.

She gave him an unsteady smile. 'I know you didn't.'

A soft silence fell between them. Harry remained quiet, not wanting to force her any further. When he heard the sound of footsteps in the corridor he turned, but couldn't see anyone.

'Don't you dare fuck him,' the man said warningly. Next came the sound of the front door slamming.

A flash of distaste crossed her face. She turned to Harry. 'That's why I don't always fuck men. Troglodytes. Women are so much more subtle.'

45

By the time Harry left Filipa fifteen minutes later, he felt as if he'd spent an entire day attending an intensive psychotherapy course. He'd used just about every psychological technique in the book to retain not just his equanimity but his authenticity, and if it was opening time he'd have been tempted to find a pub and have a pint to help him decompress.

As it was, he headed into Bath, and Chikara Martial Arts. With Lorraine's fifty thousand pounds missing along with Phil's nest egg, he wanted to check with Kevin Owen if he was missing any money too.

By some miracle he'd just nabbed a space in Sainsbury's car park, rammed thanks to the farmer's market held there each Saturday, when Libby rang.

'Are you sitting down?'

'No,' he told her. 'I'm walking through Green Park Station. There are some cracking looking quiches, but no pies.'

'Sorry, Harry, pies are the least of my concerns right now, because someone cut your brake lines.'

Harry stopped walking. 'Someone did *what*?'

'I'm just glad you weren't on a motorway. It could have been a thousand times worse.'

It transpired Libby had had her suspicions and asked the breakdown driver to take the cars to a police mechanic to check them over. Both cars were now part of Operation Armour's investigation.

'When would they have been cut?' Harry was puzzled. He'd stayed at Lorne House the night before he drove to Monkton Farleigh and the only person who knew he was staying there was Nicole, and nobody knew he'd ducked up the hill to see Vince the following morning. When he explained this to Libby, he heard her sharp intake of breath.

'Nicole?' she repeated.

'No.' He was firm. 'I know you have a beef with my ex-wife but she did *not* cut my brakes.'

'In that case, she told someone. Find out who, please.'

'I will,' he promised. 'Look, you know I told Theo about two victims missing quite a lot of money, I want to know if Vince was missing any as well.'

'I'll get on to it.'

'I'm going to ask Kevin Owen the same question in a moment.'

After they'd hung up, Harry dialled Nicole but she was out. He left a message. As he exited the market it started to drizzle. He turned up his jacket collar and increased his pace around the corner, to the judo school.

Inside, a bright young girl took his name and told him to 'take a pew and chill out', which he duly did. He took off his jacket. Watched her trot into the judo school. She returned almost at once, holding up her hand with her thumb and fingers spread, which he took to mean *five minutes*.

In fact it was closer to fifteen before Owen arrived, dressed in a white judo suit. With him was Dave, identically attired.

Together, they looked strong and imposing. Harry decided he wouldn't like to meet them on a dark night.

While Owen walked over to Harry, Dave busied himself behind the reception desk but Harry could tell he was there to eavesdrop. Harry moved purposely closer to the front door where his old friend would struggle to hear.

'What do you want?' Owen asked, pushing his hands beneath his armpits, his default position to make himself look more impressive.

'You know I'm part of the investigative team working on Operation Armour?'

A curt nod.

'The police have tasked me to ask if you've lost any significant amounts of money lately.'

Owen stared at him. 'What the hell does that mean?'

Harry explained about Lorraine and Phil's missing money in the hope it might elicit some kind of understanding, if not information.

'Nope.' His jaw was stuck out pugnaciously. 'All my money is present and correct, so you can fuck off now.'

Harry wasn't sure if it was Owen's swearing that made Dave come alert, but alert he was. He was staring at them both with what Harry could only believe was a confounded expression. How much had he heard?

'Just one other thing.' Harry's awareness was focused between the two men. 'Do you know a Hugh Lamont?'

At that, Owen's facial muscles turned from stony, to surprised. 'Yes, I do.'

46

'Hugh Lamont.' Kevin Owen shook his head at the memory. 'Slimy bastard. He tried to sell me some dodgy financial investment to do with fish farming. The brochure and patter were all very well, but when I had a look, nothing stacked up, so I sent him packing with a flea in his ear. I told him he shouldn't be in business and that I was going to report him before he fleeced someone else.'

'Did you report him?'

His mouth twisted. 'No. I forgot, to tell the truth. I should have. He was a nasty little twat.'

'What did he look like?'

The surprise returned. 'You think he's involved in my knife attack?'

'I don't know.' Harry was honest. 'But we're following this line of investigation just in case there's a link of some sort.'

Owen nodded. 'Same height as you, I'd say. Same age, maybe a bit older as he had white hair. Moustache. Wore a suit and tie. Nice shoes, brogues.'

'Accent?'

'Same as you. Same as Dave.'

'Middle England.'

He nodded. Harry tried to think what else to ask.

'He had a tatty briefcase,' Owen added. 'At odds with the shoes, know what I mean? The buckle wouldn't close properly. He had to carry it under his arm.'

'Anything else?'

Owen sucked his teeth, staring at the ceiling as he thought. 'He came across as nice, you know? I wouldn't have taken him to be a con man, but that's what he was. I remember being a bit shocked when his brochures didn't add up. He said he had a diploma with the London Institute of Banking and Finance, and a level seven QCF, but he couldn't prove it.'

Harry awarded Owen top marks for not falling prey to what sounded like a persuasive confidence trick.

Although they talked further, Harry didn't glean anything else of value, and began to take his leave. He'd put on his jacket and was walking to the door when his phone rang.

'Nicole,' he said. He could practically feel Dave's eyes boring into his back – twin lasers of jealousy. Harry didn't turn around. He stepped outside. 'I wanted to know who you told about my staying at Lorne House?'

'Oh... just Dave, I think. Why?'

'I did tell you why I didn't want to stay at home, didn't I?' His tone was hard.

'Well, yes. But it was Dave, it didn't matter, not–'

'It was a *secret*. Nobody was meant to know.'

Silence. He knew she'd be flushing with mortification, but also righteous indignation. Dave was her partner, after all.

'I now need to know who Dave told,' Harry added. 'Luckily, I'm at Chikara Martial Arts so I can do it myself.' He hung up without saying goodbye.

Back in reception, Harry leaned against the counter where Dave was filling in what looked like a medical form. Distantly,

Harry could hear guttural shouts and dull thuds that he took to be bare feet and bodies pounding the floor.

'Dave?'

'Yes?' He didn't look up.

'You knew I was staying at Lorne House.' Harry spoke to the top of his head which, he was surprised to see, had a thinning patch at the crown, reminding him that neither of them were getting any younger.

'Nicole mentioned something.'

'Did you mention it to anyone else?'

Dave scribbled his signature at the bottom of the form. 'Don't think so.'

'Because where I was staying was supposed to be confidential. I mean *really* confidential.'

At that, Dave lifted his head. His eyes were slightly bloodshot, making Harry wonder if he'd been drinking, or if he was under stress in some way. 'Why?'

'Because my life is in danger, that's why. And thanks to either you or Nicole, someone knew where I was staying and cut my brakes.'

Dave blinked. 'They what?'

'I nearly got wiped out between Monkton Farleigh and Bathford yesterday.'

'You're joking.' He didn't look shocked enough for Harry. Last year, Nicole had come to Harry saying Dave was a mistake and could they get back together? To which Harry had said no. Did Dave know this? If so, did he feel humiliated and angry enough to want Harry dead?

Part of Harry's mind split away, appalled he was thinking like this, but the other part, the survival part, was stone cold.

'Even more horrifying,' Harry continued, 'is that I nearly took a complete stranger out with me. I need to know, on behalf of the Avon and Somerset Police, who else you told about my staying at Lorne House.'

Dave stared at him, expressionless. 'Nobody.'

'Well, if neither you nor Nicole spilled the beans, then how did they know where I was staying?'

'They could have followed you,' Dave suggested. 'Or put a tracker on your car.'

With that cheery thought, Harry rang Libby and asked her to check his Rover for tracking devices. As he walked back to his hire car, he couldn't help looking around, wondering if he was being watched. It made him unsettled and tense, increasing his desire to find out who was behind the sabotage to fever pitch. If he came face to face with them, what would he do? The question kept him occupied for quite a while.

47

Harry drove to Harley Street, where he parked in his usual rented car space in the courtyard of a converted old school. He hoped whoever was after him would think he'd be at home, it being Saturday, but even so, he still took a tortuously roundabout route to the Centre, via Portland Place and St James's Square.

Trisha was in – she was burning scented candles or incense sticks – and he could hear her chatting to someone as he passed her door. Ethan had tidied up well, he saw, and although the painting job wasn't exactly top dollar, he'd done the job and the whole place looked much brighter and cleaner. He wondered if Ethan would get away with not telling his parents what had happened between him and Harry, and the anonymous, nasty message he'd received that had projected him on to a killing path.

If Ethan was forced to face them, he'd probably lie to protect Filipa. Harry sighed. It wasn't healthy for either sibling, having the secret of Filipa's rape between them. He felt deeply for Ethan. Theo had told Harry he'd been remarkably co-operative when giving his statement and seemed genuinely remorseful at his manipulability over what had proven to be a false accusation.

Ethan had, Filipa told Harry earlier, gone to stay with a friend in Norfolk for the weekend.

'I told him I wanted to have some playtime,' she'd added airily. 'He knows what that means.'

'He knows about your sexual proclivities?' Harry was appalled. No wonder Ethan hated the man who'd had such a devastating effect on his sister's life. No wonder he'd tried to knife Harry, thinking he was that man.

She does weird things. She says she can't help it. She changed that day. Irrevocably.

'Of course he knows.' She shrugged an elegant shoulder. 'We don't keep secrets. He knows I can't help it. That my behaviour's because of –' she dropped her voice to a whisper '– my rape.' She was almost coquettish as she said the words. Sly. Which made Harry wonder what else was going on in her mind.

Now Harry turned on his computer, checked his emails. Saw there was one from Theo. It was short with two spelling mistakes, which meant he'd tapped it out fast. No time to call Harry, obviously. He simply said that Richard Johnston – the man killed when his ladder had been kicked from beneath him – had been dating a university professor, Nia Mitchell, when he died.

Theo had added Nia Mitchell's mobile number along with a final note. *She's been interviewed but I'd like your input. Call me when you've seen her.*

More legwork to undertake for the police. Harry didn't mind. In fact being involved helped stem the fear of being stalked by a faceless killer.

He rang the number Theo had given him, preparing what he might say if it went to a messaging service, but it was picked up almost immediately.

'Hello?'

A warm, melodious woman's voice.

Harry introduced himself, and said how sorry he was that Richard hadn't died accidentally, falling off his ladder, but had in fact been a victim of murder.

'I'm still coming to terms with it. Poor Rick.' She sounded calm, but he heard the tremor when she said the man's name. 'I can't imagine who'd want him dead. He was so kind. I mean *really* kind.'

When Harry asked if he might see her, she didn't hesitate. 'I'll do anything to help find out who did this to him. I'm in today, if that helps.'

Half an hour later Harry was in Limpley Stoke, a village just north of Freshford, where ancient stone houses had stood for hundreds of years, overlooking a valley of green fields and sheep, and the River Avon.

The house surprised him. He'd expected a traditional dwelling but instead he was faced with a sleek, modern chalet bungalow with wide walls of glass and a wrap-around garden.

He approached the front door, curiosity rising. He'd had a quick look on the internet to see Nia Mitchell was a professor of psychology, with a PhD and master's behind her, but he hadn't delved much further, preferring to try to avoid any prejudgement and let his instinct kick in when they first met.

His first surprise was how young she was. He'd been ageist, he realised, thinking a professor would be in their fifties at least, but Nia Mitchell was in her late thirties at the most. He also hadn't expected her to look so magnificent.

Black, broad-shouldered, with closely cropped, tightly curled black hair, she had eyes the colour of honey and earrings to match. She wore a vividly coloured tunic over black leggings and her feet were bare except for the acid-green nail polish.

They shook hands. Her grip was firm and cool, her smile of welcome filled with caution.

'You mentioned you were a psychologist,' she said as she invited him inside. 'And that you did your course at Bath Uni.'

'Dr Susan Rowan was my lecturer.'

'Yes, I know Susan, but I'm sure I've heard your name elsewhere.'

They talked shop as they stepped through the house, trying to find how she knew Harry's name as well as getting a feel for one another as professionals. Harry felt a cloak of calmness drop around him as they walked and guessed it was because Nia Mitchell had decorated her house to mimic nature. Lots of greens and browns with carpets that looked and felt like moss and grass, inviting you to feel as though you were in a forest.

She brought them to an intimate sitting area with untreated wooden furniture adorned with sheepskins and felted wool. The natural light and muted murals had been chosen to create an aura of serenity. Harry wished he had a therapy room like it.

She poured them both tall glasses of water and took the chair covered with a brown and white sheepskin while Harry sat on what he thought might be a yak's hide; thick and black and very hairy.

'What do you need to know?' She was direct.

Harry went through the same questions Theo had, no doubt, until he came to asking whether Richard Johnston – Rick – had any enemies or anyone who wanted to do him harm.

'He was my architect.' She made a gesture to encompass the room and the garden view. 'A building biologist. His mantra was "if you care for the environment, you care for the occupant". He wanted to bring nature into my home, or at least the feeling it creates.'

'He did a great job.'

Her eyes closed briefly. 'I miss him very much.'

Harry gave her a moment to compose herself before speaking.

'Would you mind telling me a little about your relationship with him?'

Apparently she'd asked two architects to quote, but she fell for Rick's passion for wellness and biophilic design. At Harry's blank look she added, 'That's the name given to décor that mimics nature. Rick was convinced it could promote healing.'

Nia went on to tell Harry they worked together for barely a week before Rick asked her out for dinner. It sounded like a classic *coup de foudre*, and Nia admitted that the relationship was so powerful, so incredibly well-balanced from the start, that if Rick's life hadn't been taken so soon he could well have been her lifelong love.

'How long were you together?' he asked.

'Not long enough.' She sighed. 'Two years.'

Harry asked more questions. Nia fetched more water. He asked about her students, and it was only when she passed him a list of those she tutored that he spotted a familiar name.

Filipa Stanning Jones.

48

'She cheated,' Nia Mitchell told Harry. 'Not just once, but three times. Can you believe the cheek of her? She had absolutely no excuse and since she showed zero remorse, I kicked her off the course.'

'How did she take it?'

'She was furious. She tried to get her parents to influence me into reinstating her – they offered to build a new wing for the psychology department – but she was such a disruptive influence on the others I didn't see I had a choice.'

Harry listened to the words but he was more interested in Nia's body language which had tightened.

'You didn't like her.'

'No, I didn't. I thought she was a spoiled brat.' She flashed him a smile. 'I wouldn't say that to anyone else but a colleague, needless to say.'

'She has...' Harry paused while he tried to think of the right word. 'Issues,' he finally said, which was pretty lame but he knew Nia would understand what he meant.

'I'm sure she does, but I didn't want her acting out the aftermath of whatever it was in class. Especially when she seemed to develop a bit of a crush on me.'

It wasn't an uncommon phenomenon, as Harry knew. He'd had a bit of a crush on his own tutor if he was honest which had, in fact, spurred him on to do better than he might have otherwise.

'Did she cheat to impress you?'

'She cheated because she was lazy.'

Harry wouldn't be so sure, but considering Filipa had also cheated on Lorraine's course, perhaps Nia Mitchell was right. Harry took a sip of water and shifted his position on the dead yak, moving the questions on to include the wider picture and if Rick's finances were intact when he died.

'There wasn't anything unusual, if that's what you mean.' Nia frowned. 'He hadn't made a will so his parents inherited. They were kind to me, though, and gave me half the money they received when they sold his house.'

Harry watched a robin hop around a bird bath before it paused to take a swift drink. 'I don't suppose you know if Rick knew someone called Hugh Lamont? He's an investment manager.'

She shook her head. 'Sorry.'

Harry couldn't think of anything else he could ask, so he rose to his feet, thanking her for her time. 'I know how busy you must be,' he added politely.

'I was preparing for a conference...' Her face suddenly brightened. 'I've just remembered where I know your name from. The Swiss Psychological Association's Congress. Didn't I see your name on the list of speakers?'

'You did.' He was pleased she'd noticed. 'Unfortunately something came up at the last minute and I couldn't go.' He didn't add *because I'd been beaten to a pulp by two thugs*.

'Your replacement was...' She paused and he could tell she

was doing what he'd done earlier – trying to find the right word to convey what she wanted. 'Unconventional.'

'You're talking about Douglas King?'

'Who?'

'Douglas King. He's a colleague. He has a therapy room in the same building as me. He filled in for me when I couldn't make it.'

'Oh.' Nia looked blank. 'The person who took your slot was a woman.'

'Oh.' It was Harry's turn to go blank. 'I was sure Doug had given the talk, but I've obviously missed something.'

Which wasn't surprising, he thought, considering the state he'd been in after Clive Farmer and his pal had taken that baseball bat to him.

49

Sunday morning and Harry was in bed with Jessie. She was fast asleep, her back against his chest and his arm cradled between her breasts. He didn't know what had woken him, but he could see it was morning. A pale strip of early sunshine peeped through a gap in the curtains.

Moving carefully, he withdrew his arm and rolled over, reaching for his phone on his bedside table. Six thirty. He saw a text had come in from Doug. That's what must have woken him.

Vince's finances. We have to talk.

Knowing he wouldn't fall back to sleep, Harry slipped out of bed and shrugged on a sweatshirt and pair of boxers, padded downstairs. Put the machine on for coffee. He sipped it as he stood looking over the back garden where next door's Labrador was liberally peeing on his shrubs. Nothing he could do about it without upsetting his neighbours and potentially souring what, so far, had been a fairly decent relationship.

He tapped out a text to Doug.

I'm free now if you want to ring.

Harry's phone buzzed within the minute.

'Doug. What's up?'

'Vince's money.' His colleague's voice was higher than normal and he obviously heard it because he cleared his throat. 'It's all gone.'

'All?' Harry repeated.

'Yes. His pension pot, his investments, his ISAs. They've been cleared out.'

Harry pulled out a kitchen chair and sat down. 'Jesus.'

'Catherine's going insane. She'd banked on inheriting some money for the twins' future. Helping with university fees, a deposit on their first house, stuff like that.'

'Do the police know?'

'Yes.'

'Can they find out where it's gone?'

'Not so far.'

'What about his second home on the cruise ship? Perhaps he's already bought it?'

'I don't know. The police won't tell me anything. It's all just so *awful*, Harry, I can't tell you.'

'How much was the apartment on the ship going to cost, do you know?'

'Eight hundred thousand pounds, give or take a grand or two.'

Harry whistled. 'I bet he's bought the apartment. That *has* to be where the money's gone.'

'I don't think he has.' Suddenly Doug sounded close to tears. 'I think it's gone. I really do.'

Harry suddenly realised that Catherine probably wasn't the only one banking on inheriting some money from Vince.

He went on to tell Doug about Hugh Lamont, and Lorraine and Phil's missing thousands. Doug went quiet. 'You think this Hugh Lamont might have the money?'

'It's looking that way.'

'And you know where his virtual office is?'

'Yes.'

'The police must be able to find him. They *must*.'

In the background, Harry heard one of the twins shout, *Daddy! Hurry up!*

'I'd better go,' Doug said. 'Paton's going insane for a swim.'

'Swim?' Harry repeated.

'We're on the coast. Holiday cottage.'

Harry was startled. Vince had only died two days ago and they'd gone on holiday?

'We were going to lose the deposit,' Doug went on. 'And the twins were so excited... and since we can't do anything with Vince's place tied up in police tape, and the funeral's not for a fortnight, we decided to come down here. It's only a short break. We'll be back tomorrow.'

He sounded so defensive Harry said, 'It sounds perfectly sensible to me.'

'You're kind, Harry. Look, do you think they'll find Hugh Lamont? Do they know where he lives?'

The anxiety was back, and although Harry tried to keep Doug calm, by the time they hung up he reckoned Doug needed a double Scotch and a lie-down in a darkened room. Or perhaps that was what he himself needed. He felt wrung out and the day had only just started.

'Hey, you.'

He turned to see Jessie. She was wearing one of his shirts and nothing else. Her hair was tousled and she was blinking sleepily. She looked as sexy as hell.

'Come here.' He opened an arm and she walked into his embrace, ducking down to kiss his lips. The kiss turned into more than a kiss and Harry forgot all about feeling wrung out until he tried to sweep Jessie into his arms and carry her upstairs, when his ribs shrieked in protest.

'Ouch,' she breathed against his lips. Half-laughing, she took his hand and led him back to bed. She knew when to touch lightly and where to be tender, but when he told her his bruises and factures weren't as sore as they used to be, she became happily robust. It was her wholehearted enthusiasm that he found such a turn-on.

Later, Harry felt the released tension of the past few days wash out of his limbs. He should, he thought, prescribe a dose of sex for most of his clients. It would help them relax as well as gain a sense of perspective.

They spent the rest of the day pottering around the house, reading the weekend papers, watching a bit of YouTube – Jessie was obsessed with BASE jumper Jeb Corliss' videos – and chatting about nothing. The day was so peaceful, so *normal*, that when his phone went and Harry saw it was Tim, he expected it to be nothing more than his son ringing for some moral support over his being gated.

'Dad.'

There was something wrong with his voice.

Harry was instantly alert. 'What's wrong?'

'I've done something really stupid.'

'Okaaay.'

'I've...' Harry heard him gulp. 'Run away.'

50

Tim running away was so far removed from what Harry had expected, he felt the air rush out of his lungs.

'Where are you?'

'It was Paton's idea. She messaged me this morning. They're on holiday in Wales and it sounded so cool, on the beach and everything, and she said did I want to come. I know they're younger than me but I really like them, they can be really fun, and I was so fed up being gated on my own, that I said yes and she said to catch a bus to the train station and did I have enough money to get to Swansea? It was only a tenner and–'

'Where are you?' Harry repeated, trying to keep calm and not resort to shouting, which he very much felt like doing.

'I'm outside the train station. Paton said she'd get her mum and dad to pick me up but they're not here.' He sounded close to tears and Harry could understand why. He was only fifteen, and as far as Harry knew, hadn't been on a train on his own before. The adventure had suddenly turned scary.

'I want you to make yourself known to the station manager, or any station staff. Let them know what's happened and–'

Harry's phone buzzed, letting him know a text was waiting. He had a quick look and saw it was Doug.

Ring me. It's urgent.

'Tim, I've got a message from Doug. I have to call him back. Do *not* move. Stay where you are so I can ring you straight back.'

'Okay.' His voice was a whisper.

'Doug,' Harry barked. He could feel his heart beating at twice its usual rate.

'Harry, I'm so sorry. Paton's just told me that she, well, it's Tim... I can't believe what she's done but you have to know that–'

'Tim just rang me.'

'Ah.'

'He's at Swansea station.'

'I'll go and pick him up. Immediately. It's only half an hour from us. Then you'll know he's safe.'

'Thank you. Text me when you've got him. I'll drive straight over and get him.'

Harry rang Tim and told him the plan. He was curt, his voice filled with repressed anger.

'I'm sorry, Dad.'

Tim sounded miserable. He was undergoing another lesson in consequences, Harry supposed, but it was making him wonder when his son would actually learn something.

Next, Harry rang the school, who as yet hadn't noticed he was missing, thank God. He told them he'd deliver Tim to his house master around 10pm, who would in turn deliver him to the headmaster the next morning. Harry hung up to find Jessie had come downstairs and was watching him with arched eyebrows. 'Whatever's going on?'

When he explained, she raised her eyes to the ceiling. 'Kids,' she said. 'Who'd have them?' Then she grinned. 'He won't be doing that again, will he?'

'I hope Doug and family don't make it a super-enjoyable experience or it'll just confirm that doing stupid things can turn out to be fun.'

Harry checked on Google Maps to see it was going to take him two hours to get there, meaning a five-hour round trip if he stopped to be at least a little sociable with the Kings. He wouldn't get back until after ten in the evening, even later if the school drew things out when he dropped Tim back.

'I'm sorry,' he told Jessie. 'I was looking forward to our pizza in front of the TV.'

She brushed his apology aside. 'Just get him back safely.'

Harry called Nicole from the car, and then Theo. Even with everything going on, he was glad he'd managed to remember his friends' date night was last night. He wanted to know how it had gone.

'Rather well, since you ask,' Theo told him, sounding surprised. 'We're seeing each other again on Friday.'

'Nice one.' Harry overtook a Rover 75, one of the last made before the company entered administration, which reminded him of his own car sitting with the police, part of a murder investigation.

'How's my car?'

'Resting.' Theo's voice was dry.

'The case?'

'Getting closer.'

Maddeningly, Theo said no more.

'Come on,' Harry said. 'It's me here, your police-friendly shrink.'

'We have an IP address for our website nasty. Well, we've identified the host, its network interface, and the location of the host in the network.'

'Which means?'

'Our techies believe the location of the computer where the website was created is in the Bahamas.'

'Does that mean you get to go there?'

'I wish,' Theo said dryly. 'Last thing. Libby tells me there were no trackers on your car.'

Which meant the only people who knew Harry was staying at Lorne House were Nicole and Dave.

51

'Any luck with finding Hugh Lamont?' Harry asked Theo.

'Not yet.' Now, frustration entered the DI's tone.

'Doug and Catherine are devastated about Vince's missing money.'

'Hmm.' Theo was noncommittal.

'What is it?'

'There's no indication Vince had a large sum of money, at least not in the past seven years. The bank only has records that far back and since then, he's been living off his pension.'

For some reason, this blindsided Harry. 'I don't understand. I thought he had at least half a million tucked away.'

'He had fifteen thousand available in his bank account, but that's all we've found so far.'

After they'd hung up, Harry pushed on past Bristol, his mind taken up with considering Vince. Perhaps he'd lost the money, and hadn't been able to bear telling Catherine? But why talk about the apartment on the cruise ship?

This puzzle kept Harry occupied while he crossed the Severn Bridge – the muddy banks gleaming silver-wet in the sunshine – and continued along the M4 to Swansea. The directions Doug had given him were for the Gower Peninsula, where Harry's parents used to take him on holiday. He had fond memories of sandy bays, clifftop walks and beachside sausage sizzles.

A sign *Seabreeze* indicated he should turn left towards the coast – just as Doug's text instructed. Harry hoped that Tim wasn't overly revelling in his adventure but after Doug telling him that his son had joined the girls on the beach, he rather thought the whole escapade had probably done nothing but encourage the boy.

Harry followed a narrow single-track lane down a steep hill, hoping he wouldn't meet another vehicle coming the other way. Weeds grew through cracks in the tarmac and the potholes were deep, indicating not many people came here. It was barely forty minutes from Swansea but it felt secluded and remote, way off the beaten track.

The track led Harry to the rear of the property. He parked next to Doug's Volvo and another car he didn't recognise – a silver 4X4 Mitsubishi with alloy wheels and a bull bar. Climbing outside, Harry relished the biting salt breeze. He stretched and walked around the side of the house, the sound of the sea hissing in his ears. *Seabreeze* was at the far end of a tiny cove, and as the ad had declared, it was perfectly located to embrace the beach lifestyle. Harry stepped along the outside terrace and peered through the glass doors to see the wood burner and open-plan living was all there, as promised.

He called out *hello* a few times, but nobody answered. He looked up and down the beach, frowning. He could see several towels, a couple of buckets and spades, and a half-built castle with a double moat that was Tim's trademark.

Where was everyone?

Harry walked back to his car, checking his phone, but as Doug had warned him, there was no signal. He peered into Doug's Volvo. Crisp packets and sweet wrappers, a dog cage with newspaper and a blanket on its floor. He moved to look inside the Mitsubishi. A tatty brown messenger-style leather briefcase lay on the passenger seat. It gaped open, the brass buckle unclasped.

A chill swept over Harry as Kevin Owen's voice echoed in his mind.

He had a tatty briefcase. At odds with the shoes, know what I mean? The buckle wouldn't close properly. He had to carry it under his arm.

52

Adrenaline surging, Harry ran back to the house. This time he was shouting Tim's name.

He swept through the living room, eyes scanning sofas and armchairs, the detritus of kids – a Scrabble board on the rug in front of the wood burner, a couple of Jacqueline Wilson books, chocolate wrappers, socks and fleeces tossed here and there – and then he was in the kitchen, still shouting, 'Tim!'

Empty plates were on the table, dirty knives and forks laid haphazardly. It looked as though they'd had cheese on toast followed by pots of fruit yoghurt. A yipping sound started on the other side of the table. It was the puppy. She was shut in a pet travel backpack set on the floor and was squeaking and scrabbling to be let out. Why was Daisy here? Why wasn't the puppy with Catherine and the kids?

Panic rising, Harry was going to charge up the stairs when suddenly, Doug was there, calling his name.

'Thank God,' Harry said when he saw his friend. 'I was getting really worried. Where is everyone?'

'They've gone to get ice cream. There's a café at the top of the bluff.'

'Not Tim too?' Harry was dismayed. Getting home before midnight was now looking highly unlikely.

'Sorry.' Doug looked shamefaced. 'But we didn't know exactly when you'd get here.'

Harry rubbed his hands over his head. 'When will they be back?'

Doug looked at the kitchen clock, shaped like a sailing boat, which hung on the wall. 'They won't be long. Fifteen minutes?'

Harry inhaled and exhaled, trying to regain his composure. His fingertips started to tremble as the adrenaline left his body.

'What can I get you while we wait?' Doug asked. 'Beer? Tea or coffee?'

Harry would have loved a beer after his scare, but having to drive put paid to drinking alcohol. 'A coffee would be great. Thanks.'

'I'll join you.' Doug filled the kettle with water.

Harry bent down to the puppy. 'Shouldn't she be with the kids?'

'Too tiring. She's only eight weeks old.'

Daisy kept squeaking, her paws paddling against the mesh, her eyes frantic.

'Can I let her out?'

Doug considered. 'I don't see why not. It's not like there's any traffic out here.'

As soon as Harry released the puppy, she scampered straight outside, tail upright and ears cocked.

'I'll join you in a minute.' Doug smiled. 'Go and enjoy the view.'

Harry stood on the terrace overlooking a blue sea that crashed onto the sand, spume flying. A handful of seagulls stood in the lee of a sandy bank while two more wheeled overhead, calling. It was wild and beautiful and Harry felt his equanimity settle even further. Thank God Tim was safe. That the family were all safe.

Doug arrived with two big mugs of coffee and a plate of biscuits. Harry ate a chocolate digestive, sipped his coffee. Mulled things over. They talked about Vince's money for a while, then some of the case. Harry yawned. He must be tired after the drive. He closed his eyes, enjoying the feeling of sunshine on his eyelids.

'Who owns the Mitsubishi 4X4?' he asked.

'Why do you ask?'

There was something in Doug's voice that made Harry open his eyes. 'There's a briefcase inside. I thought I recognised it.'

Doug looked at him with interest. 'It's mine.'

'What, the car? Or the briefcase?'

'The briefcase is mine.' Doug got to his feet. 'But the car's a rental.'

'What?'

'Wait there. I'll explain.'

Harry watched Doug walk around the side of the house and disappear briefly to return with the briefcase. Harry felt a sinking sensation in his stomach. Doug wasn't holding the brief-case by its handle. It was tucked under his arm.

'This briefcase?' Doug said. He gave it to Harry. Harry's fingers fumbled with the brass catch, which was broken. 'Open it. You'll find what you want inside.'

Mouth dry, Harry folded back the lid. Opened the case wide.

'What the...' He pulled out a silver-white man's wig and a matching moustache.

'They're made out of real human hair,' Doug told him. 'Really expensive. Nobody guessed.'

Harry turned them over in his hands.

No, no, no. This isn't happening.

'Few people think beyond hair colour or a beard, or a moustache, when describing someone,' Doug said conversationally. 'Even the colour of people's eyes, for instance, unless they're very noticeable like bright blue or green, tend not to be noticed nearly as much.'

'You're Hugh Lamont.' Harry's voice was faint.

'Technically I'm Doug King, but yes, I took on another persona.'

Harry worked his mouth. Managed a single word.

'Why?'

Doug leaned back. Looked out over the ocean. 'Because I needed the money.'

'You ripped all those people off,' Harry said disbelievingly.

'I *needed* the money.' Doug's tone turned steely. 'Vince didn't. He was just sitting on it, doing nothing with it. By giving it to me, he was helping his family. Helping Catherine and the girls.'

'When did he give it to you?' Harry's voice was hoarse.

'Nine and a half years ago.'

'How much?'

'Half a million.'

'He thought you were investing it for him.'

'I was. He was investing in his *family*.'

'But you spent it.'

Doug didn't deny it.

'Doesn't your job in Zurich pay you enough?'

Doug didn't respond. Just stared out to sea. 'You won't understand.'

'But I want to.' Harry leaned forward, expression earnest. 'Tell me, Doug. Make me understand.'

Doug looked back. Held Harry's gaze. 'You'll hate me, and I can't have that. Sorry.'

Harry stared at Doug as more thoughts crashed into his mind. 'Vince wanted his money back, didn't he? He wanted to buy his apartment on the ship.'

'What was he thinking?' Doug cried, suddenly springing to his feet. 'Why did he want to start cruising? He was in his eighties, for God's sake. He should have been thinking of his *family*, not spending it willy-nilly. How selfish could he be?'

'You pushed him.' Harry stared in horror at Doug. 'You pushed him down the stairs.'

53

'He wouldn't listen,' Doug said. His fists were clenching and unclenching at his sides. 'I tried to explain but he just kept on and on, wanting his money back, but I didn't have it any more. What else could I do?'

Harry was gazing at his friend, struggling to make sense of it all. 'What about Lorraine? Did she demand her fifty thousand back too?'

Doug looked away. 'It wasn't as though she needed it right away.'

Harry's horror grew. 'And Phil Petty?'

'He was so *rich*.' Doug made it sound like a dirty word. 'He could afford it.'

'But he's going to have to sell his house.'

Doug shrugged. 'He doesn't have a mortgage on it. He'll just have to downsize like a normal person.'

More things fell into place. The hoody-wearing youths, brandishing knives and phones, laughing, taking videos.

'You used the students as assassins.' Harry stared at Doug, his skin crawling.

'Between you and me,' said Doug, 'they were pretty useless.

Initially I thought it was a great idea. How could the police possibly tie me in to the attacks? More importantly they're fit and young, and as you know, I'm not particularly physical. Not like you, punching people whenever you fancy it. But it turned out they're not really killers. They were in it for the thrill. They only killed Lorraine by accident.'

A ball of anger rolled through Harry. 'Rick Johnston wasn't an accident,' he gritted out. 'Whoever kicked his ladder from beneath him meant business.'

At that, Doug frowned. 'Yes, I suppose you're right. But that was different. That was–'

'Oh my God.' Harry reared back. His mind was ablaze. 'You're the hit and run driver.'

Doug looked irritated. 'The students were so useless, I was forced to take extraordinary measures.'

'You hired that 4X4. The one outside. The Mitsubishi.'

'Well, I wasn't going to use my car,' Doug snapped. 'That would be stupid.'

'Why did you hire those thugs to beat me to a pulp?'

'I just needed you put out of action, that's all. I didn't mean for them to break your ribs.'

Harry thought of Doug and Catherine's modest house in Bloomfield Rise, their thriftiness, rarely having holidays, only going out to eat on birthdays. With Vince's money on top of whatever Doug earned in Zurich, they should have been rolling in money.

'Where did the money go?' Harry asked.

'On the family.' His tone was weighted, as if to say, *where else*?

'But why are you always so short?' Harry took a breath. 'Doug, please don't get angry with me when I ask this, but do you have a problem with gambling?'

Doug surveyed him steadily. Harry couldn't tell what he might be thinking.

'No.'

Warning icicles shivered through Harry's veins but he couldn't stop trying to grasp what was going on. 'Is it because you have cancer? You're worried you won't be able to take care of your family if you die?'

Doug's eyes darkened and at that moment, Harry didn't see his friend. He saw a desperate man with his back against the wall. Fear surged up Harry's spine, spreading out along his arms and into the tips of his fingers. 'Talk to me, Doug.'

After a long moment Doug seemed to give a shudder and Harry watched as his gaze became distant. He was moving through options, picking up and discarding ideas and plans until finally, he found the one he wanted.

The surf hissed and surged on the beach. Doug got to his feet once more. 'Come inside.'

When Harry rose, a wave of dizziness swept over him and he had to put a hand on the back of his chair to steady himself. His fear increased.

'What have you given me?'

Doug didn't answer. 'Tim's inside,' he told Harry. 'With the girls. Why don't you go and join them?'

Alarm shot through Harry like a thunderbolt. They weren't getting ice cream? Of course not. Not with Doug confessing. The reality of the hideous situation crashed through. Oh, sweet Jesus. What was Doug planning?'

'Where's Tim?' Harry demanded. 'Where's my son?'

'Upstairs.'

Adrenaline surging, Harry pelted inside the house, clipping the glass door and nearly falling. Windmilling his arms, he regained his balance. Charged up the stairs.

The first bedroom obviously belonged to the twins, with stuffed toys, girls' clothes and sparkly accoutrements scattered around. It was empty.

The second bedroom, a spare room that didn't look as though it was in use, was also empty.

The third bedroom, overlooking the cove, was the master bedroom. For a moment Harry thought it was empty but then his eyes came to rest on the king-sized bed.

Catherine lay in the middle of the bed, seemingly fast asleep. Her arms were around her children. Paton and Mia also looked as though they were asleep.

Harry raced over. They were warm. They were breathing. He tried to wake them.

Urgency like he'd never known descended on him.

'*Tim*!' It was a scream that came from the depths of his soul.

54

Harry tore out of the master bedroom and into the corridor. He was shouting Tim's name so loudly his voice was cracking.

He crashed into the next bedroom. Saw his son laid out on the double bed, his hands folded across his chest.

Harry's mind became a single long shriek of panic.

He raced to the bedside.

Tim's skin was warm. He was breathing.

Harry put one arm beneath Tim's knees, the other under his shoulders. Ignoring the agony blazing in his ribs, he lifted him in one smooth movement. As he turned, he staggered slightly, his head turning muzzy.

Do not stop. Have to keep going.

He made it out of the bedroom and into the corridor. The walls seemed to breathe in and out as he staggered for the stairs. Where was his car key? He couldn't check his pockets now. Had to hope it was on him. Sure it was. Sure it was it was was was.

What had Doug given him? How much? Thank God he hadn't drunk all his coffee. If it was a drug like Rohypnol, or another type of benzodiazepine that acted on the central nervous system, he'd lose consciousness in the next fifteen or twenty minutes. In half an hour, he'd be out cold.

He managed to twist his wrist to see it was 7.05pm.

You can do this, Harry told himself. He was halfway along the landing when he stumbled, crashing to the ground, Tim folding on top of him. He ignored the pain riding his body. Welcomed it, to help keep him conscious. He was about to lurch forward, to bring his legs beneath him and keep walking, when Doug appeared. He was carrying a bright green plastic fuel can in each hand.

Immediately Harry dropped his head, letting it hang loosely. He opened his mouth. Let himself drool.

'Didn't get far, did you?' Doug sounded satisfied.

Harry made an agonised groan.

'I'm sorry you got caught up in all this.' Doug sighed. 'But you were getting too close.'

Harry watched Doug walk into the master bedroom. Heard sloshing sounds. He hefted Tim fractionally, making sure he was ready to move. That was when he smelled it.

Fuel. Petrol.

Doug was going to burn down the house with his wife and children inside. And Harry and Tim, if he didn't get them out of here in time.

7.07pm.

Precious seconds ticked past.

Doug came out of the bedroom, pouring fuel behind him. He walked up and down the landing, dousing the carpet. When the jerrycans were empty, he jogged downstairs.

Thank God he hadn't started the fire up here first, Harry thought. Small mercies.

When he heard more sloshing sounds below, he pushed himself to his knees, Tim against his chest. He straightened up, ribs shrieking. The landing began spinning. He leaned against the wall, waiting for it to stop.

Move.

He staggered to the top of the stairs. Knocked into the banisters but he didn't lose his grip on Tim. He couldn't hear anything from below. He concentrated on walking slowly down the stairs. As quietly as he could.

Mustn't fall. Must keep going.

He was halfway down when he heard a muffled *whump*. It sounded like a gas fire being lit but Harry knew that wasn't what it was. Doug had just put a flame to the petrol. Another *whump* and then came the sound of flames, crackling.

55

A waft of grey-black smoke drifted over the bottom stair. The crackling intensified.

Where was Doug?

Harry paused, desperately listening, but he couldn't hear any sounds aside from flames hissing and sputtering.

He carefully made his way down the stairs, hugging Tim closer to his chest at the bottom. Waves of giddiness swept through him, but he kept moving.

Smoke swirled all around. The curtains on either side of the glass walls were already ablaze. The sofa and rugs were burning, and the bookcase was alight, flames reaching for the ceiling and the petrol-soaked carpets above.

He began walking across the living room. Steadily, purposefully, Harry made it onto the terrace. No Doug. He didn't stop there but kept walking around the side of the house. The relief he felt when he saw the Mitsubishi had gone was so strong he nearly fell.

Thank God. No Doug.

Harry stumbled for his car. He hadn't locked it. He opened the back door and heaved Tim across the back seat. Closed the door. Dug in his pocket and found the key. Put it in the ignition and drove the car up the lane until he thought it was far enough away that should the house explode, it would be unaffected.

'Shee ooo,' he told his son. *See you.*

Harry tried to run back down the road but his movements were becoming more and more unco-ordinated and he had to slow to a walk. He checked his watch.

7.11.

This time he entered the house through the kitchen. The smell of burning had intensified and a cloud of black smoke was belching from the sitting area. He was coughing against the bitter stench of burning plastics, the toxic fumes pouring from chemicals in the carpets and soft furnishings.

He wanted to run a tap and drench himself in water but he was running out of time. The Rohypnol would knock him out any minute now. No point in soaking himself to get burned alive.

The bookcase crashed to the ground, exploding into a ball of fire. Blue waves spread across the ceiling. He had to hurry.

He hauled himself up the stairs using the banister. One step at a time, refusing to stumble.

Down the landing. Turn left.

Harry swore when he saw the curtains in the master bedroom were alight. He wanted to carry both twins but even though they were light and felt as fragile as birds, he'd be better off carrying them out one at a time. He'd move faster.

The room whirled when he picked up Mia. He fought an overwhelming urge to collapse on the bed and fall asleep with them. Tucked Mia against his chest instead. Moved as fast as he could out of the house. Very nearly dropped her thanks to tripping over a wetsuit that had dropped to the floor. Stumbled to the Volvo and thrust Mia inside.

He looked at his watch. Couldn't focus on the dial. Probably a good thing or he might panic.

Another tortuous trip through the house. His co-ordination deteriorated. He staggered up the stairs, bumping between the banisters and the wall. He reached the top to find the landing was alight. The carpet was burning and flames were licking the walls. Great tongues of flame were pouring out of the master bedroom. He had seconds to decide whether to risk it.

Before he could change his mind, Harry hurled himself through the flames and into the room.

The carpet and walls were blazing. The heat was so fierce he nearly turned back but Paton and Catherine were still there and he forced himself across the room and grabbed Paton, flung her over his shoulder in a fireman's lift and swayed down the stairs.

A wall of flame was now roaring through the sitting room and Harry tried to move faster but his body wouldn't respond. He felt an immense pain on his ankle and glanced down to see his trousers were on fire.

He lurched outside. Shoved Paton into the Volvo.

Sorry, love, can't waste time on niceties.

His ankles were scorching with pain and he bent over to slap at the flames and as he slapped a tidal wave of black began to form at the edge of his mind, but he forced it back.

Catherine.

The wave grew.

Harry stumbled for the house.

Catherine, Catherine, Catherine. Her name was a howl in his heart.

The wave began to swell, cresting black from a great height in a night sky with no stars.

No, he told it. I'm not ready. I've got to get Paton and Mia's mum. I have to save her.

The wave crushed him.

56

Harry awoke with a shout on his lips. He didn't know why, but he was filled with panic. He was in danger. Everyone was in danger.

'Harry, my love.'

He felt a woman's cool hand in his.

'It's me, Jessie. You're safe. The twins are safe.'

His eyes snapped open.

'Doug,' he said.

'He's not here.'

Jessie wore a puffa jacket over a pair of pyjamas with little koalas dotted all over them. Her bare feet had been shoved into a pair of mud-spattered trainers. Her curly hair stuck out in all directions and she had mascara smeared beneath one eye.

'You look lovely,' he said sincerely.

'And you're a hero.'

He frowned. 'What?'

'You saved Tim and the girls.'

Tim. Anxiety coursed through him. He began to struggle up.

'He's next to you. He's still asleep.'

Harry swung around to see his son's head relaxed on a pristine pillow, his eyes shut. His fair hair was tousled, his skin a healthy pink. Tears came to Harry's eyes. *My boy*.

'The doctor says he'll be okay but they're keeping an eye on you both.' She squeezed his hand gently. 'You saved his life. Saved the girls.'

'I did?'

All he could remember was drinking Doug's coffee, and their conversation on the terrace. Doug giving him the briefcase so he could see the silver-grey wig and moustache. Doug confessing to being Hugh Lamont.

Smoke, Harry recalled. Had there been a fire? He coughed, suddenly becoming aware how ill he felt. His mouth tasted foul and his stomach roiled, as though it had been filled with acid. He also had the headache from hell.

'You managed to get the kids out of the house as it went up in flames. You drove Tim up the hill to make sure he was well out of the way before you returned for the twins...' Her voice wobbled for a moment before she cleared her throat and continued to tell him what had happened.

Harry listened but she could have been talking about someone else doing those things. Apparently a young couple at the far end of the cove had seen the house was on fire and raced to find a signal so they could call the emergency services. The fire brigade arrived twenty minutes later. The firemen then called the ambulances and the police.

'The firemen realised it wasn't your normal fire when they came across Tim in your car... The medics here say you were all given Rohypnol.'

Which was why he couldn't remember anything. Due to the combination of sedation and anterograde amnesia, Rohypnol was also known as a 'date rape drug', and because it was odourless, tasteless and dissolved in liquid, it went undetected by the victim. Harry had had no idea Doug had drugged him until he'd started moving about. Thereon, his memory went blank.

'They told me you'll feel very hungover for a while, and your memory will be shot. But you'll recover.' Jessie pressed a kiss on his hand before getting to her feet. 'I'll get a nurse to check you over.'

He looked past the end of his bed to see he and Tim were sharing a hospital ward with four other men. One was watching TV with headphones on, but the others appeared to be asleep.

Nurse Qureshi was small and neat and built like a shot-putter. Mutely Harry let her check his vital signs while Jessie hovered.

'You've got second-degree burns on your ankles and lower legs,' she informed him. 'You'll be sore for a bit as you've blistered. We'll send you home with some antibiotic cream but the best thing is to let the burns air. Oxygen is a great healer.'

'I can't feel any pain.'

'That's Rohypnol for you,' she said cheerily. 'You and your son will both see the doctor in the morning. And then you'll go home.'

'What time is it?' he asked. He'd lost all track.

'Just after midnight. So technically it's morning now. Easter Monday.'

As he was about to ask another question, she added, 'Swansea NHS Trust. You and your son were brought in at eight thirty this evening, along with two girls.'

'The twins.'

She nodded.

'How are they?'

Nurse Qureshi glanced across at Tim then back. 'They're all doing fine.'

'What about Catherine?' He pushed himself up. 'Is she with them?'

The nurse glanced at Jessie who said, 'I'll tell him.'

Nurse Qureshi nodded. She gave Jessie a little pat and walked outside.

Harry's anxiety returned. 'What is it? What about Catherine?'

'I'm sorry.' Jessie's face crumpled. 'But she died in the fire.'

Misery washed over him. 'I didn't save her.'

'You couldn't. You'd lost consciousness, but you tried, Harry. You tried your hardest because they found you already part-way to the house. You'd put the twins in the car and were in the process of going to get her.'

He pushed his distress aside for the moment to concentrate on the now. 'Who's with the twins?'

Jessie blinked. 'I don't know.'

'Go and see. Make sure there's someone they know when they wake up. If there's nobody there, Jessie, will you stay with them? They know you. They'll feel safe.'

'Of course.'

'Oh, and one more thing. It's a big ask, but it'll be really important for the kids.' When he told her, she didn't baulk, just said, 'I'll get on to it first thing tomorrow.'

With Jessie gone, Harry leaned back against his pillows. Closed his eyes. Please God the effects of Rohypnol were going to wear off soon. He'd never felt so ill.

57

'Harry, mate. Are you there?'

Harry struggled to open his eyes. 'Whaa–?'

'It's me. Theo.'

'Shit,' Harry managed. 'I feel like–'

'Shit,' repeated Theo obligingly. 'I'm not surprised.'

Theo passed him a cup of water. Harry drank it straight down. Pushed it back for Theo to refill. Drank that one down, then another.

'Better.' He collapsed back on his pillows. 'Thanks. What time is it?'

'It's 2am.'

Theo pulled up the chair Jessie had occupied earlier and sat down.

'Where's Jessie?' Harry asked.

'With the twins.'

Harry didn't think he could feel any worse but as dread rose, so did his nausea.

'Oh, God,' he said. 'Where are Doug's parents?'

Theo sighed. 'He killed them.'

Harry closed his eyes. He couldn't bear to ask how. Poor Neil and Marjory. They'd been so proud of their son.

'Their house was burned to the ground,' Theo told him. 'Two bodies have been found inside.'

'When?'

'He would have gone straight there after leaving you and his family.'

'Where is he?'

'We've put out an APW. All Ports Warning. We'll catch him, Harry. I promise you. But if you can give us a pointer as to where he might go, it would help. You knew him best.'

But Harry hadn't known Doug at all. He recalled musing after Lorraine's funeral that he hadn't known of her attachment to the village of Colerne, which made him wonder how well he thought he knew people. People only let you know what they wanted you to know. People lied. Dissembled. Told untruths to make themselves look good.

'I have no idea,' Harry told Theo. He felt inordinately tired.

'A guess will do.'

Theo waited, seemingly patient on the outside, but Harry knew he'd be chomping at the bit to get some information to pass on to the team and *catch him*.

Harry tried to get his mind to function. 'He speaks German reasonably well. Maybe he'll head for Switzerland. Zurich. He'll feel comfortable there.'

He thought further. 'He was Hugh Lamont. He conned people into giving him their money by pretending he was an investment manager. He might have some ID with that name.'

'Cheers.'

After Theo had left, Harry managed to find the energy to send a text to Jagoda and Trisha telling them not to go to the Wellbeing Centre until he'd spoken to them. That done, he fell back to sleep.

Some time in the early hours Tim woke up and Harry dragged himself out of bed and hobbled over. Called the nurse to check on his son. After she'd given him the thumbs-up, Harry talked to Tim. Hugged him. Tried not to weep with relief.

Soon afterwards Nicole arrived. Pale and drawn, horrified.

She spent time with Tim, soothing and calm. Managed to make him smile. Harry watched, thinking what a great mother she was. Selfless and dedicated as far as her kids were concerned. He loved her for that and, he guessed, he always would.

After Tim fell back to sleep, she came to Harry and cupped his face in her cool palms and kissed him gently on each cheek.

'For saving our son.'

He held out his arms and she curled on the bed, let him hold her as she wept tears of relief against his chest.

58

Late the following morning, while Tim was being discharged into Nicole's care, Harry was fighting to take the twins home with him.

'They have to be with people they feel safe with.' He was in a room the size of a shoebox trying to keep his temper with the woman from social services, a skinny twenty-something with a steely disposition. 'I don't want them to be placed with strangers while their father's being hunted. Not after what they've been through. It would be unforgiveable.'

Clara Mackey drew herself tall as the volume of Harry's voice rose. 'I'm afraid it will be a court who will appoint a guardian of its own choosing. If there are no close family members, then they'll look at grandparents and then cascade down aunts and uncles–'

'There are no aunts or uncles,' snapped Harry. He wasn't going to mention that the twins' grandparents had just been murdered.

'We have to make sure that's the case. Besides, there might be a cousin who–'

'While you're studying the family tree,' he said acidly, 'what happens to the twins? They get shuffled off to a foster parent they don't know? They're already deeply traumatised, it's our job to do what's best for them. Which is to place them with people they already know. Paton and Mia know my house, they know Jessie and trust my boys and, crucially, we all understand how the twins have been raised.'

'It's not my decision to make.' Clara Mackey's tone was stiff.

'Ring the decision maker.' Harry thrust his phone out to her. 'Do it now.'

'I really think–' She paused when the door opened and Nicole stepped inside.

Nicole's expression stiffened as she looked between them. 'Whatever's going on?'

Harry quickly explained, finalising things by saying for what felt like the thousandth time: 'Until Doug's found and can tell us what he wants done, the twins should be with us. Me or you, but not with strangers.'

'It shouldn't be a problem.' Nicole turned her charm onto Clara Mackey. 'We're Paton and Mia's guardians.'

'We are?' Harry was floored.

'When Catherine heard the potential pitfalls of not making a will, how the twins could end up with the wrong people if she hadn't designated guardianship, she did it immediately.'

'Good on her.' Harry's voice was faint.

'I did tell you, darling.' Nicole smiled sweetly at Harry before turning the smile onto the social services representative. 'I will go home and get a copy of the will and bring it back, and then we can move things forward.'

Which sounded simple, but it was, apparently, still going to take another twenty-four hours to get the will verified, and for social services to cross various t's and dot some i's as well as make sure that the twins were happy with the decision. Once she'd seen the will, however, Clara Mackey agreed Harry could take the twins home with him until everything was confirmed.

Harry just about collapsed in relief.

In the corridor, he asked Nicole the question with raised eyebrows.

'It was after their christening when Catherine decided.'

Harry vaguely remembered something but not exactly what.

'Doug kept avoiding the subject of wills so she went ahead and did one for herself. I don't know if Doug knew she'd done it. It's so rare both parents die together, but she wanted it covered. Just in case.' She considered him briefly. 'I'm so glad you're taking them home. I would, but–'

'I have lots more room.' He smiled. 'And a garden. And a shed.'

She gave him a rueful smile back. 'Let's share, like we do with the boys, until we know what Doug wants. But in the meantime, let's say you're their prime carer.'

Which suited Harry just fine, and come the end of the day, Paton and Mia were being hustled into the back of a taxi while Clara Mackey became a decoy for the media, who had finally sniffed out what had happened and were camped in the hospital's reception.

The twins were subdued and seemed smaller, diminished, and didn't say anything during the journey. Mia was sucking her thumb, a sure sign of distress. Harry didn't go for any false bonhomie. First thing that morning he'd taken on the job of telling them of their mother's death, keeping it simple and sticking to the facts.

He said they'd all fallen asleep when a fire broke out. Luckily, he'd saved them but not their mum. Their father was fine, Harry added, saying he was sorry he didn't know where he was.

They seemed to accept what he said and he thanked God they were with him so as soon as they felt stronger, they could start asking questions. Not that he was going to tell them that their father had wanted to murder them. That would come later.

When the twins climbed out of the car and looked around, their expressions were stunned, as though they'd never been there before.

Then the front door opened and Jessie stepped outside. She was bent over and clicking her fingers.

The next second a small bundle of black and white scampered out, tail bolt upright, ears cocked.

'Daisy!' squealed Paton.

The twins exploded into a run, skidding to kneel so the puppy could jump up and lick their faces.

'Thank you,' Harry mouthed to Jessie.

She smiled and opened the door wide, and they all went inside.

59

Theo dropped by just after 8pm. The twins were watching *Shrek 2* on the TV, a movie they'd watched countless times already but wanted to watch again no doubt for the reassurance it brought. Jessie was sharing the sofa with them and they'd snuggled close to her, wanting the comforting touch.

Harry took Theo into the kitchen. Closed the door. He poured himself a whisky and was going to fetch a Black Sheep beer for the policeman when Theo said, 'I'll have one too.'

He sank onto a chair at the old oak table and knocked his shot straight back.

Harry poured him another.

Theo turned his glass in his hands. 'Good news.'

'You've got him?'

'A sharp-eyed passport officer spotted him as he tried to board a ferry to Cherbourg. He's being transported back to Bristol. The evidence is so solid, the CPS may well charge him straight off.'

Harry's legs suddenly felt weak. He put the bottle of whisky on the table and took the chair next to Theo. Downed a slug of the spirit. Concentrated on the burn as it trailed down his throat.

'Well done on taking in the twins,' Theo remarked.

Harry nodded. They sat in silence while they sipped their drinks.

'Why?' said Harry. He didn't expect Theo to have an answer, but he couldn't help asking.

Theo was staring into his glass. 'He didn't want to get found out.'

'Embezzling people's money, you mean?'

'It's more than that.'

Theo reached across for the bottle and topped up their glasses. 'Everything you think you know about Doug is a sham.'

Harry closed his eyes. 'Go on.'

'Let's start with the University of Zurich. His main place of work. No one there has ever heard of him.'

Harry's eyes snapped open. 'You're joking.'

'His psychology degree? His diplomas and accreditations? The awards he's won? Non-existent. The Swiss Psychological Association's Congress, on the other hand, is real enough, but they've never heard of him either.'

Harry was opening his mouth to say *he covered for me* but then he remembered Professor Nia Mitchell saying a woman had taken Harry's place.

'But I met him at uni,' Harry said. 'He was a fellow student.'

'Was he really?'

Harry tried to think back. He could remember drinking with Doug at the pub, seeing him around campus. Had he seen him in the lecture hall? He honestly couldn't remember. He could remember Dave, though...

'That's crazy. He's lied to me about *everything*?'

'He's only been to Zurich three times.'

Harry's mouth dropped open. 'But he comes back with gifts for the girls all the time, toys, chocolates...'

'Which you can probably buy anywhere, including on the internet.'

Which explained those parcels being delivered to the Well-being Centre.

Harry suddenly remembered touching a nerve with Doug about the odd timings of one of his trips to Zurich, and how Doug had overreacted.

How dare you pry into my affairs. Do I ask where you are for every second of every day?

'Did he have a job *at all*?'

'It doesn't look like it.'

'I don't get it. Ages ago, he told me he wasn't eligible for child benefit because he earned more than the threshold of fifty thousand.'

Theo just looked at him.

'He lied.' Harry sighed. 'But what about his practice? His clients? He seemed to know what he was talking about.' Even as Harry spoke he realised he was looking at the past with a different eye. Had Doug really understood psychology? He thought over their decompression sessions in The Chequers. Doug was a great listener. Which was the main prerequisite for a therapist, but if you weren't one, could work just as well.

Then there was the fact that Doug never kept clients for long, and over the past few years seemed to have used his therapy room purely as an office.

'Dear God,' Harry whispered as the realisation hit him. 'He took Vince's money for him and his family to live off. And when that ran out, he tried to persuade others into giving him their money.'

'It looks that way.'

Harry gazed unseeingly past Theo. Why hadn't he spotted anything? He was a trained psychotherapist, how come he hadn't seen any warning signs?

But I did. I saw them all, but each one seemed to have a logical explanation. So I excused them.

His stomach roiled. He'd failed Catherine, he realised. He'd failed the twins. The magnitude of what had happened washed over him. He closed his eyes. Dear God, how could he square his history with Doug, with what Doug had done? Was it possible? Was there any way to turn the horrific event into something that didn't possess him? He didn't want the rest of his life defined by this. He didn't want to be wracked with guilt. There had to be a way through this.

Harry toyed with his glass, thinking. 'Can I talk to him?'

'What about?'

'I'd like to know the whole story. Who was Douglas King, really? A loving father? A good friend? A liar and a killer? He's all these things but I want to know more. I want to *understand* him.'

Harry leaned forward.

'I also want to know why two thugs beat me up. Why Nia Mitchell's partner was killed six months before the next attack. If Catherine knew. Did he send that message to Ethan to get him to come after me? Why? What threat was I then? How did he know I was staying at Lorne House? There are so many gaps, Theo. I want them filled.'

'I'll arrange it.'

Harry gazed past the bottle of whisky at a photograph of the boys and Lottie having a water fight. He could almost hear their joyful shrieks coming through the picture frame.

'Does he know the twins are alive?'

'We haven't told him yet.'

'Don't. Not until I see him. My guess is, if he knows they survived he'll clam up.'

Theo frowned. 'How come?'

'I think he wanted to kill anyone he thought would be disappointed in him. Like his parents, who were so proud of their son getting a degree and jetting off to Switzerland. His wife and kids who loved him, admiring the successful professional who brought back presents from abroad. He couldn't bear for them to find out the truth. That he wasn't who they thought he was.'

60

Before Theo left, he warned Harry that although the hospital staff were trying to keep a lid on where the twins had gone, their whereabouts wouldn't be under wraps for long.

'As soon as we're blown, we'll go elsewhere.' Harry kept his voice down as he walked Theo to the front door. 'Paton and Mia need time to adjust before they're thrown into the melee.'

'We'll do what we can to help.' Theo gripped Harry's shoulder.

While Jessie sorted the puppy out, putting it in a cage she'd bought earlier along with some water and a pet blanket, Harry took the twins upstairs to choose their room.

'Tim said you can have his, and Ben too, but you might prefer Lottie's.'

Paton and Mia took the offers seriously, peering through the windows at the views outside and checking the pictures on the walls, but what tipped the balance for them was the fact Lottie's room had a bunk bed.

'I want the top,' said Mia.

'Me too.' Paton pushed her lower lip out.

'But you always get the first choice!'

Tears and tantrums hovered, making Harry step in quickly. 'How about you draw straws for the first night? Then whoever loses can have the top bunk tomorrow?'

Instantly distracted, Paton trotted downstairs for some straws while Mia checked out the pyjamas Jessie had bought them earlier. 'I like the pink ones.'

'Then they're yours.'

Jessie came up with Paton and after drawing straws – Paton won, much to Mia's annoyance – helped put them to bed. They left their door open and the hall light on. When Harry checked on them ten minutes later he wasn't surprised that they were both fast asleep. Thank God, because now he could go to bed. He was dead on his feet.

He fell asleep with his lower legs outside the duvet – *oxygen is the greatest healer* – and Jessie spooning him, her breath rolling in gentle waves over his shoulders.

The next morning passed in a reasonably ordered fashion thanks to Jessie taking the day off. Harry had cancelled his least-pressing appointments, keeping only the handful of his most vulnerable clients who he'd either visit in their own homes, or have them come to his.

His head was muzzy, his balance still not quite right, but he felt a hundred per cent better than he had twenty-four hours ago.

Harry had spoken to Jagoda and Trisha, and as he'd guessed, where Trisha had taken him at his word not to go to the Well-being Centre until they'd spoken, Jagoda's curiosity had over-ridden his text and she'd gone to work as usual. She informed him the police had gone through the building *like stormtroopers*. Harry had to pray they hadn't taken his computer along with

Doug's but knowing the police, they probably had. He supposed all bases had to be covered.

He was looking up the number of the twins' school so he could talk to the headmistress when a text from Ethan came through.

Got something I found in the Wellbeing office. You need to see it.

Harry texted back. *See what?*

When are you coming in?

Ethan obviously didn't know the Centre had become a crime scene. *I'm not.*

How do I get you to see it?

Bring it to my house. He added his address.

Ethan arrived barely fifteen minutes later.

'That was quick,' said Harry as he invited him inside.

'I was at uni.'

Which was, Harry knew, barely four miles away.

'How was Norfolk?' Harry asked.

Ethan looked surprised. 'Norfolk?'

'Filipa told me you'd gone there for the weekend.'

'Oh.' His face did its trick of going blank, telling Harry something was wrong but that he didn't want to talk about it.

'You didn't go to Norfolk?' Harry pressed, intrigued to see how far Ethan would let him go. 'Filipa told me you'd gone to see friends there.'

When Ethan didn't respond Harry added, 'I wonder why she said that if it wasn't true?'

For the first time since Harry had known Ethan, he saw him grit his teeth. There was anger there, he realised. Hot and hard and unresolved.

'Why did she lie?' Harry continued in the same neutral tone.

Ethan's breathing was coming faster as he battled with himself. When he spoke, he could have been firing bullets.

'It amuses her.'

'In what way does lying amuse her?' Harry realised he was pushing far harder than he normally would but he was so interested in the siblings' relationship he couldn't help himself.

'It gives her power. Control over others.'

'Power and control over you too?'

At that, Ethan looked straight into Harry's eyes. It was as though Harry had never seen him before. His carapace of smooth-talking rich boy fell away and in his place was a wounded young man holding a secret he should never have been made to hold.

'Yes.' The admittance seemed to exhaust him and Harry decided to back off.

After giving Ethan a moment's space, he said, 'What did you want me to see?'

Ethan took a deep breath, obviously steadying himself. 'It was in Dr King's office.' He looked uncomfortable for a moment. 'It fell out of a cupboard I was moving so I could decorate behind it. I wasn't prying, honestly.'

Ethan reached into his back pocket and withdrew a clear plastic bag sealed with a clip. Harry stared at what was inside.

A knife.

'It's mine,' Ethan said. 'It's the one I had when I thought you were Filipa's... well, you know.'

'What was it doing in Doug's office?' Harry asked, but he already knew. Doug had snatched it up. He'd hidden it so that if Ethan was challenged, there would be no proof. Harry wondered if Doug had positioned himself to video the attack but had forgone that plan when Harry started punching Ethan.

Harry remembered Doug's appraising look after he had chased Ethan into George Street.

I didn't know you were quite so physical.

Which showed Doug hadn't known Harry particularly well

either, because Harry had never been one to shy away from standing up for himself.

'Why does he have the knife?' Ethan looked baffled. 'It gave me one hell of a shock when I saw it.'

'Give it to me, please.'

Ethan handed it over.

'I'll give it to the police. They already have your statement, so this will be added to your case file.'

Ethan swallowed.

'I really admire you for showing me this. It shows humanity, courage, and integrity.'

At that, the young man straightened. His gaze firmed.

'You did the right thing,' Harry added for good measure. For every action there was a consequence, and he wanted Ethan to feel the effect of doing the right thing when handing in the knife was probably the last thing he wanted. 'Thank you.'

Ethan flushed again, this time not from embarrassment but from pride.

61

As Harry walked Ethan outside, Mia appeared. She looked Ethan up and down. 'Who are you?'

'Ethan Stanning Jones.' He held out a hand for her to shake. 'Who are you?'

'Mia King.'

'You're Dr King's daughter?'

'Yes,' she said proudly. 'I'm a twin.'

Ethan dropped to his haunches so he was at eye level with Mia. 'Are you indeed? How very special.' He smiled and Harry saw yet another side to Ethan. Kind and gentle.

'Why do you have such a long name?' Mia asked.

'Because Stanning was my great-grandmother's name and Jones my great-grandfather's. Because he was poor and she was rich, and he had control of her money when they got married, she was allowed to keep her name to show it was originally her money.'

Harry listened to them talk about equality between the sexes before he finally extricated Ethan and took him outside. 'There's something you need to know,' he said quietly. 'The twins are here because their father is in custody. The Wellbeing Centre is a crime scene. I can't say more at this stage but please, if you do one thing for me, keep the twins' whereabouts secret. The press are going crazy trying to find them, apparently.'

'He's been arrested?' Ethan stared at Harry. 'Shit. If he took the knife, does that mean he sent me that horrible message about you?'

'Possibly.'

'Mia's *father* manipulated me into attacking you?'

Harry thought of the website Executor of Justice and the disparity between his own attack and the others. How the other students hadn't had personal messages delivered to their phones but bid for each attack on each victim directly with the website.

'I'm not sure.' Harry was honest. 'You were targeted directly where nobody else was. It's bothering me.'

'It's sick,' Ethan said fiercely. 'The whole thing is *sick*.'

Harry walked with him to his Golf. Watched him drive away.

Only then did he go and get ready for his trip to Bristol to see Douglas King.

Libby collected him at midday. She wore jeans and a denim jacket over a pink T-shirt. Converse trainers.

She hugged him tightly. 'You bloody hero.'

'I'm not,' he disagreed. 'I should have recognised what was going on sooner. Then I could have stopped it all.'

'You're not clairvoyant, Harry. You're a shrink.'

'But I should have–'

'He was a *friend*.' She shook his arm. 'We don't expect friends to turn into family annihilators.'

He supposed she was right. He hadn't considered Doug to be anything but the nice, even-natured man he'd met at uni all those years ago. Quiet, measured, never the centre of attention but always *there*. Like the beech tree in his back garden.

Harry was quiet as she drove, trying to get his thoughts in order. He knew he wanted the gaps filled, but it was more than that. The details of Doug's embezzlements, how he'd sustained his double life for decades would come out eventually, but what Harry wanted to know was what he did with his days when he wasn't in the office. Where he went when he didn't travel to Zurich, Bristol or Edinburgh.

Where did he go?

What did he do?

What did he think about?

Who was he, really?

He followed Libby through the police station to the interview rooms at the rear. Into a plain room with three chairs and a table bolted to the floor.

Libby picked up one of the chairs and took it to a corner. 'I'll just sit here. Blend into the décor.'

Harry remained standing. His pulse was up, his head spinning. He suddenly wondered how he'd react when Doug arrived.

I hope I don't hit him.

The door clanged back, and then Doug stepped inside.

62

Doug already had a weird pale look about him, as if he'd been in prison for a month. His body seemed to have shrunk and he looked frail, strangely pathetic. He wore tracksuit pants and a sweatshirt that clung to the rolls of fat at his waist. He didn't look at Harry but kept his eyes on the floor. He hadn't even acknowledged Libby was there.

'Hi, Doug,' said Harry.

No response.

'I brought my friend Libby with me. You haven't met before. She's here to stop me punching you.'

At that, Doug flashed Harry a glance.

Harry sighed noisily. 'But I have to be honest –' *liar, liar* '– I don't want to punch you. You're my friend. In my view what you've done isn't criminal so much as the actions of someone driven to the edge of reason. You've been through so much, Doug. Not being able to talk to anyone about your situation. Nobody knowing what you're going through. It must have been terrible.'

Doug shuffled further into the room.

Encouraged at Doug's response, Harry continued in the

same vein. 'What happened is a tragedy. I feel for you from the bottom of my heart. You've carried your burdens for so long, you must feel really tired.'

Doug was nodding. 'That's true. I am very tired.'

'Come,' said Harry. 'And sit with me.'

After Doug had settled on a chair, Harry brought another chair over so they sat together rather than across the table. He didn't look at Libby or give any indication that she was there.

'I'm sorry this has happened,' Harry said.

Doug nodded again.

'I hope you have the courage to talk with me about it. I'm your friend, remember?'

Liar!

Doug's body shuddered. 'I adored them. I loved them *so much*.'

'I know.'

'I wanted them to go to a better place. Not to have to suffer.'

'Not to have them suffer,' Harry echoed, wanting Doug to know he was listening and empathising. He realised that Doug saw himself as a victim of the tragedy and not a nasty little con man who duped people and shoved his father-in-law down the stairs.

'I did it for them. Everything.' His gaze turned distant. 'They were so happy on the beach, playing.'

'You planned that holiday specially,' Harry said. 'Giving them Daisy as well. You wanted them to be happy one last time.'

'Yes.' Doug finally met Harry's eyes.

With a chill, Harry saw Doug's eyes were as cold and emotionless as a pair of pebbles. Had they always been like that? Or was it only now he saw the murderer in Doug that he saw the real man?

Carefully, feeling as though he was stepping alongside an icy crevasse which he might tip into if he made a mistake, Harry talked with Doug. He learned he'd started his course at university but when he failed his first year he'd dropped out. Unable to bear his parents' disappointment, he pretended he'd excelled and continued going to the university, and that was the precise moment when the fork in the road showed itself to him and he realised how much easier it was to lie.

'I thought you'd got a first,' Harry said, unable to prevent his incredulity from showing and making Doug close in on himself.

Shit, Harry thought. He'd lost contact with Doug. Time to reconnect. 'Everyone thought you did,' he added, shaking his head as if in admiration. 'That was really clever of you. How on earth did you manage it?'

'Very few people actually check, you know. A couple of people mentioned my name wasn't on the lists but I said there was an administrative mistake and it was being rectified. Nobody said anything more.'

It was the same for his diplomas, apparently.

'Nobody asks to see them, and if they do...' Doug gave a self-conscious shrug which reminded Harry of the time when he'd expressed surprise at hearing that Doug was president of the congress.

I don't like making a big deal of it, he'd said. He'd then quickly turned the conversation to Harry, asking what his presentation was about and deflecting any further interest in the subject.

If anyone asked to see his diplomas or degree certificates, Harry guessed that Doug would change the subject and if it was a new client he'd simply make up an excuse not to take them on.

His parents had supported him through university and when he 'graduated', bought him a flat in Bath as well as a car. When his father fell ill, he made a lasting power of attorney, a written authorisation for Doug to represent him in all his private affairs, including finances. How they didn't smell a rat as their savings gradually disappeared Harry didn't know.

'Where did they think their money was going?'

'I told them I was investing it, and providing the money was left untouched, it would continue to multiply so they'd have a massive nest egg at the end of the day.'

Doug's aunt also 'invested', helping him buy his first house in Bloomfield Rise. Which was when he met Catherine through a mutual friend.

'When she asked me what I did,' Doug confessed, 'I told her I was a psychotherapist working out of Zurich. She was really impressed.'

'You've been to Zurich three times in fourteen years,' Harry said, trying to sound fascinated rather than appalled. 'How did you manage to carry off the subterfuge?'

There was no security on the University of Zurich campus gates. Doug simply walked inside and filled his briefcase with every free piece of paper he could find: brochures; campus maps; codes of practice; reviews; programmes. He printed his own letterheads and business cards using the university logo and littered his home and office with them.

'Where did you go if you didn't go to Zurich?'

'There's a little B&B I like in the Lake District. I go walking. I read a lot. Newspapers, magazines, psychotherapy journals. I learned French, a little Spanish.'

He went on to say that when he was in Bath, he'd come to the Wellbeing Centre, but when he was on a 'conference' in another city, he'd use it as a mini break, strolling around Edinburgh or Birmingham, enjoying cafés and museums. In the evenings he'd get room service and eat supper in his hotel room watching TV.

It was an extraordinary story of immense duplicity that dozens of people had fallen for and which left Harry feeling betrayed, appalled, and faintly sick.

'You don't have cancer, do you,' Harry stated.

'Sorry,' Doug mumbled.

'It was clever of you to say so,' Harry mused. 'Eliciting my sympathy while giving me a reason to give you space.'

And to explain any unusual behaviour Doug might be exhibiting.

They'd been talking easily, body language in synch, when Harry thought it was time to turn the talk to the website, the student assassins.

'You hired those thugs to beat me up so I couldn't go to the congress and find you out.'

Doug nodded. 'Sorry.'

'How did you find Clive Farmer and his pal?'

Doug bit his lip. Frowned as he thought.

'Was it through the website?'

His frown cleared. 'Yes.'

'Executor of Justice dot com?'

'Yes. They were only too happy to mete out justice to a paedophile.'

Harry had to force himself to keep his pulse level and not let Doug see his surge of anger.

Calm, calm.

Doug closed his eyes, his shoulders drooping.

Realising the man was now deeply tired, Harry went for the question that bothered him the most. Which was why Doug had wanted Nia Mitchell's partner, Richard Johnston, killed. Theo hadn't found a connection between them but Harry suspected it had something to do with Nia being a professor of psychology. Was it jealousy, perhaps? Harry thought he'd ask the question by coming in sideways, rather than head-on.

'Why was Nia Mitchell's partner, Richard Johnston, killed six months before the others?'

Silence.

'Doug, did you have help with the website?'

'What, you think I couldn't do something like that myself?' He drew himself up, obviously insulted.

Doug pushed back his chair and got to his feet.

He went and stood by the door, arms folded. He refused to say another word.

When Harry left, Doug met his gaze. It was like looking into the blank eyes of a shark.

63

When Harry checked his phone outside the police station, he saw he had half a dozen missed calls from Ethan. Not wanting to disturb his thoughts about his meeting with Doug, he made a mental note to call him back later. He was glad Libby didn't talk much on the journey home. He needed time to absorb what he'd learned.

As Libby turned the corner into Harry's road, she said, 'Shit.'

Cars were double-parked outside his driveway. There were white vans with satellite dishes on the roofs, and journalists talking among one another while sound men with big fluffy microphones hung around.

'Shall I go around the back?'

'No,' Harry said. 'I don't want them to know about the lane. We might need to use it.'

Libby eased past the queue but as soon as she turned into Harry's drive the journalists flocked around the car like noisy starlings, bright-eyed and avaricious.

'Dr Hope, how does it feel to be a hero?'

'What's it like having a monster as a friend?'

'Didn't you have some inkling he was lying?'

A flurry of camera flashes made Harry blink, at which point Libby buzzed down her window and shoved out her warrant card. 'Back off,' she said at the same time as she pressed the accelerator.

Journalists and cameramen parted to let them go but the second they climbed out of the car, they crowded on the driveway shouting questions, flashbulbs popping.

Harry and Libby strode towards the house. Harry slammed the door behind them, leaning against it as though he'd been chased by a dozen sword-wielding hoodlums from the Dark Ages.

'Christ,' he said.

'You swore!' Paton popped out of the sitting-room door, looking delighted.

'I only do it under immense duress.'

'Like Daddy.' She nodded sagely before turning to Libby. 'Who are you?'

'I'm Detective Sergeant Libby Harding.'

Paton frowned as she studied Libby's jeans-clad form. 'You don't look like a police officer.'

'That's because I've been undercover,' Libby whispered.

'What, like those men in *Spooks*?'

'Should you be watching stuff like that?' Libby looked shocked. 'It's really violent.'

'Daddy's got the boxed set.' Paton pulled a face. 'It's boring. It's for grown-ups.'

Jessie appeared, looking harried. 'Hey, Paton. Go and sit with Mia and Daisy, would you? I need to talk to Harry.'

'Okay.' Paton trotted off looking remarkably sanguine, which Harry knew was entirely normal. Young children needed to experience their grief in small doses, which was why the twins would feel sorrowful for a while and then they'd suddenly want to play.

'I'm sorry,' Harry said. He gave Jessie a hug.

'Can I have one too?' Libby said brightly.

Jessie laughed and hugged the police officer, who grinned at Harry over Jessie's shoulder.

'How was it?' Jessie asked.

'Bizarre,' Libby responded. 'But your boyfriend here was a complete genius. Got him to open up like you wouldn't believe.'

'That's good, right?' Jessie looked between them.

'It helps us understand a few things.' Harry was reticent. He needed more time to digest his session with Doug before he started talking about it. 'When did they get here?' He jerked his thumb behind him to indicate the media melee.

'They've been here all afternoon. It's been shit.' Her lips quivered.

'Oh, love.' Harry put his arm around her waist. 'I'm so sorry.'

'I'll survive,' she said bravely but he could tell the effort it took.

'How have the twins taken it?'

'They've been really scared. I drew all the curtains and blinds, which freaked them out even more, but I didn't want them photographed. I've been playing with them, distracting them, which has helped, but every time one of them knocks on the door or shouts something, we all jump and I can't help it that I feel unnerved as well.'

'I'll get a patrol car to sit outside,' Libby said. 'Keep them off you when I'm gone.'

It wasn't ideal. Harry wanted the twins to be enjoying the garden, playing hide and seek with the puppy and feeling as normal as possible in what was a horrendously abnormal situation, but he guessed it was the next-best thing. When a journalist began calling through the letterbox that his newspaper would give six figures for an exclusive, Libby yanked the door open and told him to *back off or I'll arrest your arse for harassing minors.*

Everything fell quiet.

'Come and have a coffee,' he told Libby.

'You're making it, right?' Libby looked at Jessie, who nodded. 'Great. I'll have a coffee.'

'Are you saying I make crap coffee?' Harry asked.

'Don't feel insulted,' Libby told him. 'Your coffee's fine, it's just that Aussies make it so much better.'

Which made Jessie smile, which in turn made Harry feel a bit better. Thank God she could smile. He felt as if he might not smile for months. Listening to Doug had taken more out of him than he'd bargained for. It made him question his ability as a psychotherapist. It had, he realised, shaken his professional foundations to their core. How could he have been deceived for so long? What about other clients of his; had they misled him too?

He went and sat with the twins while Libby and Jessie chatted in the kitchen. They'd been playing with Lego, building one of Tim's old pterodactyls, but when he went into the sitting room and sat on the sofa, they came and sat with him. They all looked at Daisy, who was happily chewing on a piece of dinosaur.

'Where's Daddy?' Mia asked. 'Will he be coming here soon?'

Harry felt waves of exhaustion wash over him but he knew he couldn't ignore this opportunity to broach the subject of their father.

'Daddy won't be coming here because he's in prison. He's talking to the police. But Jessie and I are here and we're going to make an extra special supper just for you guys.'

'What kind of supper?' said Mia at the same time as Paton said, 'Why is he talking to the police?'

'He's helping them with their inquiries into the fire at the cottage in Wales. We're having pesto spaghetti because we know you love it.'

'It's my favourite.' Mia beamed but although Paton was slower to respond he was glad she also took up the refrain.

Slowly, between assuring them their need for protection would be taken care of, Harry made them aware that Doug wasn't coming home any time soon.

'Like when he's in Zurich?' Mia said. 'He's away for ages then.'

'It's longer than that, but yes, it's similar.'

After a while, the twins returned to play with Daisy. He'd dropped into a light doze when someone began banging on the front door and shouting, 'Harry, let me in, will you? It's like swimming with fucking piranhas out here!'

Harry opened the door to Ethan who fell inside like a drowning man reaching the shore. He was pale, his hair sticking up oddly and his eyes were wild.

'What's wrong?' Harry asked.

'I nearly killed her,' he gasped. 'I very nearly killed her.'

64

'Killed who?' Harry asked.

Ethan ran his hands through his hair. 'Christ almighty. I had no idea. Absolutely none. I lost it when she told me.'

'Told you what?'

Ethan opened his mouth, then shut it again, biting his lips. 'I've thrown them all out. Wren, Cabe and Filipa.'

Harry watched him carefully.

'They all *knew*. I feel so...' His voice trailed off and he balled his fist, making a sharp, angry gesture that indicated he felt like punching someone.

'You're upset,' Harry stated.

'Of course I'm fucking upset!'

'Shhh.' Harry pointed down the hallway. 'We've kids here, remember.'

Immediately, Ethan was shamefaced. 'Sorry.'

'Look, this isn't a great time as I'm sure you can understand. I'll be only too happy to see you and talk about what's upsetting you, but not today. You might have noticed the media circus out there?'

At that, the anger left Ethan's body. 'God, I'm sorry. You must think me a selfish shit…' He trailed off as he looked at something past Harry's shoulder. 'Hello there.'

Harry turned to see Mia peeping around the sitting-room door.

'Mia, isn't it?' Ethan asked.

She smiled shyly. 'You're Ethan something Jones.'

'Stanning Jones. Yes, that's me.' He smiled and Mia came over.

'Would you like some Ribena?' she asked.

Ethan looked at Harry over Mia's shoulder. Harry nodded.

'I'd love some.'

Harry followed them into the kitchen where Libby was watching Jessie washing up their coffee cups. It was the one room that didn't have any blinds or curtains and it felt good to be in natural light after being beneath electric lighting everywhere else. How the hell they were going to cope with the media camped on their doorstep indefinitely he didn't know, but cope they would.

Ethan was halfway through his glass of Ribena when he pulled out his phone, answered a call. 'I don't want to talk, okay?' he snapped. 'Ever. Again. So you can fu–' He swallowed the swear word as Mia jerked her head around and hurriedly amended it. 'Go away and leave me alone. I'm going to block you now, so when you call again…'

Harry didn't think he'd ever seen anyone lose colour so fast. He moved swiftly to Ethan's side, thinking to make him sit down but Ethan backed off. His mouth was open in horror. 'No,' he said. 'No, Filipa. No, I didn't mean it like that. No, absolutely not. Please, no, stop…'

He pulled the phone away from his ear, glanced at it, then dialled. 'Shit, *shit*.' His eyes were wild. 'She's not answering.'

Libby, Jessie, Mia and Harry were watching him, transfixed.

He looked back, his mouth working in distress.

'She's threatening to...' He suddenly looked at Mia and managed to stop himself mid-track.

'I've got to go.' He strode out of the kitchen.

Harry strode after him. 'What's she threatening to do?'

'She's taken a whole loads of pills.' Ethan was frantically digging in his pocket, looking for his car key. 'I could hear she was running a bath... She's going to *open her veins*, is how she put it.'

'Where is she?'

'Back at home. Combe House. She broke in after I kicked her out. She was crying. She never cries.'

Harry took hold of Ethan's arm. 'I'm coming too. But we can't go out the front. We have to go out the back.'

'But my car's at the front.'

'We'll use Jessie's. She parked it along the lane, in case we needed a getaway.'

Together they returned to the kitchen where Libby, Jessie and Mia were watching them curiously. 'I've got to go and help Ethan's sister,' Harry told them. 'I'll use your car, Jessie. I'll be back soon, Okay?'

Then they were outside, and jogging across the garden to Harry's back gate. Jessie's car was a six-year-old Mini Hatch with Crunchie bar wrappers in the central console and lots of dried mud in the footwells. Harry drove fast down the weed-filled lane, the little car bravely bouncing over potholes.

'Talk to me,' Harry said.

'It was you. What you said. It made me look at me and her.'

Harry accelerated down the hill, grasses and untrimmed shrubs brushing the paintwork on either side.

'I told her that although I loved her, sometimes I didn't like her very much. I told her I didn't like her lying about me for fun. That I hated it when she brought men and women home, banning us from the house while she did God knows what with them. I told her I hated the way she'd kept her rape a secret from Mum and Dad and that I didn't want to keep the secret any more. That I was going to tell Mum and Dad, and then I was going to move out and find a place of my own. Without her.'

Bloody hell, Harry thought. Talk about a shitstorm of self-realisation.

'We then had a huge row. She screamed at me and I yelled back. And then she said something so awful...'

Harry hustled the Mini through Batheaston and along London Road. The rush hour traffic was, luckily, going the other way and they were making good time.

'I nearly killed her.' His voice was filled with wonder. 'But I didn't. I slapped her, though. Really hard. I threw all her stuff outside and bolted the doors. She's so upset, she's going to kill herself.'

They were skirting the bus station and heading towards Wellsway.

'What about your housemates?' Harry asked. 'Why did you throw them out too?'

Ethan made a groaning sound and leaned his head back, against the headrest. Harry risked a quick glance across to see he had his eyes scrunched closed.

'They all lied to me.'

65

'What did they lie about?' Harry asked, but Ethan had turned his head to the window and refused to answer.

As Harry drove swiftly up Bloomfield Road he thought of Doug's house on the Rise, no doubt taped up as a crime scene, and then they were sweeping along Englishcombe Lane and diving left onto the unnamed road, plunging into the other-worldliness of the woods and through the Combe House gates.

Just one car on the gravel. Filipa's bright red Mazda sports car.

Ethan ran for the door, Harry hot on his heels.

They had to navigate the explosion of clothes, books, boots and shoes that lay on the steps. Two suitcases lay on their sides, their contents spilling out. Harry saw a make-up bag and a shattered bottle of shampoo. Ethan meant what he'd said when he'd thrown his sister out.

The door was locked. Ethan fumbled for his key, put it in the lock and turned, pushing the door wide. He tore inside, shouting his sister's name. 'Filipa!'

He was barely halfway across the hallway when Filipa appeared. She wore faded jeans and a silk shirt the colour of raspberries. Her feet were bare, her hair loose around her shoulders. She was holding a bottle of champagne. Her right cheek blazed vivid red from where, Harry guessed, Ethan had struck her.

She stared in astonishment at Harry. 'What the fuck are you doing here?'

And why aren't you sitting in the bath, slitting your wrists? he thought, but right then, as Harry looked at her, her exquisite face and huge expressive eyes, he knew.

'What's the champagne for?' he asked.

'Ethan, of course. And me, because I have some fantastic news.'

Ethan's mouth was opening and closing. He looked stunned.

'Come see what I've been doing.' Filipa took Harry's hand in her own, cool and slender, and was about to lead him towards the stairs but he withdrew his grip. He ignored her pout.

'What do you want to show me?' He kept his tone stiff.

Putting the champagne down on the hall table she walked ahead of them and up the stairs into a room with gold-flecked wallpaper and a view over the front drive. Paper was everywhere. Great drifts of it. Notes, printed pages, charts and graphs surrounded an iMac. She swept her hand to encompass the room.

'All my own work.'

Harry glanced at Ethan, who simply stood there, hands at his sides, looking shell-shocked. Harry wasn't surprised. Ethan had expected to find his sister's corpse in a bath filled with watery blood and here she was, not just vibrantly alive, but in an ebullient and celebratory mood.

Filipa laughed. 'I've just signed a book deal for two point three million pounds.'

This seemed to pierce Ethan's consciousness. 'What?'

'My literary agent did the deal.'

'How long have you had one of those?' His stare was fixed on his sister, disbelieving.

'She's also sold the film rights for another million,' Filipa squealed. 'Now you can see why I had the bubbly.'

Even Harry stared. 'How come?'

'I'm writing Douglas King's story.'

For a light-headed second, Harry wondered if he'd heard correctly.

'Before he went to Wales, your friend Doug gave me his computer.'

Harry wanted to say Doug wasn't his friend, that the computer should be with the police, but kept his mouth shut.

She looked at him from beneath her lashes. 'He didn't tell me his plans for his poor family or of course I would have done something to stop him.'

Liar.

'He begged me to write his story. I didn't know why it was so important to him until I found his website. It's called Executor of Justice.'

Wanting to see where things led, Harry kept quiet as she brought the website up on her computer screen and led them through its layers, explaining how it worked.

Ethan's skin turned waxy as she talked. He didn't say anything. He looked too shocked.

'Douglas King is an exceptionally sick and twisted individual,' Filipa said. 'The public are going to love this story. They'll lap it up. It'll be on the front pages for weeks. I'll be doing author tours, talking on radio, TV. I'll be on *The One Show*! I love *The One Show*! I'll be famous at last. I'll be on the red carpet in Hollywood...'

She beamed.

'I'm going to become the expert on Doug King's kind of psychosis and everyone will want my opinion. I'll even make

Professor Nia Mitchell sit up and take notice. She'll have to eat her words now.'

Filipa's expression tightened. 'Finally, she'll see me as an equal, that I can be as brilliant as her, and she'll invite me into her house and we'll drink wine in her garden and she'll let me fuck her. She is so fuckable, that woman.'

'She rejected you.' The words were out before Harry had the chance to think and as he spoke, he had a rush of realisation that came from the back of his mind, powering like a speeding train down a tunnel, roaring, shrieking, until it exploded into his consciousness, and as he looked at Filipa he knew that she'd seen him make the connection.

'It must have been hard,' he said quietly. 'Having a crush on your tutor. Especially since she wasn't interested. She was in love with Rick.'

Her eyes darkened and in that second, Harry smelled danger, hard and bright as steel.

'She didn't realise what a jerk he was,' Filipa said contemptuously. 'So up himself, eco blah-blah, save the fucking planet. It was because of him she stopped having me round. We would have been together if it hadn't been for him.'

Harry held her eyes as he said, 'Who killed Rick?'

She considered him at length. Then she leaned over and tapped on the computer keyboard. Harry moved to view the screen to see she'd just sent a text, but before he could read who it was to, she'd brought up the video, instantly distracting him. Being on a large screen with a higher resolution, the film sprang at him, much clearer and brighter than he remembered.

Harry watched the video and studied the figure striding towards the ladder. Jeans, hoody. Same width of shoulders.

Briefly, he closed his eyes.

'It's Doug.'

66

F ilipa squinted at the picture. 'Don't be ridiculous. You can't possibly identify who it is.'

'It's Doug. You filmed it. You created the website, using this as the first video to encourage others. You *got away with it*. You told others they could too.'

Ethan made a strangled sound at the back of his throat but Harry didn't look at him.

'You met Doug at Lorraine's creative writing class. You struck up a... friendship.'

Filipa's head was on one side. She was totally focused on him.

'You wanted Rick gone. Doug wanted...'

She raised her eyebrows.

'He wanted everyone he'd stolen money from killed.' Harry took a breath. 'He thought if they were gone, he could keep going, keep his secret safe. But it was too late.'

Harry thought further.

'He knew things were coming to a head, didn't he? With Vince wanting his money for his cruise-ship apartment, his parents going into care, Doug had his back against the wall. He was buying time, wasn't he?'

Filipa's eyes widened fractionally. He took that to mean he was on the right track.

'Did he give you a list? Tell you who he wanted killed? And when the time was right, in return, you could write your book?'

Long silence.

'You were a team.'

Harry's words dropped like stones.

'You can't prove anything.' She was dismissive. 'It'll be your word against mine. There's absolutely no evidence.'

Harry could hardly breathe as he began to get the measure of her.

She wasn't damaged. She wasn't psychologically wounded. She was exactly who she was. A supremely confident, manipulative and unscrupulous young woman.

'Ethan found out you'd lied, didn't he?'

She gave a careless shrug, but he could see she was nettled by the way her eyes flickered between him and her brother.

'Lied?' she said.

'You were never raped, were you,' Harry stated. It wasn't a question. 'You made it up for the attention. The drama. To keep your big brother in your control, looking after you, protecting you.'

Ethan stared at Harry, stunned. 'How the hell did you know that?' Then he swung to Filipa. His colour went from pale to a furious red. 'Did you tell him too? Did you tell *everyone but me*?'

'No,' Harry quickly interjected. 'She didn't tell me. I made a guess, that's all.'

It had been the sly way she'd said the word *rape*, he realised, that had alerted him. There had been something salacious and sensual about it, not an attitude a rape victim would necessarily assume.

'Well, clever old Dr Hope,' Filipa purred. She stepped so close he could smell her perfume; wild musk and rose. 'Let's put you at the top of the class.'

Ethan's words trailed through Harry's mind. *She's never been quite right since, a bit off the wall, a bit crazy. She does weird things. She says she can't help it. She changed that day. Irrevocably.*

'You used your supposed rape to cover your true personality.'

'Which is?' Now she was openly curious, her mouth slightly parted, her aqua eyes gleaming.

But Harry wasn't going to get drawn into that particular chasm of darkness. 'I don't make off-the-cuff diagnoses.'

'Oh, come on.' She twirled coquettishly around in a circle. 'Aren't you going to say something along the lines that I'm enacting a false self to avoid experiencing the pain and hurt of my childhood?'

'Hey,' Ethan interjected. 'There was nothing wrong with our childhood.'

Filipa sent him a cutting look.

'Except for the normal hang-ups, of course,' Ethan muttered. 'Dad not being there much, then Mum's career taking off. Jesus, Filipa. Did you really create that website?'

She shrugged.

Another thought obviously crashed into Ethan's mind because suddenly, he stepped right up to his sister, towering over her.

'What about me? Did you send me that text? To get me to kill Harry?'

'What if I did?' Her tone was edged with defiance.

Ethan bunched his fists, rage on his face. 'You *bitch*. I wish you'd run that bath and slit your wrists.'

He strode outside. Harry listened to his footsteps on the stairs, the front door slamming.

67

H arry said calmly, 'I'll go after him. Calm him down.'
'He'll be fine.' She was unconcerned. 'He's like a boomerang. He always comes back.'

I doubt it, this time.

'Still, he's had some shocks.' Harry began to back away. Cautiously, as though he was distancing himself from that tigress he imagined three days ago.

'You do realise,' Filipa said conversationally, 'that if you say a word about this, I will go after your pretty little Jessie.'

She meant it, he saw, and at the same time he realised he would do anything to protect Jessie. Psychotherapist or not, he was still a man who would pretty much do anything to defend those he loved.

'You touch her,' he said in the same conversational tone she'd used with him, 'and I will kill you.'

Filipa blinked. 'Really?'

'Yes.'

Her eyes widened. Good, he thought. She knew he meant it.

Keeping her within his vision, Harry made for the door. He expected her to try to stop him, to talk further, but she'd moved to the window. She was looking outside. She put her hand on the glass, then gave a thumbs-up.

Harry didn't wait to see who'd arrived. He was jogging downstairs. He had Jessie's car keys in his hand as he approached the front door. His heart was thumping. He put his hand on the door handle at the same time as someone turned it from the other side.

Harry sprang back as the door swung in.

The instant he saw the large figure, the baseball bat swinging at his side, Harry turned and ran.

He raced across the hall and down the corridor, past the kitchen to the back door. He yanked it open and dived outside. At the same time something large, *huge*, was rushing at him and then it hit him and he tried to fight it off but something punched him very hard on the side of the head. Harry felt a falling sensation engulf him, as if he'd been thrown off the top of a building in the dead of night, making his stomach swoop with nausea and his vision shatter.

He felt himself hit the ground and his ribs exploded in shards of white-hot glass. He wanted to get up but the pain billowed from his core, engulfing him into silence.

When he came around he was sprawled half on, half off the back seat of a car. Pain bloomed through his body and he thought dully: *here we go again.*

He could hear himself uttering a sickening groan each time he tried to breathe in and for a moment he wondered why the hell he bothered trying to help others when he simply ended up getting trashed.

Get up, he told himself. *No point lying around feeling sorry for yourself.*

Belatedly, he realised his hands were tied with rope but the good news was that they'd been bound in front of him. With inordinate care, Harry levered himself upright. Sat there, head hanging, until he felt a semblance of control against the roaring pain pulsing in his head, his ribs.

To his immense relief, he saw they were parked outside Combe House. The engine was running. Harry looked at the wide-shouldered man in the driver's seat and almost wished he hadn't.

Clive Farmer.

68

Harry could taste blood in his mouth and when he gently probed with his tongue, counted two gaps where there shouldn't have been any.

Harry saw Filipa striding for the car, a strapping man just behind her. He was tossing a baseball bat from hand to hand.

As she approached, Clive Farmer buzzed down his window.

'Your son,' said Filipa, obviously infuriated, 'says he won't kill him.'

'We don't go around killing people,' Clive Farmer said. 'We threaten them. Don't we, Andy?'

'Yeah.'

Andy. Filipa's bit of rough who'd been on the staircase when Harry turned up. He hadn't seen his features at the time thanks to the sunlight pouring through the windows behind the man.

Well, that's part of the puzzle solved, Harry thought muzzily. He bet Doug asked Filipa how to stop Harry from going to the convention in London and finding him out. And, hallelujah, she just happened to know a tame thug or two who happened to hate paedophiles. Had Filipa shown Clive and Andy the website? Encouraged them to bid the one hundred pounds to bring supposed justice to Harry? It made sense considering Clive Farmer's wife had shown Harry the same doctored photographs that had been on that very site.

'Hasn't he got a family we can frighten?' Clive Farmer asked. 'Wife and kids?'

'You can forget it. He's not the type to give in. He'll promise the world while we're around but the moment we let him go, he'll head straight for his cop friend, and we're in the shit.'

Got it in one, Harry thought. *I want to see you hung from the highest fucking rooftop and left to dangle.*

'Cop friend?' Farmer twisted in his seat to look at Harry. 'What cop friend?'

'DI Theo McCannon,' Filipa told him.

'He's a fucking *friend* of yours?'

Harry shook his head then wished he hadn't. A ringing sound started up in his head, pealing in time with his pulse. For a moment the pain was so acute he thought he might be sick.

'Shit,' said Andy.

Filipa put her hands on her hips. 'If you dispose of him, you'll get half a million quid. If you don't, you'll go to jail.'

Trying not to attract their attention, Harry moved inch by inch towards the door. He didn't think he'd get far in his state, but dammit, he had to *try*.

'Half a million?' Clive Farmer repeated. 'For real?'

'Two hundred and fifty grand to you, two fifty to Andy.'

'Shit.'

'Money to burn, or jail. Your choice.'

Small silence.

'We can't do it here,' Farmer said.

'Wales?' suggested Andy, still hefting his bat. 'Loads of bogs there to swallow up a body.'

Harry twisted slowly and put his fingers around the door handle.

'I know someone with a boat,' said Farmer. 'We wait until night, wrap him in chains with a sodding great weight attached and chuck him overboard.'

'I don't care how you do it,' Filipa snapped. 'Just *do it*.'

Harry pulled the door handle gently, pushing the door with his shoulder but it was locked. He'd always thought child safety locks were a brilliant invention, but not today.

'Okay, love,' said Andy testily. 'Keep your hair on.'

'Sorry.' She raised a hand to her temples. 'I'm just so stressed at the moment. Forgive me.' She offered a trembling smile to Andy, who appeared to melt.

'Don't worry, babe.' He scooped her close, kissing her on the lips. 'We'll sort him, okay? And then we can go and have fun.'

'Fun.' Her eyes danced. 'Now we're talking.'

Infinitesimally slowly, Harry eased himself down on the seat. Closed his eyes. Let his head droop.

'Okay,' said Farmer briskly. 'Let's go.'

Harry heard feet crunching on the gravel and then he heard the rear passenger door open. Fresh air drifted over his face. He kept his muscles relaxed and his eyes closed.

'He's out cold.' Andy sounded surprised.

'You hit him hard enough.'

'Yeah,' Andy said with relish. 'Fucking hard.'

Harry felt fingers on his neck, checking for a pulse.

'Not dead yet, though.'

'Get the dust sheet out the back. Cover him up.'

Harry heard the boot pop and then felt the dust sheet settle over him. The door slammed shut. He listened to Andy settling in the front passenger seat.

The car slipped into gear and Farmer began to drive.

69

'What are you going to do with your share?' Farmer asked.

'Buy a fuck-off house with a pool.'

'Like, where?'

'Spain.'

Exquisitely slowly, Harry began to edge himself into position.

'Who do you know with a boat?' Andy asked.

'Frank Jones.'

'Frank as in Furnace Frank, in Swansea?'

'That's the one.'

'Then why aren't we heading for the M4?'

'We are.' Clive sounded irritated. 'But there's a sodding jam on the A36. Look at it. Red all the way. Google's got me cutting over the bridge and going up via the racecourse.'

'Nice one.'

Harry knew he'd only get one chance with this, and that he had to make every move he made work. He didn't want to die, have his body buried at sea, his flesh eaten by fish, eels to slither through his eye sockets. He couldn't bear the thought of Jessie having to suffer his disappearance. Not knowing where he'd gone. Then finding another man. Because she would; she was too gorgeous to be on her own for long. He wanted to be her man. For ever. Full stop.

He was aware he was drifting. Andy had indeed hit him hard on the head. He had concussion, for sure.

Concentrate, he told himself sternly. Rehearse your moves. Just three moves to make but they have to be smooth, and they have to be perfect.

'What sort of boat does Frank have?'

'A big one.'

'D'you fancy buying a boat with your share?'

'Waste of money.' Clive grunted. 'Just sits there, gathering bird shit.'

'I'd like a boat,' Andy said wistfully.

'More fool you.'

'Perhaps Filipa–'

Andy never finished his sentence because Harry erupted from the back seat. Gritting his teeth, he tossed back the dust sheet and went for the driver. Clive Farmer.

Three moves.

One: he pushed himself upright and along the seat so he was behind the driver.

'What the...'

The shock of Harry's sudden appearance resulted in a wild swerve across the road.

Two: he rose and brought his bound hands over Clive Farmer's head.

'You fucking...!' Andy yelled.

Three: he yanked his bound hands backwards and into Clive Farmer's throat.

Andy had twisted round and was yelling at Harry.

Clive Farmer pulled at Harry's hands. He was shouting frantically, 'Get him off me!'

Harry yanked his hands harder. Jerked rhythmically with all his strength. Clive Farmer stopped shouting. Started making strangling sounds. Harry felt something give as he kept wrenching, but he didn't relent.

The car was careering erratically. Horns blared.

Andy picked up his bat and tried to bash Harry's hands but there wasn't enough room to manoeuvre. He launched himself over the central console and belted Harry's hands, but Harry didn't stop hauling Clive Farmer's head back towards him.

'Brake!' Andy suddenly screamed. 'Dad! Brake!'

Harry felt the car surge forward and realised Clive Farmer had missed the brake and shoved his foot on the accelerator.

A truck horn blew, filling the air.

Rubber screeched.

The horn continued to bellow.

Harry glanced up. He saw Windsor Bridge. They were on the wrong side of the road. A truck bore down on them. They were about to get pulverised.

Harry let go of Clive Farmer and ducked behind the driver's seat, closing his eyes.

A huge bang. An immense sound of tearing metal filled Harry's head.

The car swung wildly sideways.

Second car crash in less than a week, he thought idly. Harry put his arms over his head.

Another huge bang and the car leaped into the air.

For a second, nothing happened.

They were, Harry realised, falling.

Then they hit the river.

70

The car slammed onto the water, throwing Harry to the roof before flinging him into one of the doors. Andy Farmer tumbled around but Clive Farmer was wearing his seat belt and stayed put.

Brown water immediately began squirting through cracks in the doors and windows. The car's bonnet dipped as it started to sink, heavy end first.

They had seconds to get out.

'Open the windows!' Harry yelled.

The car's bonnet dipped further. They were going down.

To his horror, Harry saw the waterline had risen past the front windows and was about to engulf his own.

'Won't open!' Clive Farmer hollered.

'Open the doors!' Harry shouted. 'Or we're going to drown!'

A clunk. Harry tried to open his door but the water pressure was too great against him.

Harry punched the side of his fists against a side window to no effect. He twisted and used his feet but the glass held.

Clive and Andy Farmer were yelling as the car rolled.

The car was filling up with water much faster than Harry

expected. It was dark and he was disorientated. He couldn't tell which way was up. Panic rose.

Keep calm, he told himself. *If you succumb to panic, you'll never get out.*

All he knew was that he had to break a window and *get out.*

His hands were still bound, but he wasn't going to let that stop him. He pulled out the head restraint in front of him. Twisted around and pounded the metal struts against the rear window thinking that if he succeeded, at least it was bigger and easier to get out of. He kept bashing.

It cracked. He kept hitting it. Another crack appeared. Water dribbled through.

Suddenly, the car shifted position. Clive and Andy Farmer screamed as water rose up their bodies.

Harry kept bashing the rear window and suddenly a hole appeared. Icy water poured inside. Another belting and Harry was hit with a flood of water.

He punched and punched again, widening the hole. He felt glass tear his skin but he didn't stop.

If I get out, I'm going to ask Jessie to move in with me. Marry me. Go to France with me. Timbuktu. Wherever.

The car rolled violently to one side. Harry braced his feet against the front seats. Belted the rear window some more. It finally crumpled. Harry took a huge lungful of air and pushed the glass aside, forcing himself up and through the water, wriggling and thrusting himself through the window double-handed, feet lashing out.

A final kick and he was free. Which way was up? It was murky, no obvious light to head for. Desperately he looked at the bubbles. Pushed off the car and followed the direction they were going. How deep was the river? He had no idea.

The next second, he popped into the air.

Gasping and coughing, he trod water. Unable to use his arms it took a huge effort to stay afloat. Frantically he looked around.

The surface of the river was churning behind him. Bubbles rose, breaking on the surface.

The cab of a lorry hung over the crumpled metal railing on the bridge. A crowd of people gazed down, mouths open, eyes wide.

Harry kept kicking hard, keeping his head above water. He was opening his mouth to yell for help when a man called down from the bridge.

'Is there anyone else down there?'

'Yes.' Harry tried to shout but his voice was hoarse and didn't carry, so he flippered his feet to raise his hands, sticking up his thumbs to indicate *yes*.

The man stripped down to his underwear, climbed over the railings and jumped. Began to swim for the roiling area. Another man stripped and jumped in too.

To Harry's relief, the second man swam hard and fast, straight for him.

71

The man reached Harry in seconds. Thirties, serious expression.

'Your hands are tied.'

'Yes.'

He had a quick look. 'Can't untie them, sorry. Rest on me.'

'You're kind.'

Glad the man didn't ask any questions he put his bound hands gratefully on the man's shoulders. It was a relief not to have to tread water any more.

The man began to swim for the shore, but although Harry tried to cling on, his hands kept slipping.

'Mind if I tow you?' the man asked.

'No.'

'I'm Mark, by the way.'

'Harry.'

Moving so he was behind Harry, Mark put an arm around and over Harry's shoulder, grasping him under his opposite armpit.

'Buddy tow method,' Mark told him. 'All you have to do is relax.'

The kindness of strangers, Harry thought.

Mark pulled Harry to the river bank, but it wasn't a bank at all. It was a ten-foot-high wall of concrete on both sides, which had sheer edges and no hand holds. It appeared to go on for ever. He'd walked along the riverside path several times and couldn't remember if there were any rungs or steps to lead one in or out of the water.

'Here! I'll help get you out!'

Harry craned his head up to see a crowd of people looking anxiously down at them. A young man was on the ground, on his stomach, trying to reach them, but they were too far away.

'Find us some rungs!' Mark yelled. 'Quick!'

Immediately there was a flurry and people started jabbering. Several began running along the riverbank – some going west, others east – pausing every so often to peer over the edge before jogging on.

Cold had seeped into Harry's marrow and he started to shiver.

'It won't be long,' Mark said. 'We'll have you in the warm with a hot drink soon.'

Eventually a shout came from upriver.

'They've found somewhere for us to get out,' said Mark.

'Great,' Harry managed.

It felt as though hours were passing as Mark pulled Harry through the water, rather than minutes. When they came to a set of steps, several people came to help. Harry felt their hands and arms holding him. When their skin touched his, they felt incredibly warm. Their voices swirled around him, concerned.

'His hands are tied.'

'They're bleeding.'

'Who's got something to cut him free?'

'We've got to get him somewhere warm.'

He didn't see who cut through his bonds. He tried to say

thank you, but he had no strength. The crowd virtually carried him up to street level and to the nearest road.

'What's your name?'

'What on earth happened?'

'How many were in the car with you?'

Harry couldn't respond. He felt dazed and numb, but even through his exhaustion there was an immense gratitude that he was alive. That he wasn't still in the car with his stomach and lungs full of river water. He saw several people filming him on their phones but had no energy to protest.

He was surprised to see an ambulance on the roadside, rear doors open. Paramedics came over and after a brief inspection, gently helped him on board.

'Shortest trip I've ever had,' one of them said as they helped him into A&E. 'Three minutes exactly. Wish more were like that.'

'Can I...' Harry struggled to speak. 'Use your phone?'

'I'm sorry, but it's not something–'

'I need to call the... police. Stop a criminal from... getting away.'

'Put like that,' the medic said, 'how can I refuse?'

Harry called Theo. He strove to make sense, finishing by repeating, 'Get Filipa. Just get her and her computer.'

72

Harry spent two days in hospital thanks to his concussion, and when he was eventually discharged, he still wasn't right. His ears continued to ring and he was dogged by headaches.

'Post-concussion syndrome,' the doctor told him briskly. 'See your GP if you still have symptoms after three months.'

Harry had never been so pleased to be at home. Paton and Mia were quiet and solicitous – they'd been given strict instructions by Jessie – and they'd come and snuggle up with him on the sofa from time to time, saying, 'Hugs make you better.'

He couldn't agree more.

Aside from a trip to the dentist to assess replacing his two missing teeth, knocked out by Andy, Harry conducted his life over the next week from the comfort and security of his sofa. He invited his rescuer, Mark, around for a beer to say thanks, which turned into a happy consultation with Jessie about the best surf beaches in Sydney since he was going there in a couple of months.

Harry watched movies. Read a bit. Listened to music and a selection of podcasts. In between, he talked to people who visited. Jessie and Theo, Ethan, Jagoda, Angela Petty, Nicole and Dave.

He learned that the first man who'd stripped and dived off Windsor Bridge for the submerged car had managed to haul Andy Farmer to safety through the rear window, but not his father, who'd drowned after getting tangled in his seat belt.

Harry felt no remorse for what he'd done. Clive Farmer had been going to kill him. Dump his body at sea. Harry had done what he had to do in order to survive.

Andy Farmer had been hospitalised briefly, and was now in police custody.

When Theo and his team turned up at Combe House, barely an hour after Harry had made the call, they found Filipa sipping champagne in the garden with Cabe and Wren. Despite the quantity of film footage caught on people's phones, none of them had the slightest clue about the drama unfolding less than two miles away. They'd been too busy celebrating Filipa's good fortune.

With Doug's computer and Harry's statement, Theo had enough to arrest Filipa but what clinched her not getting bail was that Andy Farmer decided to do a deal and turn witness against her. Mrs Farmer, his mother, went public with the story, earning a fat fee from one of the tabloids, the sum of which made Harry's eyes water.

The public loved the salacious story of the beautiful, privileged student and her BDSM predilections. Photographs of Filipa's stunning face and body graced the front pages every day and would, Harry predicted, for weeks to come.

Filipa was famous at last, just not in the way she'd expected.

The students who'd been involved in the knifings were rounded up, thanks to the police having Doug's computer. They were arrested, the three who'd thrown Lorraine into the canal charged with her murder.

Phil Petty came out of his coma. His wife, Angela, told Harry that he'd agreed to be a witness for the CPS.

'He fell for Hugh's... I mean Doug King's patter.' Some colour had returned to Angela's face, Harry was pleased to see, and she had started to smile again. 'He sucked us in by giving us fabulous returns on our money to start with, then telling us to leave it with him for longer so we'd get even better returns.

'It makes us sound greedy, doesn't it? But it seemed so easy, leaving it all to someone we trusted. It was only when we decided we wanted to help our son buy a house that it all came unravelled. Phil wanted his money and Doug kept putting it off until Phil, who was getting pretty angry by then, asked if he treated *you* like that.'

Jagoda told Harry that the police had given the go-ahead to the Centre to reopen. She went on to say that Kevin Owen's wife Susanna had separated from her judo instructor husband, and when he threatened her physically, enraged at what he perceived to be her 'unwarranted expectations of a marriage', took out a restraining order against him and had him thrown out of the house.

'She is more calm,' Jagoda said. 'Still jumpy, yes. But her eyes, you know? She never looked at me before. Always too scared. She is very pretty. I never saw it before.'

Susanna had dropped into the Centre to give Jagoda the latest Booker Prize winning novel, which she wanted Harry to have. *To help with the boredom*, apparently.

But Harry wasn't bored because between his visitors, he was taken up with what he should do next. When he was better, of course. Because after what had happened, how could he possibly continue as a psychotherapist?

73

When Nicole and Dave came to see him, Harry was deep into researching a new car. He very much liked the look of the Volvo XC60 but not necessarily the price tag. When Jessie led them into the sitting room he looked up from his laptop, surprised to see them both.

Nicole read his expression. Her face was grim. 'You've got it right,' she told him. 'I strong-armed him to come here.' She sent Dave a fierce look. 'Tell him.'

Dave bit his lip, looking sheepish. 'I told Doug where you were staying that night. At Lorne House.'

Harry was floored. 'Why?'

'I'd invested some money with him. Ages back. He didn't approach me as Hugh Lamont, though, because I knew him as your friend, Doug. I thought he wanted to discuss it.'

Harry stared. Who else had Doug lured into giving him money? Would it ever stop?

'When he rang, he sounded frantic. He wanted to know where you were. You weren't answering your phone and he was desperate to track you down because one of your patients was threatening suicide... I insisted I couldn't say, that it was a secret, but he was a *friend of yours*.'

'I said don't tell *anyone*,' Nicole spat. 'What part of *anyone* didn't you understand?'

Dave held up his hands. 'Guilty as charged, but seriously–'

'I don't think I can forgive you,' she said tightly. 'Let alone trust you again.'

'Nicole.' Harry was gentle. 'You can understand why Dave told him. He thought someone's life was in danger.'

'You nearly *died*!' Suddenly she was close to tears. 'And it was Dave's fault!'

'It was Doug's fault,' Harry pointed out. 'He was the one who cut my brakes.'

Nicole pressed her lips tightly together.

'You did me a favour,' Harry told Dave. 'I needed a new car, and this is what I'm thinking of getting.' He spun the laptop around so Dave could see the screen.

Dave's face lit up. 'Hey, good choice. Wasn't it World Car of the Year not so long ago?'

'Yes, but it's bloody pricey.'

'What about the Mazda CX-5? It's a cracking family SUV and there's loads of second-hand ones around. Great value.'

Nicole rolled her eyes. 'Men,' she said. She sounded as though she didn't know whether to be relieved or disgusted at their behaviour.

'Lose much?' Harry asked him innocently. 'With Doug's investments?'

Dave grimaced. 'Too much.'

Harry resisted the urge to gloat and when they finally left, he was glad the atmosphere between the three of them had been equanimous. A good result, he thought, considering everything that had gone on before.

74

Harry would have gone to see Ethan, but since Jessie had returned Harry's car to the hire agency – he couldn't drive until his concussion had gone – Ethan came to him. He looked dreadful. He'd lost weight and his skin had broken out in spots. His normally thick head of floppy brown hair was lank and greasy, his clothes crumpled.

'I'm so sorry,' Harry said.

'I don't know if I'll ever get over it.' He stood with his back to the fireplace, expression haunted.

'Ever is a long time.'

'What's *wrong* with her?'

'Nothing. She is who she is.'

'But who is she?' Ethan wailed.

'I can't say for sure, but I'd guess she suffers from NPD. Narcissistic personality disorder.'

Ethan's eyes bulged. 'What?'

'It's a mental condition in which people have an exaggerated sense of self-importance, and an excessive need for attention and praise.'

Ethan sat down on an armchair as though his limbs had suddenly collapsed. 'Bloody hell.'

Harry had spoken to Libby, who had told him what the police psychiatrist had suspected. As it happened, Harry agreed with the diagnosis.

'People with NPD expect to be recognised as superior, even when they don't have any achievements that warrant it,' Harry went on. 'They take advantage of others to get what they want. Insist on having the best of everything.'

Ethan swallowed. 'Holy crap. That's her all right.'

'Has she struggled to maintain relationships?' Harry asked.

'She doesn't have any close friends, if that's what you mean.'

'Yes.'

'They're all acquaintances.' Ethan's gaze grew distant. 'Even Cabe and Wren keep her at a bit of a distance. She can be a real bitch sometimes.'

'It's because of her lack of empathy for others,' Harry agreed. 'But I'm guessing that behind her mask of extreme confidence lies an incredibly fragile self-esteem. This makes her vulnerable to the slightest criticism. Which is why when your sister isn't given the admiration she believes she deserves, she can turn exceptionally nasty, like creating that exceptionally nasty website.'

Ethan closed his eyes. He looked as though he was at the end of his tether.

'But there are positive things about being a narcissist,' Harry added.

Ethan's eyes snapped open. 'Like what?'

'Well, they have immense charm and charisma. They're persuasive. They break the rules, which is good when old practices, for instance, hold back progress.'

'Mum and Dad are devastated.'

'I can understand why.'

Ethan's left leg started to jiggle.

'She hates jail.'

I'm not surprised.

'She blames you for everything. She says if it wasn't for you, everything would have gone according to plan.'

Harry studied the pain etched at the corners of the young man's eyes, his mouth, the way he was holding his waist, as though he was trying to keep the grief from expanding.

'You blame me too,' he said softly.

Ethan closed his eyes. 'Yes. Sometimes, I hate you.'

'Sometimes,' Harry said feelingly, 'I hate myself.'

75

Six weeks later Harry and Jessie were on holiday in Normandy, sitting on a low wall and watching the twins playing on the beach at St Malo. Although Harry still got the occasional headache, he was pretty much recovered and was, at last, enjoying being able to function as a relatively normal human being. Whatever 'normal' meant, that was.

'I'm not going back to work,' he told her.

She looked shocked. 'What do you mean?'

'That I won't be practising psychotherapy any more.'

A silence fell. She frowned and kicked her legs against the wall.

'But you're so *good* at it,' she said.

'Who says?'

'All your clients, for starters.'

'I don't know about that.'

He watched a seagull float overhead. 'I can't treat anyone, having failed so spectacularly to identify Doug and Filipa as being a potential danger to others. How could I possibly ask a client to trust me after what's happened?'

'But, Harry–'

'There's nothing special about me,' he cut in, not wanting her to protest any further. 'I'm just a person, like anyone else, with a handful of qualifications framed on the wall. At the end of the day, have I really made a difference? Am I really able to help anyone at all?'

'Of course you are, you're–'

'Jessie.' He turned to look into her green eyes. 'I can't go back after this. Okay?'

She ducked her head. 'Okay,' she murmured. 'But personally, I think it sucks. It's such a *waste*.'

Paton and Mia had teamed up with two other children and were busily building what looked like a town out of sand. Daisy the Jack Russell was staying with their neighbour and the Labrador. At last, the Labrador was of some use.

'Will you move in with me?' he asked.

She swung her head around and stared at him.

'I'd really like it,' he added, suddenly petrified she might say no. 'And it's not because I need a nanny for the twins. It's nothing like that. It's because I love you.'

Her whole face was alight. It was as though the sun had burst from behind a cloud.

'You love me?'

'Totally.'

'Well, Harry Hope. It's your lucky day because I love you back.'

She flung her arms around his neck, making them overbalance and tumble onto the sand.

'I take it that means yes.'

'You betcha.' She was laughing into his face. 'So, Mr Unemployed, what thrilling career are you going to be taking up when we get home?'

He hadn't actually decided but it suddenly came to him, and at the same time he felt a sensation of being unshackled and set free.

'Pastry chef.'

THE END

Printed in Great Britain
by Amazon